THE NEW HOUSE

Persephone Book N° 47
Published by Persephone Books Ltd 2004

First published 1936 by Victor Gollancz Ltd
© Leo Cooper
Preface © Jilly Cooper 2003

Endpapers taken from 'Rope and Dandelion',
a block-printed velvet designed and
printed by Margaret Calkin James for her new
house, 'Hornbeams' in Hampstead
Garden Suburb, in 1936.
© Elizabeth Argent

Typeset in ITC Baskerville by Keystroke,
Jacaranda Lodge, Wolverhampton

Colour by Banbury Litho

Printed and bound by Biddles, King's Lynn

ISBN 1 903155 371

Persephone Books Ltd
59 Lamb's Conduit Street
London WC1N 3NB
020 7242 9292

www.persephonebooks.co.uk

THE NEW HOUSE

by

LETTICE COOPER

****

with a new preface by

JILLY COOPER

PERSEPHONE BOOKS
LONDON

PREFACE

✳✳✳✳✳✳✳✳

Proust had a theory that people fall in love where they want to go in life. I'd always longed to be a writer and was therefore in heaven in 1961, when Leo Cooper asked me to marry him. Not only was he immensely kind, witty, darkly glamorous and worked in publishing, but also most of his family were authors.

His father Leonard, for example, wrote excellent novels and biographies, his Aunt Barbara, as well as working for the revered *London Magazine*, produced poems and novels (including one topically entitled *Sweet Chariot*). Most famous of all was his Aunt Lettice, a talented biographer, journalist and children's author, whose widely acclaimed novels were both page turners and of great literary merit.

There must have been something about that rich, dark West Riding soil which produced both the four Brontës and these three brilliant Coopers.

I had in fact heard of Lettice long before I met her because our families were inextricably entwined. We all lived in the West Riding, and my mother and two of my aunts went to Queen Margaret's School in Scarborough, as did Lettice's sister Barbara and also Leo's mother, Stella Jupp, a charming Southerner who became Lettice and Barbara's sister-in-law when she married their brother Leonard.

✳✳✳✳✳✳✳✳✳✳

My mother, a voracious reader, loved Lettice's novels and would regale me with tales of how she and Barbara suffered mutual humiliation at Queen Margaret's as they pounded down the gym in their blue serge knickers and failed to get over the buck or the horse. Later Barbara invited my mother to stay for a dance in the Coopers' splendid dark grey house near Leeds, and assured her that if she played her cards right, brother Leonard might ask her for the supper dance. As it turned out Leonard didn't offer. As compensation my mother met and was enchanted by Lettice.

When I became engaged to Leo, I was thrilled but terrified at the prospect of meeting such a distinguished novelist, but Lettice could not have been sweeter or more welcoming. She and Barbara used to invite me and Leo to wonderful parties at their flat in Hampstead where I met a stream of famous writers, Rosamund Lehmann, Sybille Bedford, Francis King, and Maureen Duffy and where Lettice, a dashing cook, served delectable stuffed eggs and chocolate Charlotte Russe.

By this time, Lettice had written a dozen novels but chose as an engagement present to give me a copy of *The New House* which had been published twenty-five years before, but which she and many others thought was her best novel.

More than forty years later, I still remember how enraptured I was by *The New House*, staying up all night to finish it. For like Charles Dickens and Robert Louis Stevenson, whose biographies Lettice later wrote, she was above all a story teller, not of action-packaged sagas, but of adventures of the heart.

All that outwardly happens in *The New House* is over one long day a family move from a large imposing secluded house

✳✳✳✳✳✳✳✳✳✳

with beautiful gardens to a small one overlooking a housing estate. But all the characters and their relationships with each other are so lovingly portrayed that one cares passionately what happens even to the unpleasant ones and shouts, 'yes, yes, yes' to acute observations on each page.

I also remember biting my nails over whether Rhoda, the loveable, immensely sympathetic heroine would finally cut loose from the apron strings of Natalie, her querulous, tyrannical mother, who was making such a fuss about the move.

I, on the other hand, rather identified with Natalie's distress as six years earlier my own family, after a boardroom coup, had been ousted from a large, beautiful house in Ilkley with seven acres where my pony roamed freely, to squeeze into a tiny flat in Earls Court. Lettice's wonderful description of the West Riding with its mills, four-square houses, obsession with making brass and fierce appreciation of the arts made me incredibly homesick.

The New House reminded me as well of my favourite author Chekhov, who so influenced Lettice's generation of writers. Like him, she had perfect social pitch and could draw an arriviste developer as convincingly as a steely Southern social butterfly. Like him she seldom judged her characters and found humour and pathos in every situation.

To digress briefly, in the early years of my marriage, I worked for a small publishers in Fitzroy Square and Lettice and I lunched frequently in an Italian restaurant in Charlotte Street, where we devoured delicious chicken marsala and a great deal of wine and talked our heads off.

Lettice was always splendid looking, a flamboyant dresser with luxuriant white hair and bright brown eyes that swivelled everywhere but never quite met one's own. This is usually construed as shyness, but in writers, I suspect, is a reluctance to reveal the amount of material they are absorbing.

At one of these lunches in 1962, Lettice gave me the proof of her latest novel, *The Double Heart*, which I started reading on the bus home. By the time I'd reached our flat in Kensington, I realised it was based on the break-up of Leo's first marriage. Dialogue and events were so true to life that one had a vision of Lettice plus notebook perched on the end of several beds.

None of the protagonists in *The Double Heart* emerges very attractively. My charismatic, forceful Leo is portrayed as a wimp called Lewis. I become a ghastly mousy-haired drip called Sherry who rushes home most uncharacteristically in the lunch hour to put in slow cooking casseroles for Lewis's supper. Laura, Leo and his first wife Diana's enchanting four year old daughter changes sex and becomes adorable Toby. Most incensed was Diana, who is depicted as the beautiful Belle, when her lover was described as 'sliding his hand down under her vest'.

'I never wear vests,' she stormed, 'they're so dingy.'

It was only when I read *The New House* a second time in order to write the foreword to a new edition, which I'm delighted Persephone is publishing, that I realised this novel is even more based on the Cooper family than *The Double Heart*.

In *The New House* for example, two sisters Rhoda and Delia

and their brother Maurice are, like Lettice, Barbara and Leonard, all intellectuals who care about books and ideas.

Their mother, Mrs Cooper, like Nathalie the mother in *The New House*, was a self-centred histrionic bitch, who evidently tried to stab her kind husband when she learnt she was pregnant and who, once widowed, annexed the sweet, biddable Lettice to look after her and cater to her every whim.

Nathalie's kind husband, although already dead in *The New House*, is clearly based on Lettice's father, whom she absolutely adored. A genial steel magnate who 'liked people who interested him and grudged no man his rise', he also spoilt his capricious wife rotten.

The real tension in the novel, as I pointed out earlier, is whether Rhoda will escape Nathalie's clutches and forge a new and fulfilling life in London. In fact it was not until 1939, three years after *The New House* was published that Lettice broke free from her own mother and joined the London-based magazine, *Time and Tide*.

In the story, Rhoda and Delia's brother Maurice was the only one married, increasingly unhappily, to Evelyn as Leonard was to Stella Jupp. Southern Stella, according to my mother, was an absolute charmer, immensely popular at school. I also found her a welcoming and delightful mother-in-law. But in *The New House*, probably because Lettice was on the side of her beloved brother Leonard, she perhaps unconsciously portrays Stella as the spoilt, self-centred manipulative, Southern Evelyn. Maurice, depicted as a far more sympathetic character, lacks Leonard's endearing eccentricity and coruscating wit.

The tragedy was that Leonard and Stella were two attractive people with totally different values who, except for producing three delightful children, should never have married. Like Stella, Evelyn in *The New House* reads few books and prefers pretty clothes and houses to ideas.

Maurice, by contrast, nobly but rather irritatingly feels: 'What did it matter if they had their drawing room redecorated when so many people had only just enough food to keep them miserably alive.'

When Evelyn points out that people treat you differently when you're doing well, Maurice snaps back:

'Who gives a hoot about those sorts of people', and Evelyn sees he is 'on a platform of his own.'

Finally, Maurice and Evelyn have an adorable daughter, Tatty, whom I'm certain is based on Leo, who was born in 1934, who like Tatty had a shock of black hair and who, as a first-born, was doted on by aunts, parents and grandparents alike.

'A small child in a family was an island where belligerent powers could meet.'

The New House is, however, a far greater novel than *The Double Heart*, perhaps because Lettice was younger, more fearless when she wrote it and felt more able to flesh out the characters, whereas in *The Double Heart*, possibly reluctant to hurt, she pulled her punches.

Happily, because Stella, like Evelyn, didn't read books, she probably never discovered how she'd been portrayed and she and Lettice remained on comparatively cordial terms all their lives. We also forgive Lettice totally for drawing so ruthlessly on her family because her compassion continually shines through.

Part of her genius as a writer is to realise that humans are never consistent and, as Rhoda observes, that 'hard people will suddenly be tender and gentle people hurt you.'

Every time the reader becomes outraged at the monstrous egotism of a character, the kaleidoscope shifts and they do something spontaneously, unexpectedly kind.

'I never meant to be a selfish woman,' cries Natalie in a rare and touching moment of self-knowledge, but an adoring husband had made it so easy. 'I wish he'd shaken me and told me not to be a little fool.'

Like Chekhov, Lettice is also wonderful on lost love. Only twenty-one when the First World War ended, she and Barbara must have found young men in very short supply. Both Rhoda and her maiden Aunt Ellen in the novel turn down men whom they love and who love them because they put duty first and are not prepared to abandon their dominating mothers.

But before either of them can adjust their haloes, Lettice (or Rhoda) points out:

You lived to be good not happy. . . . It was better to forego your own wishes and enjoy the rarefied happiness from being on the side of the angels.

Jealousy is also brilliantly depicted. Thus we see Rhoda frantic to escape her mother's clutches yet unable to hide her resentment that maiden Aunt Ellen, during the move, is suddenly better at calming and looking after Natalie than Rhoda is.

While Natalie, having totally enslaved Rhoda, is unable to hide her jealousy that an old school friend, who writes to wish Rhoda luck on the morning of the move, may be loved by Rhoda more than herself.

As Auden recognised, we all want 'not universal love but to be loved alone.'

The New House doesn't date and reads as freshly today because above all it is about the shifting balance of power within any family. In our twenty-first century, the grand old house would probably be saved as a listed building and the NIMBYs would be out protesting against anything being built in its place.

Unlike them, but like Rhoda, Lettice was a true socialist, who although sad to leave a large, beautiful home, felt her conscience eased because it seemed right that such places should be knocked down to make way for lots of little houses for the poor.

During her life Lettice supported her sister Barbara and many other writers. At their parties along with the literary lions were always lame ducks: Turks who longed for British passports, pale spinster poets who couldn't get anything published.

Among Lettice's many other activities was to be one of five women members of the Writers' Action Group, which helped to establish Public Lending Right. For this, she was awarded the OBE and many writers were able to carry on working when the PLR cheque arrived each spring.

✺✺✺✺✺✺✺✺✺✺

Although Lettice wrote so well about jealousy, it was not a deadly sin from which she suffered. She was continually encouraging young writers, and when my first short story was published in 1967, she immediately wrote saying how much she'd enjoyed it. Six months later another story called 'Christmas Stocking' appeared about a girl who spends Christmas hiding her fat legs from the boy she loves. When she puts on the black fishnet stockings he has given her for Christmas, however, she discovers to her ecstasy she has 'real ankles' after all. Lettice fired off another letter saying she'd rushed out and bought some black fishnet tights and I was right, they had improved her ankles no end.

It was this wonderful sense of adventure and fun that made Lettice so loveable. Before another Christmas, she rang in fits of laughter to say she had been admiring the decorations in Regent Street when a nine foot wide steel snow flake had clanged to the ground, nearly slicing her in half, but she had been revived on the bus home by overhearing a woman saying to her friend: 'I'm not going Christmas shopping tomorrow, I'm going to spend all day in John Lewis's.'

A lot of Lettice's wonderfully true dialogue was picked up on the top of buses.

Nor will I ever forget her kindness. When I was going through a bad time and couldn't finish my novel, *Polo*, Lettice rang to say she and Pamela Frankau, another wonderful novelist, always cured their own writer's blocks by quoting to each other from Kipling's *Thorkild's Song*: 'There's no wind along these seas, Out oars for Stavanger!'

This meant that the fishermen would never get home

before the arctic winter set in, unless they got out their oars and rowed.

Having pencilled in the quote above my desk, I managed gradually one word after another, to slog my way to the end of *Polo*, which did better than any other book I've written.

I tell this story because Lettice's prose is so exquisite, so blissfully easy to read, that few people realised how long and hard she laboured to achieve it. Like Chekhov again, she was a naturalistic and symbolic writer. Beautiful descriptions of nature are never shoved in for effect, but invariably for additional meaning.

When weary Rhoda takes refuge during the move in the neglected garden of the new house she finds like predatory self-made developers that:

Nasturtiums had sown themselves all over, covering carnations, pansies, and the edge of the grass with their green umbrellas, and with a generous profusion of gold and tangerine trumpets.

She also notices: 'Insidious strands of convolvulus wound their green coils up the stout stalks of the hollyhocks,' symbolising the stranglehold both the slender Evelyn and Natalie have on Maurice and herself.

Whilst in one of the most beautiful passages in the book, Rhoda, wrestling with her conscience, as she heats up her mother's hot milk and water bottle, catches sight of Micky the kitten:

****

His black head pressed against his mother's side. Relaxed by sleep, shorn of his bold daytime personality, with limp paws and slack body and soft cheeks, he was a little kitten again.

Like the human family today, Micky is going to a new home tomorrow, to be bumped around in a horrid cat basket. 'You won't like it,' Rhoda tells him,

> but you'll get to a house, and hands will stroke you and there will be a saucer of milk. You'll taste it, and it will taste the same. You'll sniff all the furniture with your black nose, and you'll look all round the room with your big green eyes, and then you'll see something, a string hanging out of a drawer or a bit of paper on the carpet, and you'll pounce and spring and play, and it will be all the same to you. You won't remember your mother, and she'll look for a new tomcat to sing to her in the dark, and fight other cats for her, and then she'll have another family of kittens and she won't remember you! Cats were all right, they lived in here and now.

To Rhoda, the kitten, un-hampered like humans by a sense of duty or a desire to hang onto material possessions, has become a symbol of freedom.

The New House was published by Victor Gollancz who published all Lettice's novels and to whom she was steadfastly devoted. He was clearly very fond of her and would frequently

****

take her to lunch at the Savoy. She said it was uncanny how he always ordered for her and it was exactly what she would have ordered for herself.

This seems to sum up Lettice's acceptance and enjoyment of food or anything else life set in front of her.

The only tragedy, because she had such a huge circle of friends, was that she never wrote her memoirs.

If a bomb had fallen on the Saville Club on the night of her ninetieth birthday celebration, literary London would have been wiped out. Leo and I had an exciting evening sitting with Margaret Drabble and Antonia and Harold Pinter. As well as the rest of the Cooper family, among the other guests toasting a radiant Lettice were Roy Fuller, Francis King, Nina Bawden, Jasper Ridley, Penelope Fitzgerald, Hilary Spurling, Maureen Duffy, Kathleen Nott, Josephine Pullein-Thomson and Michael Holroyd.

In her last years, Lettice joined her beloved brother Leonard in Norfolk, where Leo's sister Rosemary Nolan and her husband David looked after them just as devotedly and kindly as Rhoda had Nathalie.

Lettice, although going blind, continued to plan another novel. A cast of characters and jottings for plots were found among her papers when she died in 1994. I'm sure in Heaven the angels are nagging her to finish this novel, not least because they are longing to read it and curious to see how she has portrayed them.

Jilly Cooper
Gloucestershire, 2003

THE NEW HOUSE

CONTENTS

PART I

MORNING

"Pray you, Sir, whose daughter?"
"Her mother's, I have heard."

LOVE'S LABOUR LOST

CHAPTER I

THE WINDOW, bare of blind or curtain, was reflected
in the long mirror of the wardrobe on the opposite side
of the room, so that the bed lay between two barred
oblongs of light, pale grey at first, then pinkish, deepening
at last to the triumphant gold of the September morning.
Rhoda opened her eyes. Slowly, as a boat rises on the
water of a lock, she rose out of the warm sea of sleep that
had engulfed her, and floated on the surface, holding the
moment of tranquillity, knowing already that it was
threatened by the returning world. Her dreams, which
had been pleasant, slipped away from her, bright fish
slipping back through her fingers into the water. She
blinked, stirred, and was suddenly wide awake.

She had always awakened like this on the day on which
she went back to school, not slowly and pleasurably, but
with a jerk, coming face to face with disaster. At least that
was over. This was a different departure. It meant leaving
her home, but it did not mean leaving herself. The worst
part of going back to school had been the sensation of
losing the real Rhoda, of going off with an automaton who
for twelve weeks would work and play games and live by
regulations. Sometimes, as she was going to sleep in her
dormitory, she had imagined the real Rhoda still at home,
reading a book, or grubbing about in the garden. To re-
enter herself on the first day of the holidays had been an

exquisite relief. She knew that Maurice had felt the same, although neither of them had ever spoken of it. In those days it had so often been unnecessary for them to communicate by speaking.

She jerked herself up on her pillow and looked at her watch. It was quite early, but she thought that she would go down and make some tea. Cook and Ivy had worked up to midnight, helping to put everything ready for the men. They were sure to be tired and late. It would be as much as they could do to get breakfast and clear it away before the vans came. She had a fancy that she would like to go downstairs, now, while everyone was still asleep, and she could be alone with the house to say good-bye.

She sat on the edge of her bed, pushing her feet into her slippers. How large her room looked with the carpet up and the walls bare, large and light and full of sun ! She had slept her last night in it, and this was the last time she would wake in the morning and see the high boughs of the copper beech rise above her window-sill as she sat up in bed. The moment had no sharpness. It was so often like that; anticipation or foreboding were vivid, but the climax was blunt, almost muffled. You expected something, happiness or pain, to stab you with a sharp point, and it hit you a dull thump, as though it were padded. Probably you were looking forward to the feeling instead of to the thing itself. There was a kind of dishonesty in that, and, anyhow, it would be better to-day to waste no time on feelings.

She went out of her room on to the landing. It was light, for the heavy curtains had been taken down from the staircase window. They were to go into the sale since they were no use to Evelyn. Very few of their discarded

possessions had proved to be of any use to Evelyn, who
had always known exactly what she wanted for her house,
and, by the end of four years of married life, had mostly
succeeded in getting it. Maurice had wanted to have some
of the furniture from his old home. He had pleaded with
unusual pertinacity for at least a few of the things that he
had grown up with, heavy chairs, solid tables, even those
oil paintings in gold frames which he had condemned and
laughed at when he was at Oxford. Maurice, who had
said in those days, " Can't we put those revolting things
in the boxroom ? " now wanted them in his own dining-
room. They would have looked incongruous in his house,
and Evelyn was quite right to be firm. Rhoda thought
that, and tried to feel it, knowing that she could not have
done it herself in face of Maurice's distress and her
mother's pained surprise at the rejection of each offered
treasure. She would rather fill her house with Victorian
furniture than hurt two people.

But then, she reminded herself, she did not mind so
very much what furniture she lived with. She liked things
that were easy and comfortable and had been used. She
had no schemes for a perfect house in her mind. For her,
only the people who lived in it, and the rhythm of the life
they lived, seemed really important. She lacked the power
of seeing that rhythm in terms of concrete surroundings.
Delia had it. Delia knew what she wanted for her flat,
despised Evelyn's pouffes and cretonnes, and meant to
have plain, pale wood, with bowls of jade and orange, or
great heaps of cushions, raspberry red, silver green, and
the deep, blue-purple of anemones. She had been talking
about it last night as they went up to bed. At the thought
of Delia lying asleep upstairs Rhoda's spirit lightened.

Dell coming home for the move had made all the difference, had introduced an element of picnic and holiday.
If your sister was also your great friend, there was nothing
else like it, and you had one piece of luck whatever else
you missed.

Rhoda unfastened the chain and opened the front door.
She did not often let the morning into the house, and she
found it exhilarating. The cool air swept over her and past
her, stirring the flowers still left in a bowl on the hall
table. Last night she had emptied all the other vases, but
this one had been forgotten. A fat, waxen rose drooped its
full-blown head over the rim, and two creamy petals fell
on to the dark wood. Rhoda stood for a moment in the
doorway, looking out across the lawn to the herbaceous
border and smelling the September morning, smell of
damp and dew, earth and autumn. A leaf from the copper
beech danced up the steps towards her, brushed her bare
instep, and drifted across the carpetless stone floor of the
hall. It was a good hall, with its wide doors, and generous
hearth, and gracious, shallow staircase. It was a pity to
pull down a house whose beauty was so solid and suitable,
so right for its purpose; but perhaps it was not as suitable
now as it had been for the generation who built it—a
generation with more conviction and stability, well on top
of life. It was when you remembered that they put their
servants to sleep in attics without windows that you saw
the justice of a housing estate blotting out their garden.

Rhoda moved from room to room, throwing open the
doors and windows. Last night, when she had gone round
locking up, she had felt the house thick with the ghosts of
their past life in it. They had come back, obscuring her
more recent view of it as a burden, something that had

to be kept clean and habitable with a staff too small for
the work, so that it drained her time and energy. Lately
it had been her enemy, but last night she had forgiven it.
It was astir with all her experiences. Her father, laughing
and playing with her; her mother, busy, exacting, sometimes tender; games in the nursery; lessons in the schoolroom; preparations for Christmas. The house was crowded
with memories of those very early days, memories that had
kept a depth of colour and pungency of flavour different
from the more coherent and detailed memories of later
years, of Barry coming home with Maurice one long vac,
her own first grown-up evening frock most fortunately
ready, and life suddenly in flower; of Delia home from
school, eager and full of plans; of letters from Barry, his
last visit, hearing the car going down the drive; of Maurice
bringing home the stranger, Evelyn; the difficult week-
end, trying to find contact and finding none, seeing
Maurice changed and hating Evelyn for it; of her father
dying, asking for help with his eyes, fighting for breath.
They had all come back to her last night, filling the house
with the past. They seemed to disappear, almost reproachfully, as she let in the hard, clear daylight.

On the table in the drawing-room, Delia's gloves and
little hat lay where she had thrown them the night before.
Rhoda picked up the hat and turned it on her hand.
Even lying there discarded it looked alert and lively, not
just a hat, but Delia's hat, flavoured with her personality.
It was not only that Delia was pretty, but that she added
to life, just as Evelyn subtracted from it. With Delia you
yourself were more of what you could be. In her company
there was more in everything, more spirit, more meaning; in Evelyn's, less. Was that why Maurice had faded,

become what most people called " settled " and lost some
essential quality ? Nobody except Rhoda seemed to have
missed that quality, and perhaps she was weighing something intangible against the solid values of wife and home
and child.

In the kitchen, she lit the gas-ring and filled the kettle.
It was a walk from the gas-stove to the tap ! Whatever
else they might regret, none of them would be sorry to
leave these kitchens, built for the days of scullery-maids
and of a jack turning before the fire. As Rhoda unfastened
the shutters, the cat and the kitten, Mrs. Robins and
Mickey, stirred on their separate chairs. Mrs. Robins
stretched herself with slow grace, got down to the floor,
and padded to the back door, asking to be let out; but
Mickey, when Rhoda stroked him, curled the black and
white ball of his person against her hand, and purred the
loud, vibrating purr of a much-petted kitten. It had been
so dull all night, and he liked life and attention. He looked
up, alert and curious. His nose was a black smudge in
his white face; his eyes, turning from blue to green, were
full of light. He saw a jinny spinner on the wall and sprang,
pouncing with his big white paws. Rhoda picked him up
and cuddled him against her cheek, but he would not
purr for her again; he wanted the jinny spinner. She put
him down, and heard his feet scamper along the passage.
He was going to-morrow to his new home. Two cats in one
little house would be rather a nuisance, but they would
miss him as they missed Tatty after she had been for a
week-end, another young, lively creature, seeing the
world full of possibilities.

Rhoda sat on the edge of the table, waiting for the
kettle to boil. All the kitchen china was arranged on the

top of the dresser, ready to be packed. The window curtains had been taken down and folded in a pile on one of the chairs. A big clothes-basket on the table held a collection of odds and ends, a mincing-machine, some tin canisters, cookery books, a blue china dog that had adorned the mantelpiece ever since she could remember. A camp was struck; an army was preparing for the march. A faint thrill of excitement warmed her blood. You could put up with a good deal so long as there was drama in it. Human nature liked more than anything else to have things happening.

The trouble is, thought Rhoda, that so little has happened to me. She looked back at her grown-up life and saw it slipping past her like a film. There was no day or week that she could remember on which she had cried " Stop," held up the reel, and made the picture hers, living so ardently that time was defeated. She had been nearest to it, perhaps, that last week before Barry left. One movement of her own then would have made her part of the film, fused her with the picture. When she hung back, she had thought only of waiting a little longer. She had expected her opportunity to wait for her. She had not learnt the blank and simple fact that opportunities do not wait. It was the fairy-tale over again, she discovered: the girl with the magic purse whose contents decreased if she bought nothing, but grew with every purchase. An opportunity accepted always made more, but, if you let one go, you lost others with it. It seemed that it was an inexorable law, yet, except for that one failure, she could not quite see how or why it had caught her.

The kettle interrupted her thoughts by boiling over. She jumped off the table, and filled the teapot. The scent of the tea, homely and aromatic, made her feel more solidly part of the daytime world. She arranged her mother's tray, and filled cups for herself and Delia. She realised that she was hungry, but it was too late now to cut any bread-and-butter, the tea would be cold by the time she got upstairs. Her mother always had bread-and-butter with her early tea, and would probably complain. Rhoda felt impatient, steeling herself in advance against the complaint, and against her own feeling of being remiss. Too many conflicting emotions attached themselves to such small things. She saw that it made life exhausting, but had not found out how to stop it. She looked down at Mickey, who had come back into the kitchen, and was lifting up ardent eyes to the tray in hopes of milk.

" Not just yet, Mickey. Not for you."

She carried the tray upstairs.

CHAPTER II

Natalie Powell awoke from a distressing dream, turned in the big bed for reassurance, and saw that the pillow next to her was empty. The dream had been true. In that moment of waking, not only what she had lost, but what she was going to lose, came back to her. Her heart sank like a stone, and she stared before her, her face bewildered and incredulous. It could not have happened ! All through Tom's long illness she had felt that this could not be true; it could not be happening to her. Other people's husbands were ill. You were sorry, and at the same time faintly pleased and interested. You sent flowers, and telephoned inquiries. When it was your husband, you did not believe it. Other people lost their husbands, and again you were sorry, and sent more flowers, and somebody went to the funeral. It was all real and probable, but there had been no reality or probability at all about that flurried half-hour in the middle of the night; about Tom, an old man, struggling painfully for breath, with his head against Rhoda's arm; about Maurice coming in with the raindrops on the shoulders of his coat, then voices, footsteps, the doctor, a glimpse of Tom's still face, the taste of something in her mouth, and a heavy sleep. She felt that all that could not have happened. Before she had had time to make it part of her experience she was asked to accept a new improbability. They were leaving Stone Hall.

That was even harder to believe. It hurt a pride in possessions that was very strong in her blood. Tom, who on the whole lost more than he made, had never really shared that pride, had argued that it's what people are that matters. Natalie, grandchild of old John Lister, who had started with nothing and made a fortune, was more inclined to think that it is what people have. In her limited way, she knew her world better than Tom. He was long-sighted about life, but her short sight was keener. Besides, the house was part of her. She had come to it as a bride, borne and brought up her children in it, worried and fussed over it, sacrificed time and pleasure for it. It was hers by right of the energy she had put into it, and because it had held the whole current of her life for thirty years. She could not be leaving it. Someone or something, she had felt sure, would prevent this from happening. Now the day was here, and it seemed that nothing had prevented it. A helpless, hopeless rage possessed her. She was angry with Tom, who had not managed to leave her well off; with Maurice and Rhoda, who had explained to her that she could not afford to go on living here. All her life she had contrived to get her own way by being angry or crying, but this time neither had done any good. Providence itself had failed her.

When Rhoda knocked and came in with the tea, her mother was lying high up against her pillows, staring before her. The look on her face, so resentful and bewildered, hurt Rhoda, but her pity was mixed with a certain dread. I can't go over it all again, she thought. She felt physically incapable of explaining for the hundredth time just why it was necessary for them to leave. She had borne the brunt of the arguments, after Maurice had lost patience and gone off home; she had had to go all over it again each time, assuring her mother that Maurice wasn't wrong, that he had looked into it all, that he wasn't rushing them any more than was necessary. Rhoda put the tea-tray down by the bed and remarked cheerfully:

" Awake, Mother ? It's a lovely day ! "

The unreal, distressing brightness of her tone grated on her own nerves. She turned away to pull the curtains back from the far window, hoping with a fervency that was like prayer that her mother would not want once more to be reasoned out of her objections.

Natalie propped herself on her elbow and reached over to the tray.

" Is it late, dear ? Isn't Ivy down ? Why did you bring the tea ? "

" They didn't get to bed till after midnight, you know, Mother. They had their own things to pack when they'd finished in the kitchen. They must have been tired out."

" Still, I don't like you to bother about me ! " And that, Rhoda thought, was not quite true, although her mother didn't know it. She thought that she tried to arrange everything so that Rhoda should have a good deal of time to herself. She always urged Rhoda to go away for week-ends, or to go out to friends for an afternoon or evening. She said, " You'll enjoy it, dear. I want you to accept. I like being alone " ; but when Rhoda was setting off she always said, " You won't be coming back late on Monday, I suppose ? " or " What time do you think you'll be home, dear ? I shouldn't think you'll be late." A strong, invisible current, proceeding from her real wishes, reached Rhoda and pulled at her, cutting short

week-ends and spoiling parties. She would remember
how unselfishly her mother had spared her, and would
be sucked back under the compulsion of a morbid conscience. This conflict, not so noticeable before her father's
death, had grown more acute in the last year.

Her mother sipped her tea.

" I expect Aunt Ellen will be coming round to help
this morning."

" There won't really be very much to do until they
begin to get the things in over there."

" There'll be everything to look after."

" I expect the men will get on much better if we leave
them to themselves."

Rhoda thought that her mother was making a fuss
where none was necessary; her mother that Rhoda was an
irresponsible girl who had never had a house and did not
understand her religious sense of duty towards her household goods.

Tears came into her eyes as she thought of those household goods broken up and scattered, some of them gathering dust in a sales room, others in strange houses, knocked
about, misused. She began to complain.

" I did think Evelyn would have liked to have the settle
for their hall. They've nothing but that rather unsteady
little table. And those big double linen sheets would have
cut into beautiful single sheets for her spare-room beds.
She hasn't any linen to touch it. I suppose it was too
much trouble to cut them, although I offered to have Mrs.
Willey in to hem them for her. And the oak Cromwell
table, Rhoda, and all that carpet ! It seems a shame to
let them go when that carpet Evelyn has in the dining-
room is wearing now where Maurice always rests his

feet, and anyhow, it's not a very good one ! A lot of their
things are such poor quality ! It seems a pity to keep all
that cheap stuff and let our good old things go for
nothing."

" It's her house," said Rhoda, trying to be fair, the
more so because any condemnation of Evelyn soothed a
quivering nerve.

" Yes, but it's Maurice's house too. Not that he has
much say in it ! I know he wanted to have some of the
family things, poor boy ! "

" Oh, Mother ! " Rhoda exclaimed. "If he wanted
them he should have said so ! "

The impatience that crept over her at the thought of
Maurice giving in to Evelyn was older than his engagement and marriage. It was the impatience that she had
felt when her father gave in to her mother, letting her
tears and tempers keep him from doing this, turn him
from doing that. She was a little girl again, playing unobserved in a corner of the drawing-room, while her
mother tried to persuade her father not to ask some people
to dinner. " Dormer was very kind to me when I went
there on business," he pleaded. " And now his wife has
come up here with him, I should so much like to ask
them ! " Rhoda, small child as she was, knew that he
would not ask them. She heard her mother advancing
the cook's holiday, her own bad headaches, until she came
to temper—" You're very inconsiderate when I'm not
well "—and finally to tears—" I won't have them. I
don't want to entertain your queer business friends ! "
Squatting by her dolls' tea-service, spread out on the
low stool, Rhoda was indignant with her mother, and a
little scornful of her father. She wanted him to show

fight. She had not then discovered the difficulties of a campaign conducted so near home. She knew more about it now, and sometimes felt a little scornful of her own surrenders.

" Maurice should stand up for himself," she said.

Her mother's voice ran on.

" Your Grannie and Grandpapa would be so distressed at my leaving here. They always loved this house, and enjoyed coming here so much. They were so fond of the garden. One of the last things Mother said to me was about the lilacs. She wanted to know if they were in flower. I never dreamed we should have to leave the place. I always thought your father and I would live here to the end of our lives."

Rhoda stood silent. Dragging up consolation from herself this morning was like trying to draw water from a dry well. A part of her was impatient of the demand for it. Her mother had had the best of everything all her life ! To go from an inconvenient big house to a convenient small one was hardly a tragedy in a world where so many people were short of necessities. Her mother was not going to do without anything that really mattered. But then, she thought, perhaps you could not say that, " What really mattered " in itself meant so little; it was what really mattered to each person. A part of her was warm with sympathy for her mother, whose roots were being torn up after thirty years, who was losing so much of what she cared for. This part of Rhoda felt tender, wanted to soothe and comfort, but was withheld by an instinctive fear of giving in. She achieved an unsatisfactory compromise. She said brusquely :

" You know we couldn't have managed here. It's far

too big for us. We shall be much happier in a little house."

She looked at her mother, thinking that the face between the grey plaits of hair was a young face. Its lines and wrinkles, the marks of years, were only on the surface. Nothing had sunk into her, no acceptance of change nor knowledge of the inevitable. She was a little girl cheated of a party, and unable to believe it.

" I've left Dell's tea outside, Mother, getting cold, and I must go and get dressed."

She bent down and kissed her quickly, and went out of the room with a feeling of escape.

When she had gone out, Natalie put the cup of tea down on her table. The tears welled up and ran down her cheeks. Rhoda was young, or at least had never been married and had a house and children. She did not understand. She did not know how all your life was threaded in and out of the house where you had lived it. To leave it was like losing your husband again, and seeing your children leave you and go out into the world. It was like cutting yourself off for ever from the Natalie Powell who had been a mother and wife and housekeeper for so many years. Not only that, but it seemed like cutting yourself off from her forerunner, Natalie Lister, who had driven to dances in a cab, and danced through many a little pair of satin shoes, and coaxed Ellen to bring her her breakfast in bed next morning. Natalie Lister had been so pretty that it had seemed natural that Ellen, five years older, should spoil her. Natalie Powell had expected her husband to go on with Ellen's good work, and because she charmed him, and had the potency of someone who never questioned the absolute rightness of her own wishes, he had done so. He often felt vaguely guilty towards her. He had caused her to bear three children, a business which she took hardly, but there was more than that. She made him feel that in marrying her he had intruded upon her fastidious privacy, and that he owed her some reparation.

To Natalie, who had passed from Ellen's spoiling to Tom's, the world had grown cold. At least, she thought, I have Rhoda. She tried forlornly to picture herself and Rhoda together in the new house. Her spirits rose a little. It might not be so bad. Rhoda was not always sympathetic; occasionally she was cross; but, then, it had been trying for her lately. She had had far too much to do in this big place, and there had been so much to arrange and clear up before the removal. Besides, she had never got over her father's death; she had always been his darling; too much so, Natalie thought resentfully. She pushed that thought away. A wave of tenderness flooded her. Poor little Rhoda ! When they were settled, she would send her away for a holiday. She should go and stay with Ursula and Giles. She had not had much fun lately; she would need a holiday before they settled down for the winter. Perhaps after all they would be very cosy together in the new house.

It's such a good thing, Natalie thought, that Rhoda has never got married, or gone to work in London like Delia. I should have been so lonely ! She heard a clock strike, and wondered anxiously whether cook and Ivy were late this morning. She began to listen for any sounds from downstairs.

CHAPTER III

DELIA AWOKE lying in the shadow. A broad, single bar of light, slanting between the curtains, warmed and enriched the apricot folds of the dressing-gown thrown over the corner of her bed, and made a pathway of gold on the carpet. Delia threw out her arms, stretching her strong young body. Her journey back to consciousness was quick and complete; the day held more for her than the night. Hardly noticing the transition, she was enclosed again in her actual life, a life that held Jim, the flat that they were furnishing, and the lab that they were equipping in the basement. It held also her work, a great many friends and ideas, and doings, and Rhoda, whom she had not seen since Easter. She jumped out of bed and ran to the window.

What a heavenly morning ! The garden lay below her, still drenched with dew, untouched and secret in the early light. A faint mist hung over the fields beyond it, veiling the open country. When they were children, this had been a country house. To go into the town had been an expedition, beginning with quite a long walk to the nearest tram. It was only after the war that the town had begun to spread and grow to their gates, pushing out ring roads, throwing up housing estates as though a mole were working underground throwing up gigantic mole-hills. The house had stood for some time on the very edge of the building, holding back the spreading city like a breakwater holding back the waves. Now they were going to sweep over it.

And a good job too, thought Delia, jumping back into bed. It's time they were out of it, for Roddy's sake ! She could see in Rhoda's face how difficult the last months had been. You could probably live quite happily in a house this size with two maids if you did not mind things being different, but with Mother, who could never understand that they were, it was impossible ! She would not have rooms shut up or silver put away; she expected everything to be the same with two maids as it had been with five. Rhoda, of course, had had the worst of it, persuading the maids to do more, and her mother to put up with less, and filling all the gaps herself. A new start in a small house was her only chance.

And yet, thought Delia, I believe she's sorry. Perhaps I should be if this had always been my home. It was so long since it had been the centre of her life. Even when she was at school she had thought of the holidays as the intervals between terms, not of the terms as intervals between holidays. School, with her friends and work and games, had been so much more interesting, she had never minded going back. Before she herself was old enough to go, she had watched with concern the departures of Rhoda and Maurice, white-faced and gloomy, unable to eat their breakfast on the last morning. Was it as bad as that, she wondered ? Half-way through her first term she perceived with relief that it was not. Rhoda and Maurice, astonished in their turn, saw her cheerfully eating strawberry ices on her way to the station. " Heartless little beast," Maurice had once called her, watching

her start on her third ice with the determination of one
who will get no more for twelve weeks.

Compared to them, thought Delia, I was. I didn't
really much mind leaving Mother and Daddy. Perhaps it
was because she was odd man out in the family. Maurice
was his mother's pride and joy; Rhoda and her father had
a much closer sympathy and understanding. Delia,
although they were all fond of her, was on her own. She
could not remember a time when she had not known this.
She had not, so far as she could remember, been jealous.
She had accepted it, and had always had plenty of small
affairs and discoveries to absorb her. It was as she was
growing up that she really began to make friends with
Rhoda as a person and not as her sister, discovering her
all over again for herself. You could not help loving Roddy,
she was so fair. She treated other people's minds with
delicacy and respect, and made no unfair demands on
them. It was a quality that Delia, at loggerheads with her
mother from ten years old, had been able to appreciate.

But I wish, thought Delia, that I could get her out of
it ! I suppose it's partly my fault that she didn't get out
before. There had always been an idea that when Delia
left school and came home, Rhoda would go away and
get a job. She had wanted to go and teach English abroad.
Delia had left school and gone up to London at once to
learn to act. She smiled as she remembered that old
ambition, and its prompt downfall. Rhoda had stayed on
at home, but at that time it had not seemed to matter.
We all thought she was going to get engaged to Barry
sooner or later. I wonder what went wrong ? It was like
Rhoda never to have told her what happened about that.
Delia's own affairs had engrossed her, and for some time

she had not really noticed what Rhoda was doing. She had gone abroad herself after breaking off her engagement to Hilary. When she came back, Rhoda, who seemed much older, was finishing a secretarial course and talking of finding a job. The beginning of their father's long illness had put a stop to that. His life had been uncertain for the last four years, and Rhoda had hardly left home.

I left it all to her, Delia reflected. She had been working at the lab in Wimpole Street during those four years, and meeting Jim. Difficult to realise that four years so packed with interest for her had held so little that was new and exciting for Rhoda. You're awfully selfish when you're happy ! There was a knock at her door, and Rhoda came in, carrying two cups of tea. Delia sat up.

" Hulloa, is it late ? Tea ! Oh, good ! Sit down on my bed and drink yours."

To go from one room to another in a house may be as complete a change of climate as to go into another country. Rhoda breathed the congenial air of her own generation, and felt a release of her spirits. In Delia's company, the shadows and hesitations in her own mind dwindled. The world seemed a plain daylight place of solid possibilities. Rhoda sat down on the end of the bed and pulled Delia's dressing-gown across her knees.

" What time does it all begin, Roddy ? "

" Half past eight the vans come."

" There won't be anything for us to do this morning, will there ? I suppose we couldn't go for a walk ? "

Rhoda laughed.

" Oh, Dell, of course we can't ? We shall have to keep our eye on everything."

It struck her suddenly that when her mother had said

that to her she had thought it fussy. Probably Dell thinks
I am now. A fright seized her—I'm getting like Mother !
She said apologetically :

" I don't suppose we shall really be any use, but Mother
would worry if we weren't about all the time."

" Yes. Probably," Delia said drily.

" Maurice will probably look in on his way down to the
office, and I expect Aunt Ellen will come round to help."

" Good Lord ! It might be a funeral ! "

" It is rather like one."

" Do you really mind very much, Roddy ? You'll be
glad to get out of this barrack, won't you ? It must have
been awfully hard work keeping things going just lately.
You'll have far less bother in the new house. Won't you
like it better ? "

" I expect I shall—only—I don't know. I think I hate
changes ! I'm rather frightened of them."

" Oh, don't say that ! "

" Why not ? "

" It shuts the door on things so. It sounds so old ! "

Rhoda said austerely :

" I feel old."

" But you're not ! It's absurd ! Thirty-three isn't old
at all. You oughtn't to feel as though it was. Why,
nobody does ! "

" It isn't old if you've done things before you get there,
Dell, but it is if you haven't. If you have, then you've
moved on to the next stage, and it's all right. If you haven't
it's like staying on and on in the bottom form with new
small children coming in every year, and then going on
past you up the school. You seem very old to the form
you're in, although you wouldn't if you moved up.

People who were born when I was at school are just
growing up and coming to the tennis club, and they count
me about the same age as their parents. Evelyn makes me
feel old, too. She just thinks I'm Tatty's spinster aunt."

" Oh, Evelyn ! Does it matter what she thinks ? "

" It oughtn't to really, I suppose, but I find it damping.
I see quite a lot of her."

" Evelyn belongs to the last generation."

" She belongs to a permanent generation."

" She's narrow and conventional. I shouldn't worry
about her opinions ! "

" Most things are decided, when you come to think of
it, by the opinions of narrow and conventional people."

" Oh," Delia exclaimed hopefully, " we shall change
all that ! "

Rhoda laughed. Delia put down her empty cup on the
chair by her bed, and sat up, hugging her knees.

" Listen, Roddy. Why don't you apply for my job at the
lab, and take it on when I leave at the end of October ?
They've got to find someone else. Vicary was talking to
me about it the other day, and asking if I knew of anyone.
You've done the secretarial training ; you'd soon rub it up.
The rest is using your wits ; you pick it all up as you go
along. It's awfully interesting—well, you know what it's
like. You've been there. Why don't you try it ? "

Rhoda stared at her in astonishment.

" But I couldn't possibly ! How could I ? "

" Why not ? "

" I couldn't leave Mother ! "

Seeing her face both stubborn and afraid, Delia said
gently :

" Why not, Roddy ? She isn't ill or disabled. She'll

have Ivy to do most of the work in the new house, and she'll do some herself. It would be much better for her than if you do everything, and make an old lady of her. Maurice and Evelyn are so near, and Aunt Ellen would always be in and out. Aunt Ellen might even live with her, or she could stay for long visits. You'd come back for holidays and week-ends. Don't you think it would be quite all right, really ? "

Rhoda shook her head.

" It would be too hard on her just now. She couldn't bear it ! "

" Do you think it's often true to talk about people not being able to bear things ? I don't, except, perhaps, cancer and a few things like that."

Suddenly Rhoda was annoyed with Delia, so confident and happy and young, dismissing the sorrow of humanity so lightly. People who were getting what they wanted thought everything was easy ! She said in a voice more hurt than she intended :

" She would miss me, you know."

" Of course she would, but I expect she'd get used to it. And she hasn't missed much so far, has she ? First her own family made a queen of her, and then Daddy. She's had a very good deal, all her life. I think it's your turn."

Rhoda was silent. She felt annoyed with Delia for making the suggestion, angry and afraid because something within her agreed with Delia. Perhaps Delia was right, and her mother could do without her. Perhaps there was something in herself holding on to her mother, aiding and abetting her mother's continual desire not to let her go. Oh, no, Rhoda thought, crushing this down, Delia isn't right. She was like someone who showed you a

small-scale model of a mountain range, and said that the
mountains were only two inches high, and you could easily
walk up them. When you were at the foot of the real
mountains, they loomed gigantic; you could not see their
top, nor their proportion to the others round them. A
flash of angry jealousy stirred in Rhoda. It was all so
easy for Delia, going to be married to her Jim in three
months' time. She had always done what she wanted.
Rhoda sat silent, playing with the tassel of Delia's
dressing-gown.

Her face, Delia thought, looks defeated. In a few more
years it will look resigned. Why didn't she marry Barry?
I wonder if she'd be happier if she talked about it? She
mustn't be resigned! My poor Rhoda, I must get her out
of this!

Yes, thought Rhoda, Delia with Jim and Evelyn with
Maurice; they were alike in one way. They had the
assurance that comes from being loved and wanted, and
they presumed on it, looking kindly on the rest of the
world and proposing to put it in order. She was annoyed
with Delia. Once, as a small child, she had wanted very
much to go on a roundabout at a fair, and had been
desperately afraid of it. Her nurse had forbidden it, so
she had forgotten the fear, and dragged on her arm as
they went round the stalls, saying over and over again,
" Why can't I go on the roundabout? " Then her father
had come to meet them, and had said that he would take
her, and all her terror had come back and she had
refused to go, and cried. He had been perplexed, and
laughed, and nurse had scolded and called her silly, but
she had been dreadfully distressed, and angry, angry with
her father for making the choice hers, so that in bed for

nights afterwards she saw the brilliant lights and whirling horses and wept for a lost opportunity. In the same way now she felt angry with Delia.

" Roddy," said Delia, " don't be cross with me ! " She swung her legs out of bed, moved down, and put her arm round Rhoda's shoulders.

Rhoda's annoyance vanished. She rubbed her cheek against Delia's, an old caress of their nursery days.

" I'm sorry, Dell. I'm not cross, really. Only I couldn't leave Mother. Not now, anyhow. Perhaps I might have done it before."

" If I'd stayed at home, do you mean ? "

" No, I didn't mean that. I mean that perhaps if I'd pushed out at once when I was young, when Daddy was alive and things were easier, it would have been all right. I couldn't do it now. She hates leaving this house, and I'm about all she's got left. It's my fault; I've let time slip over me, and now it's too late. I often think I should like to do it, but I can't."

" Are you sure you couldn't if you really wanted to ? "

" Yes. Quite sure." Rhoda swung herself off the bed. " It's time we got dressed."

She stood looking down at Delia, building herself up again in her own mind. She said to herself that Delia was still like a little girl, a quick and decisive little girl as she had been, wanting something to happen, and seeing no reason against it. She saw things without light or shade; they were all plain, and clear, and easy to deal with. In spite of her wide experience, she knew less than Rhoda; she was ignorant and brave. Probably she would always do and get what she wanted because she would be unaware of the thousand complications that entangled

other people, and so they would not exist for her. Unconsciously building up her own platform again, telling
herself that she was wiser than Delia, Rhoda felt better.

" I'm off. Be quick, Dell ! "

" All right."

CHAPTER IV

R<small>HODA</small> brushed her hair in front of the glass. It was pretty hair, dark and soft. She had had it set again three days ago, feeling that she would be able to face the removal more confidently if she was not looking a sight. She was not pretty, but she very often looked nice, especially when she was happy or amused. Her face had not the glow and warmth of Delia's; it was longer and paler. Her eyes were grey and smiled quickly. Her nose was indeterminate, her mouth full and sweet. She needed colour but did not make up, partly from distaste and partly from laziness. She loved clothes, and chose them well, but she wore them without confidence. Sometimes it seemed to her that, even when she had taken trouble about it, her appearance was incomplete. Evelyn and her friends, other young women of her age, contrived to produce the appearance of a finished article, although often with ugly and uninteresting colours and lines. Occasionally Rhoda tried to see what they did that she left undone, but more often she did not bother. She despised them a little for being dull and entirely preoccupied with their own concerns, and yet they made her feel shy and subdued, perhaps because of their unconscious attitude of kindly but indifferent patronage.

As she brushed, she marshalled in her mind arguments against Delia's proposal. It had given her a shock from which she was still trying to recover. There could be no question of her leaving her mother ! To do it now, when she was losing everything familiar, would be cruel. Delia was young and happy, and had gone away from home and made new ties. She did not understand. Whatever people might write about fixations and repressions and leading your own life—and Rhoda had read plenty of it—you had duties and obligations. She set up a Delia who denied it, and argued with her to her own satisfaction. Your own life wasn't everything. The young Rhoda had been religious, and had been taught that you lived to be good, not to be happy. An antagonism between the two states had been instilled into her very early. Enjoying yourself, doing what you wanted, implied at least a risk of not being good, anyhow of not doing what other people wanted you to do. It was better to forego your own wishes, and enjoy the more rarefied happiness that came from being on the side of the angels. Rhoda at thirty-three had grown out of all religion except a vague belief in a possible Creator, but she had not grown out of the religious habit of mind. Only once in her life had she wanted anything so much that she did not care whether she ought to have it or not, and then she had not been able to get it. It had been as impossible for her to show Barry that she loved him as it would have been for her to dance suddenly to a barrel-organ in the street.

The thought of Barry, although she had not seen him since his wedding, was like a pain that could still return if she moved a part of her body. It was not only the memory of the loss that hurt; it was the memory of the ardour and ecstasy of loving him, having to stop that. Delia said that it wasn't true that people couldn't bear things. Probably it wasn't, thought Rhoda, since something intolerable had happened to her, and she had survived it. People could bear even that wrenching pain and sorrow that left them impoverished, as though their essential self had lost blood. Only, when you had felt like that, you were careful of what you did to anyone else. She had been too unhappy herself to make her mother suffer.

She slipped her jumper over her head, and ran a comb again through the roughened waves of her hair. She laughed suddenly at her solemn face seen in the mirror. This is all a fuss ! My life isn't a bit tragic ! She thought of the things she enjoyed, her friends, books, gardening, walking in the country. People were always interesting. The world was full of things more important than her own affairs. She loved her mother and Maurice; she was fond and proud of Tatty. It had been the strain of the last weeks, persuading her mother into the move, and now the move itself, that had got on her nerves, and given her this feeling of being shut up in a box with her mother, and wanting to scream if she couldn't get out. When they were settled in the new house, just the two of them together, they would be very happy. She would begin working out her new W.E.A. lectures for the winter. She thought of walks in the autumn outside the town, crisp air, and wide distances under a windy sky. She thought of coming in to her mother, the little tea-table by the fire, a new book to read, or a long letter from Ursula. I can go and stay with Ursula whenever I like. I'm not tied, she reassured herself. She had been indulging in self-pity, she concluded, which was indecent and disgusting. She gave a last twist to the dark curls behind her ears, and ran downstairs.

CHAPTER V

MAURICE, in his newish villa three miles away, woke up and blinked at the light. Before he roused himself into full consciousness, he was aware of the flavour of a mood in his mind like a taste in the mouth. He wanted to sink down into unconsciousness again, but the curtains were drawn back, and the light of a sunny morning poured over him, reclaiming him for the outside world. There is a dressing process to be gone through before you get out of bed. The nucleus of Maurice assembled, piece by piece, the garments of his daytime personality, slipping on custom and habit, buttoning itself into the defences of the mind, assuming again its adult covering, re-establishing communications with the actual world. The complete Maurice yawned, turned over on his pillow, looked at the clock, and saw Evelyn's fair head stirring on the pillow of the parallel bed. He remembered why he felt discontented. He frowned, rolled on to his back, and lay staring up at the ceiling.

If she did not want to have another baby until next year, then of course he did not want her to, but it was a damned nuisance all the same, this business of being careful. It was not only that he minded the humiliation of constant refusals. What disturbed him more deeply was his feeling that Evelyn did not mind. She had never shrunk from him at all. She was frank and free about the

whole thing, but she was—business-like; there was no
other word for it. She made him feel that she regarded
it as a necessary part of the state of marriage, and a
preliminary arrangement for securing children. She had
been very sensibly brought up. On her wedding night
she had been much less nervous than he had, but he
almost felt as though he might have preferred her to be
the shrinking bride of Victorian tradition. That would at
least have shown an appreciation of mystery and wonder.
Nothing was mysterious or wonderful to Evelyn. You did
this, and then that happened. Maurice sometimes had an
uneasy suspicion that she discussed these most intimate
details of their common life with her mother, and the
suspicion infuriated him. It recurred to him now, and
he turned his eyes away from the fair waves of hair, so
pretty where the sun just slanted across the pillow, and
touched them to gold.

He glanced again at the clock. Firmly anchored once
more in time, he remembered what day it was, and
that his own family were removing. He felt a deepening of his tenderness for them; he was distressed to think
of his mother and Rhoda leaving their home. Of course,
they must be sad about it. He himself hated to think
that he would never go there again. They had always
been to tea on Sunday, he and Evelyn, from the first
Sunday after their honeymoon, and Tatty from six weeks
old. As the car left the road and turned into the drive
it made a different sound on the gravel—a crunching
sound which he had never heard without a lightening
of the heart. Once inside the doors, he breathed deep
the familiar atmosphere of home. He was pleased to see
his wife talking to his mother by the fire, and Roddy, his

own playfellow and companion, playing with his child
in the very room where he and she had played together.
Maurice loved continuity and tradition; he wanted things
in his house done as they had been done in his father's
house. He never admitted to himself that he did not
really like his own house, with its uniform, pale walls,
its fresh cretonnes, and its modern but not too modern
furniture. He liked Tatty's nursery best, and, when
he brought toys for her, he always brought those that
were most like the toys he had cherished himself as a
child.

Evelyn sat up, and reached out a hand for her watch,
which hung by its gold wristlet on the knob of the chair
by her bed.

" Gladys is late again."

She yawned, stretching her arms above her head. Her
firm little breasts lifted under the pale flowered silk
of her nightgown. She tilted her head back, and the fair
hair swung out from the nape of her neck. There had been
a time when to watch her wake up had been for Maurice
a tingling ecstasy, a prelude to the beginning of another
day together. Often it still gave him a troubled pleasure,
but this morning he only felt as though some stress were
coming back into his life, breaking his peace. He tightened
himself to meet it.

" Your watch was fast last night," he said.

Evelyn turned her attention to the morning outside
their window.

" It's a good thing it's a fine day ! It will be so much
easier for them removing. It's dreadful when you get a
lot of wet and dirt into the house at the beginning. Are
you going round there, Maurice ? "

" I expect I shall go this morning on the way to the office."

His tone was not encouraging. Somehow he did not want Evelyn's sympathy and interest for his family; it irritated him. He knew almost to a word what she was going to say next. He shut his eyes and turned his head away in the hope of averting it, but it came in her pretty, clear voice.

" I simply hate to think of the house pulled down, and nasty little red houses, full of common people and scream-ing children, all over that lovely garden."

Evelyn's view of the housing problem was simple. " Our sort of people " needed, and ought to have, nice houses, because they were accustomed to them. " Work-ing people " ought, she supposed, to have decent houses, but not in any place where they would spoil the view of the neighbourhood for " our sort of people." In any case, most " working people " did not want nice houses. If they were given four bedrooms, they all slept together in one. Gladys's young man had told her about a family who did that, and it showed you that it was no use trying to help " that sort of person." Another of Evelyn's articles of faith was that it was waste of time moving people out of a slum, because they turned any house they lived in into a slum. She had been told all these things, and accepted them with entire conviction. She was a shrewd young woman where the management of her own affairs was concerned; no tradesman could cheat her, and even in the first weeks of her married life her maids had not got the better of her, but on all general matters she swallowed clichés whole, and reproduced them with flat decision, a habit irritating to Maurice, whose intelligence, when not confused by his emotions, was discerning.

Gladys, late but apologetic, brought their tea, and they both sat up to drink it. It was one of the companionable moments in their life together which Maurice had always enjoyed. Sometimes he thought what a lot there was to help you in marriage. You were joined together by so many small threads that held firmly even when the tug came on the big ones. Perhaps, after all, his discontent amounted to no more than the old nursery sin of " waking up with a black dog on your back."

" Eve," he said more cheerfully. " Don't you think we'd better bring them all back here to-night for a meal ? They'll be dead tired by the time they've got the house ready to sleep in, and they probably won't have got the china unpacked. Besides, I don't think Ivy's sleeping there; she's going off for the night. They won't want to start cooking at the end of this day. I'll ask them, shall I, this morning, and we'll give them some supper about eight ? "

" Don't you think it would be a nuisance coming all this way ? I should think they'd rather have eggs or something on the spot, and get to bed."

" Oh, of course, if it would be too much trouble," Maurice said coldly.

" Don't be silly, Maurice ! Of course, if you think they'd like it, I'll do it. I should loathe it myself when I was dirty and cross and tired out after a day's removing."

Evelyn felt injured. Her opposition had been at least three parts consideration for her in-laws, even if it had flashed into her mind that she wanted to go into town this morning, and was taking Tatty out to tea this afternoon, and that the rest of the chicken would have done very well for Maurice and her for to-night.

Maurice, his head turned away from her, said in the same cold tone:

" It isn't Gladys's day out or anything, is it ? It wouldn't give you a lot of trouble ? "

" You know quite well I'm always ready to take trouble for your people."

" Well," said Maurice, still sulky, " they take plenty for us." Something inside him said, Stop it, you fool, but he couldn't or wouldn't stop. " Look how they always take Tatty when we want to go off for a week-end ! They've always been so awfully good to us ! "

He was working himself up into a state of sentimental pity and partisanship over his family. His affection and sympathy were genuine, and were given point by his instinctive perception that Evelyn's attitude towards them had altered. When his father was alive, and at the head of the business, and they were the younger couple, going back to the big house to be petted and welcomed, there had surely not been this touch of patronising kindness that was already creeping into her manner towards the widow and her daughter who would have one little maid and much less money, and no man in their house to give them dignity and consequence. She would be kind to them, but suddenly and fiercely he resented her kindness.

Evelyn thought angrily that it was the very devil, Maurice being so touchy nowadays. She had always treated his people properly. She had been to see his mother every week, as well as on Sundays, ever since his father had died, and she often asked Rhoda to tea or in the evening, although she didn't play bridge well, which

was a nuisance. And only yesterday she had taken Aunt
Ellen a pot of her crab-apple jelly ! Maurice was unfair
and bad-tempered ! Perhaps he wasn't well. She looked at
his moody face. It was still healthily red and brown from
the summer, but there were too many little lines on it.
That was the worry of business in these difficult times.
His hair was beginning to go thin on top already—the
thick, dark-brown hair which she had loved to feel crisp
under her fingers. She wished that he would look round
at her and smile, that she could see his face merry, gay,
pleased, as she had so often seen it when she went to meet
him at the station in the brief year of their engagement.
All at once she did see it. His head jerked up; the ill
humour cleared away from his eyes. He smiled; he looked
amused, alert, and tender.

" Listen ! " he said. " There's the tat-rabbit awake ! "

He swung himself out of bed, and thrust his arms into
his dressing-gown, as though the day suddenly seemed
worth getting up for. He went out of the room, leaving
the door open. From the small bedroom across the passage
Evelyn heard a joyful squeal of " Daddy ! Daddy ! " She
heard Maurice's voice, teasing and pretending to scold,
love and pride in every note of it. She heard Tatty's
chuckle, and Maurice's laugh in answer, then soft thumps
and bumps as though they were having a pillow-fight.

She lay still in bed, her muscles tightening. She often
wished that Tatty had been a boy. Maurice probably
would not have petted a boy so absurdly. A boy would
have been hers, would not have stolen anything from her.

She heard their voices in the passage, and Maurice came
in, Tatty in her blue dressing-gown bundled in his arms.
She was like him, but more like Rhoda. Maurice was

pleased whenever he noticed the likeness, but his pleasure always pricked Evelyn. She had wanted her baby to be like him, but surely he should have wanted it to be like her !

" Is there room in your bed for a large one ? " Maurice said. He put Tatty down beside her. Tatty hugged her, and thrust the hairy head of a toy dog against her cheek. Evelyn cuddled the small, warm body to her, and smelled the delicious smell of a clean child. She felt vaguely remorseful for something unacknowledged. This was her own baby, her little girl. A hardness melted in her heart ; she looked up at Maurice, resting her chin on Tatty's dark head.

" All right, Maurice. Bring them home to-night if you like. I daresay it would be less bother for them than cooking a meal for themselves. Ask them, anyhow. I expect I shall go round some time this morning and see how they're getting on."

" All right. I will. Thank you." Maurice stood by the bed looking down at his wife and child as though he wanted to say something. Why were they not always like this, happy and peaceful, the three of them together ? When such happiness was sometimes possible, it seemed as though it should be permanent ; as though it were absurd that it should so often be lost or damaged. Was it his fault or Evelyn's, or the fault of things beyond their control ? My fault, I expect, he thought. I must pull myself together.

" I'll turn your bath on when I've finished, shall I ? "

He touched Tatty's cheek with his hand, and went off to the bathroom.

CHAPTER VI

BREAKFAST at Stone Hall was a hurried meal of tea
and boiled eggs, eaten in the big, bare dining-room. The
footsteps of cook and Ivy clattered backwards and forwards on the carpetless boards outside the door. Mrs.
Powell was distressed because she knew that Delia would
rather have coffee.

" I'm so sorry, dear. I only remembered just as I was
coming downstairs that you don't like tea for breakfast.
I daresay cook could have made some coffee."

" Of course she couldn't, with all this going on. It
doesn't matter a bit."

" Have some marmalade, dear. I put some grape-fruit
marmalade out for you specially in a little dish. Oh, it's
in the cupboard. Rhoda, will you get it ? "

Rhoda reflected bitterly what a difference there was
between living at home and coming back to it. Live with
people and do everything for them, and they thought that
anything would do for you. Go away and come back
occasionally on a visit and they would turn the house
upside down to get you what you wanted. The worst part
of the whole thing was what it did to you. She did not
seriously grudge Delia coffee or special marmalade, nor
really mind when all the household plans were upset so
that Evelyn and Maurice could have an early meal with
them before going to the pictures. What she did mind was

being made to feel mean and jealous and grudging over trifles. She liked having Tatty for a week-end, but she was annoyed when her mother said, " Rhoda will look after Tatty for you. She enjoys it." She saw then very clearly how in her mother's eyes the main stream of the family ran down through herself, through Maurice and Evelyn, to their children, who would beget and produce children. Rhoda, however dear and useful she might be, was not a part of that main stream, and must contribute to its needs.

She picked up the paper and read the headlines. She glanced at the first leader, looked at the names of books reviewed, saw a picture of the opening of a new Youth Hostel in the Highlands, and another of a politician addressing a group of unemployed men. There was a very large world outside her own. It was full of great issues and infinitely worse troubles. Nations trembled on the edge of war; men were short of work and women and children short of food. Bodies were maimed and broken in road accidents; young husbands mourned for their wives and mothers for their babies. She had nothing to complain of compared to most people. She was ashamed, and turned her attention to Delia, who was talking about the lab where she worked as secretary.

" I'm learning to help with the specimens. I go in as much as I can, and pick up everything I possibly can, because it will be so useful to Jim when he has his own; only they're a queer lot ! Vicary doesn't bother with me, of course, he shoots into the place and just looks at what the others are doing, and says off-hand, ' That's sugar diabetes,' or whatever it is; and he's always right, but you couldn't learn from him; he hasn't any real mental processes. He just smells what a thing is, and when a diagnosis is right or wrong. That's why his book wasn't better; he can't say how he gets to conclusions. He's like somebody who always gets an answer to a sum, and generally a right one, but he can't say how he worked it. It annoys Jim because it's so unsound, but he *is* brilliant."

" What time is Jim coming, dear ? "

" He said he'd get the 1.30, and be here at 5.14. I told him to come straight up to the new house."

" You'll be sorry to leave the lab," Rhoda observed.

" I may go back one or two afternoons a week—at first, anyhow, before we get very much work at our own."

Yes, Delia thought, I shall be a bit sorry to leave the lab, even to marry Jim. She saw the long, low basement room with the hundreds of little bottles and retorts winking in the bright lights. She saw the moving figures of the two white-coated assistants, the square shoulders and sleek dark head of Dr. Nella Dunt humped above her high stool as she bent over a slide. Dr. Vicary burst in, a small, compact man charged with energy, shouting impatiently, pointing with a stumpy forefinger, brown with nicotine. " No, no ! That's never right ! Look *here* ! " with a thump of emphasis on the *here*. Delia was in her little room off the lab, sitting behind her typewriter, and Nella Dunt came in to talk of her lovers. She pursued free love conscientiously, making new contacts like a good but rather tired commercial traveller, careful never to acknowledge to herself that her congenial husband and two nice little girls would have satisfied all her not very ardent affections. A darned good bacteriologist if she was a silly

ass, but she distrusted Delia's anxiety to learn from her.
She thought that Delia was trying to do her down somehow, or catch her out in a mistake. She suspected everybody; the muscles of her body and mind were tight with
suspicion. She was at her best and nicest when she talked
like any ordinary young woman about her home and
clothes and children. Her scientific brain was good, but
the rest of it was a pity; it caused her to swallow
whole a good many undigested ideas, and to mess
up what would have been simple and straightforward
emotions.

How would Rhoda get on with her? Rhoda, when not
feeling shy and abashed, was very good at getting on
with people. When she came up to London for a week-
end, all Delia's friends liked her, and Rhoda herself
expanded. Her cheeks grew pinker and rounder; she
displayed a quiet gaiety, said amusing things, and put on
her hats at a different angle. She was cleverer than Delia,
read much better books, and knew a lot more about what
was going on in the world. At the same time she knew
very much less. Whatever she might read or know about,
she had the essential ignorance and innocence of a very
inexperienced person. If she could really be persuaded to
take Delia's job, she would get some shocks! But shocks
were better than not living. Up here she was hardly living
at all, doing things for Mother that didn't really need
doing, and allowing herself to be subdued, made to feel
a failure by Evelyn, who had the brains of a hen except
about food and clothes, and as much personality as her
own desirable modern residence! A pity, thought Delia
in a detached way, that that was the best Maurice could
do! She had no personal animus against Evelyn, but

found her limited and without warmth, and if she was making Roddy feel crushed, then she would be annoyed with her !

Ivy came in with the post and put the letters down in front of Mrs. Powell, beaming round at them all. Ivy was enjoying the move; it was exciting, and interrupted ordinary work. She was pleased because cook was leaving, and she was going with them to the new house. She would like being on her own, without cook for ever nagging, making a fuss if there was a bit of a mess in the kitchen, or if you just took a drink of tea out of a cup without bothering about a saucer. Ivy looked forward to doing the cooking. Cook thought she couldn't, but that was all she knew about it ! They wouldn't stick fast, that Ivy was sure. And with cook out of the way she'd have Mrs. Robins on her knee whenever she wanted, and pick up the kittens as much as she liked, little souls ! There would be some different kittens in the new house, because Mrs. Robins would go with another Tom over there. Proper bigamists cats was, but it was their nature, and so you couldn't blame them.

" All right," said Ivy to Mrs. Powell, who had just told her that the china, when washed up, must be put with the rest on the kitchen table ready for the man to pack. Ivy became aware of a disapproving gleam in Mrs. Powell's eye, bethought herself, and amended to " Yes'm." She went out of the room, reflecting joyfully that her boy's mother had said she would give her a jumper with a zip fastener next time she got to the shops.

Mrs. Powell sorted the small pile of letters rather slowly. Rhoda saw an envelope addressed in Ursula's handwriting

on top of the pile. Warmth spread through her. It was like
Ursula to remember and send her a cheering line. What
need of hers had Ursula ever forgotten since their first
meeting in a school cloak-room ? Rhoda had been stooping
down to push her gym shoes into her locker; she had
looked up and seen in front of her a sturdy child with a
long pigtail, who said, " I don't know if they've told you.
We aren't allowed to wear our tunics for the last lesson."
No one had told her, and she was so disconcerted by the
many small mistakes she had already made that she felt a
disproportionate gratitude. " It's silly, but it saves trouble
to remember," had been Ursula's attitude to a good
many minor regulations. Her robust common sense and
unblinkered mind had been the best part of Rhoda's
education. Now that she had a husband and two babies,
a flat and no maid, she had as much attention as ever to
spare for Rhoda's concerns, her generous heart growing
with every new demand on it.

Mrs. Powell held the letter in her hand for a second.
She knew Ursula's writing. That girl, she thought. She
resented a part of Rhoda's life which she could not touch.
She would never be able to break that friendship. She had
a secret suspicion that Rhoda liked Ursula better than
her mother. Any ideas of Rhoda's which did not please
her were ascribed in her own mind to Ursula. She
guessed that Rhoda shared Ursula's views rather than
her own. She would have liked to tear up the letter, yet
she felt in some other part of her mind sympathy with
Rhoda's pleasure; she was glad that the letter had come
for her.

" Here's one for you from Ursula, Rhoda." She
added, " I wonder she has time to write so often,

with two small children to look after and a flat to keep clean ! "

But that was just where Ursula was different, Rhoda thought. She would write to her friends first if she thought they were in trouble, and dust the flat afterwards. Neither her mother nor Evelyn would do that. For both of them a tidy house came before a personal relationship. Rhoda had seen them draw together in Ursula's company like true believers recognising a heretic. So few people ever really stopped to think which things were most worth while !

They all sat reading their letters, drawing into their hands the threads that linked them up with other parts of their lives. Every morning a new cobweb of threads was laid down on top of yesterday's pattern. The threads ran to Delia's Jim, now in his London hospital; to Ursula, at present feeding her babies with porridge in the room in Hampstead which she had painted deep yellow, because it got so little sun; to Cousin Annie in Australia, who had sent Natalie a picture postcard of a street in Adelaide; to Sally Gwynn, who had stopped, on a walking tour, in a little shop in Carcassonne and sent a postcard to Delia, who had been her secretary; to a clerk in a coal merchant's office who had made out a bill to Mrs. Powell, thinking all the time about the chances in a football match next Saturday. Queer, thought Rhoda, and exciting, that endless weaving of cobweb patterns all over the world, so that you would almost expect at any moment, when you looked down on it from an aeroplane, to see it covered thick with a network of criss-cross lines.

There was a crunch of wheels on the gravel outside,

and the light was obscured for a moment as a tall van passed the window.

" There," exclaimed Mrs. Powell. " I knew we shouldn't have finished before they came ! We must be quick and get breakfast cleared away. Well—fancy Annie only sending me a postcard after all this time ! "

CHAPTER VII

MAURICE got the car out of the concrete garage at the side of his house. The arrangement was that he took it in for the day when he had to go anywhere inaccessible on business; otherwise Evelyn had it. The arrangement had worked very well until a few months ago, when, like a good many other things, it had become a source of bickering. Evelyn always asked for the car when she wanted it, and did not often inconvenience herself to let Maurice have it. Maurice did sometimes put himself out to spare it to Evelyn, partly from unselfishness, and partly from a dislike for opposing her. On the other hand, Evelyn, if she had to do without it, thought no more of it, whereas Maurice was apt to be plaintive in the evening about the amount of time he had wasted in trains, and the awkwardness of getting anywhere. Evelyn often told him that they ought to get a works car; it looked bad for them not to have one. Maurice agreed that they ought, but was tired of repeating that at present they couldn't afford one; it was absolutely necessary to keep down expenses. The argument sometimes ended in a quarrel, or in sulky silence. In his saner moments, Maurice thought how absurd it was that a thing like the use of a car should be allowed to make so much disturbance in the lives of two grown-up people, but he had not yet faced the fact that the car question was the focus for a division of thought that ran all through their lives.

Evelyn talked of herself and Maurice as hard up, because they had two inexperienced young maids, could not afford to redecorate the house when she thought it necessary, and had to spend an unambitious summer holiday with her mother in rooms at the sea. Her friends, most of them other young matrons, were also " hard up," some of them a little more so, some of them a little less. One or two had no maids, or they had a nurse for the baby and did the cooking. They all cooked, made clothes, repapered rooms, and enjoyed it, boasting freely and gaily about their experiments. Evelyn joined in the talk, but she did not really enjoy it. She found very little pleasure in such activities. She wanted to have things, not to do them. She did not think it was fun to scratch up a meal for unexpected visitors. What she did, she did well. She did not, like her cheerful young friends, bake a lop-sided cake that was sad in the middle, and offer it, laughing and apologetic, to her guests. She made a good cake, but she would rather have bought an expensive one. There lay always now between her and Maurice her urgent desire that he should get on and make more money.

Maurice would have made more money if he could, but his private opinion was that they already had as much as one family ought to have, if not more. Maurice had imagination and a social conscience. The inequalities of life distressed him. What did it matter if they had their drawing-room redecorated when so many people had only just enough food to keep them miserably alive ? He had said this once to Evelyn, and she had called him sentimental. She was quite right, he supposed. It was sentimental to think and feel these things and not to do anything, but what could he do ? He was the head of a small capitalist firm built up by private enterprise, and he was beginning to have an unwilling belief in Socialism. He was uneasy because he was so much better off than a lot of other people, and his wife wanted him to be better off still. Then there was Tatty. About Tatty he had no doubts at all. He wanted her to have the best of every-thing, only he was not sure what was the best. Pretty clothes and lovely toys, an expensive school, nice friends and holidays, or a taste of the rough and tumble earlier, learning to make things do or even to do without them. He would have liked to give her the first if he could, and suspected that the second might be a better preparation for the coming world.

Evelyn and Tatty were on the path in front of the house, waiting to see him off. In the September sunshine, Evelyn's fair hair glinted and shone; the wind blew it back from her ears, and ruffled Tatty's dark mop as she skipped up and down. Maurice stopped the car, his heart suddenly warming. This was his family, to love and work for and cherish and keep against the world. Family life as he knew it, as most of England still knew it, was a solid thing that could withstand heavy stresses. It seemed to him for the moment that this was his only reality, his house, his sunny garden, his wife, his little girl. His doubts and sense of division were a dream.

" What are you doing to-day ? "

" I'm going down to town this morning. This afternoon I'm taking Tatty to Bobby Wilson's birthday tea-party."

Tatty stopped skipping. " Is it my birthday soon ? "

" You had a birthday just a few weeks ago, greedy, before we went to the sea."

Tatty wrinkled her forehead. It was a long time ago

before they went to the sea. Her mind travelled back over a vista of pools and waves and brown sand that got into everything, and recovered, out of that distant abyss of the past, presents, and a cake with pink icing and tiny, thin, pink candles standing in sugar roses. She nodded.

" Yes. I was three, wasn't I ? "

" I must get off," Maurice said, " if I'm going round by home."

An old wish that he wouldn't still call it " home " stirred in Evelyn's mind, an echo of the faint resentment that she felt when he said : " could we have bread sauce with the cutlets ? We always do at home "; or when he was pleased because someone gave them a pair of glass candlesticks like those in his own mother's drawing-room.

Maurice sighed.

" It's the last time I shall really see it looking like a house with people in it ! "

Perhaps, Evelyn thought, it was a good thing. Maurice's roots were still half in his old home; it was his standard of perfection and comparison. He thought that he had settled a friend's worth if he said, " They like him awfully at home," or " They knew him at home, and they think he's rather an ass." Not even to herself had Evelyn admitted that in the middle of her genuine regret when her father-in-law died had been a tinge of relief, because so much of Maurice's affection clung to him, and he had so readily accepted his judgment.

" Things can't go on the same for ever, you know," she said.

Her unconscious satisfaction coloured the words more than she knew. Maurice felt that she was unsympathetic. He said gloomily :

"They always change for the worse."

"Oh, not always." Her light, firm tone dismissed his regrets. "You'd better hurry up, Maurice, if you do want to go round that way. You'll make yourself very late!"

The moment of union had passed; the sense of division was there again. Maurice struggled against it.

"Well, good-bye, darling!"

He had called her "dear" and "darling" far more often lately.

"Good-bye."

He leaned out of the car and kissed her cool, fair cheek. He drove off, feeling unsatisfied. Often, now, when he left his house he felt as though he had left behind him something which he ought to go back and put right. It remained with him through the day, a teasing discomfort in the bottom of his mind.

He drove along the suburban road. It was bordered by houses like theirs, some larger, some smaller. None of them was beautiful, but all looked clean and prosperous. Their gardens were still full of flowers, roses, dahlias, chrysanthemums, late carnations. Their lawns were trim and well cut. Maurice disliked them. He thought that they looked smug. They suggested to his mind happiness without joy, prosperity without enterprise, comfort without adventure. They were full of nice young husbands who had been to Public Schools, voted Conservative, read the cricket news, and played golf at the Lawn Club. Their wives were pretty, pleasant, capable, and came to tea with Evelyn. Very often a couple or two came in after dinner to play bridge. It was all very nice, and Maurice felt that he ought not to be sick of it, but he was. He said to himself that he would like to see them surprised by a revolution. Then he grinned, realising that he was lying. He would not like to see Tatty and Evelyn surprised by a revolution, nor to have to face one himself. Why did he think about facing it ? He might be part of it. He knew perfectly well that he would not. He would be behind the barricades with the bridge and golf-playing husbands, probably less use than most of them, trying to conceal a shrinking of the flesh and a sneaking sympathy for the other side.

He felt better when he turned out of their long, quiet street into one of the main roads leading to the heart of the city. Trams and shop windows were a more cheerful prospect than suburban gardens. In front of him a stream of cars dwindled down a long hill into midget cars, vanishing under a toy bridge. Beyond, the house-tops of the city spread out like a frieze against the sky. Here a church spire soared above them; there the dome of a new cinema dominated the buildings near it. It was a city built without design, houses, works, bridges, churches, theatres, added to meet the pressing need of the moment, century after century leaving its deposit of good and bad, useful and worthless, beautiful and hideous. In the years that followed the Industrial Revolution, it had been a city of sharply contrasted wealth and poverty. The big, solid stone houses, with their beautiful gardens, had been built then, and the slums where children went barefoot. The twentieth century had reduced the contrast; there were no barefoot children, and one by one the big houses were going, turned into flats or institutes, or pulled down so that the land could be used for building. The contrasts were being reduced

in the English way, haphazard, here and there, some
by the Government, some by the town council, some by
private enterprise, all without much excitement or ill
humour. People grumbled, made jokes, adjusted themselves, and regarded the more dramatic reforms or re-
actions of foreign countries with sardonic detachment.
Sometimes Maurice admired them, feeling that their
steadiness and sanity were the best things left in a crazy
world. Sometimes he was afraid that they would be too
slow in their changes to keep up with the necessary pace.
Always he was deeply interested, aware of the times of
transition through which he was living. He talked about
them to Rhoda, and wished that he could have talked
about them to Evelyn. He never admitted it himself
how much he wished this, nor acknowledged that Evelyn
had lived through five years of stress and history in a
northern industrial town without being aware of it.
Her life, although extended by Maurice and Tatty, had
been a continuation of her life in the London dormitory
in Surrey where she had lived with her mother and sister
before her marriage.

He turned in at the gates of his old home, and drove
between the trees. The house stood square and solid,
its back to the town, its face to the open country. From
the gravel sweep in front of the door, steps ran down to
the smooth lawn. He could remember the first time Delia
had walked alone down those steps, staggering to the
bottom adventurous and triumphant, while his mother
from the drawing-room window called out to him to stop
her. He could remember sitting out there one night with
Evelyn the first time he brought her to stay with his
people. It had been fairly dark; there was a small moon

above the copper beeches, and the windows of the house behind him had been lit up. When he looked round, he could see the back of his father's head as he sat at his desk writing letters, and once, turning, he had seen Rhoda, in a dress the colour of mulberries, cross the room to the bookcase. He had not looked round much, for he had been too absorbed in Evelyn. At that time he was seeing things in a different perspective. She was very near to him, in his blood and in his eyes, waking and sleeping. The rest of the world had fallen back to a distance; they were like people outside a circle of lamp-light.

A nostalgia for the past was released in Maurice's heart, and spread through all his veins. He would never be as happy again as he had been in this house ! To come back to it had been a revivification of that happiness. Now that he would not come back to it any more, he felt as though he might be cut off from happiness. People should think what they were doing when they pulled down a house ! They destroyed more than bricks and mortar. Maurice left his car at the back, in front of the old stables, and walked round the side of the house.

A large van was drawn up before the door, and three men were lifting his mother's wardrobe into it. Maurice thought that already the place had begun to look deserted. The steps were marked by the trampling of muddy boots, and pieces of straw and paper were blowing about the floor of the hall. Men came out carrying more of his mother's bedroom furniture, each object familiar to him, and yet strange and forlorn, detached from its usual setting. He saw a large wooden workbox which he had made in a carpentry class at his prep school and given

to his mother at Christmas. He had enamelled it a brilliant
shade of grass green that had seemed to him beautiful,
but the lid had never quite shut. " Good Lord ! " he
thought. " Fancy her keeping that old thing all these
years ! "

He heard someone hailing him, and, looking round,
saw Rhoda and Delia strolling towards him from the
garden. They were both bareheaded, in tweed skirts and
jerseys, and Delia was smoking, and had her hand through
Rhoda's crooked elbow. A faint jealousy smote him—
or, rather, an envy of their close friendship. He wanted
to insist on his right to be part of the old circle, to assert
that he was still one of them, not detached by marriage
and Evelyn and Tatty. He turned towards them.

" Hulloa, you two ! " he said.

CHAPTER VIII

"HULLOA, MAURICE!" said Delia.

She thought, Maurice looks older on top but not underneath. He isn't growing levelly. His hair is a bit thinner and his body a bit thicker. There's a sort of beginning-to-be-middle-aged-head-of-the-business-father-of-the-family-Maurice painted on top of Maurice Powell, but he hasn't grown up to it. It's only a new picture laid on top of the old one. His eyes don't belong to it.

"You look gloomy, Maurice," said Rhoda.

She knew that he was often not happy nowadays, and blamed Evelyn for it, with a pleasure in the blame which she tried to suppress. It was inconceivable to her that anybody could be happy living with Evelyn; her mere presence in the room flattened, deadened, reduced life to the minimum.

"I hate all this," said Maurice, jerking his head backwards towards the vans.

"It will soon be over," Rhoda said consolingly.

"I expect you'll be very uncomfortable in that horrid little house!"

"Oh, rubbish, Maurice!"

They both laughed at him. He was not often laughed at nowadays, and he cheered up.

"It's a nice little house. Delia hasn't seen it yet. It's better than——"

Rhoda stopped herself. She had been going to say that it was better than a nasty modern villa, but had remembered in time that Maurice's house was a modern villa, and in her opinion might almost be described as nasty. An obscure impulse prompted her to make amends to what she really disliked most about his house.

" How is Evelyn ? "

" All right, thanks."

" She was going to the Crawfords' bridge-party yesterday, wasn't she ? Did she enjoy it ? "

" I don't know. Yes. I think so. Oh, yes, she won a prize."

" Oh, good ! What was it ? "

" A powder-case thing, a round flat one."

Their voices were constrained, Rhoda's too cordial, Maurice's too casual. He knew, but would never acknowledge to himself, that Rhoda disliked Evelyn. He was not safe enough to acknowledge it. He shrank instinctively from seeing his wife, even for a second, through unsympathetic eyes. He turned to Delia, who was watching them both. They are so alike, she thought. In the shifting combinations of the family, she had sometimes been detached from them, feeling that they were made of the same stuff, a finer stuff than hers, but less likely to stand wear. As a little girl she had admired her two elders, but their hesitations had puzzled her. She could remember very few times when she had not known what she wanted, and tried to get it. She had often heard people say that she was like her grandfather, Grandpapa Lister, her mother's father, who had made a comfortable fortune in ten years. As a small child she had accepted without much emotion the often repeated statement that she was naughty, and

that Rhoda and Maurice had never been as naughty as she
was. She respected their goodness, but continued to try
and get what she wanted. Watching them now, she felt
older, tougher, more experienced. She was afraid for
them, and especially for her dear Rhoda. She loved her
far more than Maurice. Maurice had not for some years
been much in her life.

" What about Jim, Dell ? When's he coming ? "

" He's coming up to-day; he'll be here about tea-time.
He's sleeping at the Carters' to-night and to-morrow
night. We thought he could probably be useful to-morrow,
helping to arrange things in the new house. Then we've
both got the rest of the week off, so we're going walking
for three days in Swaledale."

Her mind ran forward eagerly to the prospect of
showing Jim her own country, that he had never seen ;
of three whole days together, not afternoons and evenings
snatched out of the middle of work, encroached upon by
hurry and tiredness, but long, full days out of doors, alone.
They had so much to say to one another, they never had
time to talk enough, and certainly no time to be quiet
together. Delia forgot Rhoda and Maurice. Seeing her
face softened and lit by excitement, they looked at one
another and smiled, as though they saw the little Delia, so
much younger than themselves, playing alone ; as though
they had crept up unheard and found her intent upon
some secret game in her own corner of the garden. In the
minds of both was surprise that these things should be
happening to their younger sister. Rhoda felt envious,
and suppressed the feeling. Maurice felt a kind of pity, a
desire to warn her that nothing turns out as well as that. At
the moment he was almost enjoying his disillusionment ;

he made of it a platform from which he could watch
Delia. Almost anything is endurable that provides a platform from which to watch someone else. Maurice was less
unhappy than that tale of his own life which he told
himself. He suddenly felt almost cheerful as he stood
talking to his sisters in the sunshine.

" Tatty's going to a party to-day," he said. His voice
lifted, his face cleared altogether, as he spoke of Tatty.
Of divided mind about so many things, he was whole
about her. The jangled pieces of his nature fell into
harmony together when he thought of her.

" Whose party is it ? "

Rhoda sympathised with his affection, and tried not to
be meanly glad that his face now lighted up for Tatty more
than for Evelyn.

" Bobby Wilson's. It's his birthday. Evelyn bought a
present for Tatty to take, but she wants to give him her
own leather reins as well. She'd give anybody anything ! "

His tone caressed her little dark head that rose up so
easily before the eyes of his mind at any moment in the
day.

" Yes," said Rhoda. " She's a Friday child, loving and
giving."

Let's hope she'll stay like that, Delia thought, but she
hasn't got too good a chance ! It was sad to think of the
soft wax of Tatty's mind pressed into Evelyn's mould, and
limited by her rigid barriers and by Maurice's withdrawals. Tatty would be brought up in the same way as
her parents, or, rather, in a mixture of the same ways, in
the sheltered complacent world of the prosperous upper
middle class. By the time she was grown up, perhaps there

would be no such world. It would be like bringing up Miranda on Prospero's island, and then putting her down in the middle of London traffic to cross the street.

" I ought to be going," Maurice said reluctantly. He was never in a hurry to get to the office, where the usual struggle awaited him, competition with larger firms, the alternative of getting no work or getting it at prices that allowed no profit, the constant anxiety of watching the overdraft when money was so quick to go out and so slow to come in. Worse than the struggle was his growing conviction that he was fighting in a cause almost stupidly lost, like a Jacobite rising plunging down into the heart of a sober and sensible England that had grown a hundred years beyond it. To be carrying on an old-fashioned business in a new world gave him a dispiriting sense of dislocation, but he could not see how else to earn his living; he shrank from putting an end to other people's jobs, and he was still so unsure of what he thought that his new convictions would seem absurd in the company of those who did not share them. He looked at the square stone house fronting the serene garden.

" I wish I'd lived in those days ! "

" I don't," Delia said decisively. " These are much better times, exciting and full of possibilities. I like them. That was a stuffy age, Maurice ! "

" Well, if it was, it was warm and snug. This age is too draughty ! "

" It's open to the fresh air ! "

" Fresh air is draughts if you don't like it," Maurice replied firmly. " What do you say, Roddy ? "

" I don't suppose it matters much what age you live in so long as you're in tune with the best part of it."

Natalie Powell came out of the house and saw her three children together. They looked a cheerful and united group, talking and laughing. Her lips tightened, and the lines between her eyes deepened, as her ready sense of injury sprang to life. Maurice might have come in to see her first ! If his father had been alive, he would have come straight into the house to look for him, instead of staying out in the garden with his sisters. Rhoda and Delia might have remembered her, and not kept him. Once you begin to lose things, thought Natalie, you lose everything ! Tom is dead, and we're leaving the house, and none of the children really loves me, although I've done everything for them and given up all my life to them. She came slowly across the terrace.

" Good morning, Maurice. I thought you were going without seeing me."

Maurice stooped down and kissed her cheek. She let him, but did not return the kiss. It flashed across his mind for the first time that her unresponsive acceptance of his caress was like Evelyn.

" I didn't know where you were," he protested. " I was coming to look for you."

" I was only just inside the front door. I saw you go past."

Then why couldn't she call out to him ? Delia reflected. Her mother's complications of simple things had often driven her to rage before she left home.

Maurice no longer wanted to stay. The ease of the last few moments was broken. Demands and dissatisfactions had crept in again to spoil the casual intercourse. He had a real affection for his mother, but was often unhappy in her company.

" I'm going to be late," he said. " Take care of yourself and don't get too tired. Oh, Evelyn wants you all to come and have a meal with us to-night. Will you all come over when you've finished ? About eight ? "

" Oh, no, dear, it will be far too much bother. Such a lot of us ! I think we'd better not."

" Nonsense ! We want to have you. Ivy's going home for the night, isn't she ? "

" I don't like Evelyn to have all that trouble. We shall manage quite well, shan't we, Rhoda ? "

" Yes," said Rhoda. She was divided between annoyance at having to think it kind of Evelyn, and irritation because her mother was so willing to give trouble to her own daughters and so unwilling to give trouble to her daughter-in-law. She thought, Thank God that even in a family no one knows anyone else's private thoughts ! The meannesses of her own mind revolted her; there seemed to be so many of them nowadays. She felt as though they ought not to be there, as though the real Rhoda who could give and receive, be generous and tender, was stifled under them. She looked at Delia, and Delia smiled at her. The warmth of a positive feeling, loving Delia and Delia loving her, released a spring of generosity in her heart. It *was* very kind of Evelyn.

" Let's go, Mother," she said. " It would be fun, don't you think ? And we shan't be able to find any of our own knives and forks."

" Jim too ? " Maurice smiled at Delia. He was pleased because he would have all his own family in his house this evening.

" Yes, thank you, Maurice. Jim would love it."

" Now I must go."

" I'll come round with you to the car." Rhoda and Maurice walked round towards the old stables.

On an impulse Rhoda said:

" Delia wants me to try and get her job, and take it on when she leaves at Christmas."

Maurice stopped.

" At the lab, do you mean ? In London ? "

" Yes."

" But you couldn't, could you ? Go and live in London, I mean ? What about Mother ? "

" I know. I don't see how I could possibly leave her. Now, especially. Do you ? "

Maurice began to walk on slowly.

" I don't know. I'd never thought about it. I didn't know you had any idea of going."

" I hadn't. At least, I didn't know I had, until Dell suggested it this morning."

" I suppose Mother would be miserable without you." Maurice was considering. " Do you want to go, Roddy ? "

" I don't know. No, I don't think I do."

" I shouldn't think you'd like it much ! It would be awfully hard work, wouldn't it ? And all among strange people, and living alone, perhaps in uncomfortable lodgings, or some beastly club. It's different for Dell."

" Why ? "

The urgency of her tone pulled him up, and made him think. Why should it be different for Delia ? Because she had always plunged into things and out again ? Look at the way she had insisted on going to that College of Dramatic Art as soon as she left school, and had then discovered before the end of a year that she couldn't act, and had taken a secretarial course and got herself a job with that novelist almost before her family had drawn breath ! And then she had got engaged to that dreadful fellow who wrote plays, and called everything " dim " or " dreary " or " bourgeois." And then that had been off and she had gone to Germany, and then there had been Jim, who was a little better than the other fellow but still an object of suspicion to Maurice, tom-cat enough not to like other tom-cats in the family, and then there had been this new job ! You felt that Delia could knock about anywhere and it wouldn't matter. She would get into scrapes and get herself out again. Rhoda was different. Rhoda was like himself. They did not get into so many things, but they got into them head first and stuck there.

" Oh, well," he said, " Dell's knocked about such a lot, hasn't she ? "

" If I were going to get married, nobody would think I ought not to leave home."

He was not stupid, and he was fond of her. He stopped and looked at her.

" If you want to, I should do it. Do you want to ? "

She began to laugh.

" I don't think I do really. I think I'm being silly. It's this queer feeling to-day of being suspended between two lives. It makes you feel rooted up. Delia suggested the idea and I felt unsettled. I thought if I talked to you about it I should settle my own mind ! "

She had been sure that Maurice would be against her going. She knew his conservative temper, his dislike of any change. She had expected that as the head of family he would feel responsible for his mother's welfare, and anxious that Rhoda should look after her. He surprised her by saying in a disturbed voice :

" I believe we ought all to do more of the things that we want to do, and damn the consequences."

Rhoda forgot her own problems for the moment and looked at him. What did he want to do, or regret not doing, that made his face look so harassed, at once younger and older than it should have been, a boyish face under a fine net of worry and nervous strain ?

He saw the inquiry in her eyes and withdrew.

" I must go now," he said. " You needn't decide anything to-day, need you ? "

Rhoda was not sure. If you were a prisoner being transferred from one prison to another, your best chance of escape was on the passage. That was absurd and melo-dramatic ! She was not a prisoner at all. She was free to arrange her own life. It was foolish, she told herself, to think of making an important decision to-day when there was so much to do, when she was jerked out of her ordinary routine of living and could not think quietly or see anything steadily.

" Oh, no," she said lightly. " It's a bad day for deciding things. I mustn't keep you now, Maurice. See you later."

Maurice drove off, thinking of what she had said. He was surprised at the suggestion. Funny that Delia should have thought of Rhoda leaving home and going to her job ! Very funny that Rhoda should have considered it ! He had always thought of her as permanently at home, necessary to his mother, and happy ? He wondered. He had been so much absorbed in his own affairs that he had not thought about it; had just been glad to see her when they met and enjoyed talking to her. When they did not talk generally, about books or politics, as they often did, they talked more about his affairs than about hers. It struck him suddenly that Rhoda had no affairs. She had everyday doings, of course, friends and occupations, her lectures, and she messed about with committees and societies, but she had nothing of her own to which she was necessary, as he had his work and his family. Maurice perceived that even a business that worried you incessantly might be better than none. He did not think so clearly that even a wife with whom your temperament clashed might be better than no close ties; he was not going to look into that part of his mind; but some unexamined conclusion made him feel better pleased with his own lot.

As he turned out of the drive into the road he saw Aunt Ellen coming towards the gate, a basket in her hand. He stopped. He had for Aunt Ellen the indifferent and rather patronising affection of a young man for an elderly, poor, and unmarried aunt. At the same time he felt that ease in her presence which an uneasy person feels in the presence of uncritical kindness. For some years before he was married he had not bothered about her much, but now that she often did little things that pleased Tatty—cutting out paper ladies for her, and making tiny cakes for a dolls' tea-party—he felt grateful, the warmest feeling in his life begetting warmth. He stopped the car, leaned out, and waved to her.

" Hulloa, Aunt Ellen ! "

Aunt Ellen stood by the car, smiling at him. She was taller than his mother, and thinner. Her movements had more freedom and activity, but far less grace. She had been called Gawky Nell, when she was growing up, by rude schoolboy cousins, and the quality that had earned the name had outlasted it. Her face, long and sallow where Natalie's was pink and white, was yet unmistakably like her sister's.

" Well, Maurice, dear, I'm just going up to see if I can be of any use. How is your Mother ? "

" Oh, I think she's all right. They seem to be getting on quite well."

" It's a horrid business, removing, isn't it ? How's little Natalie ? "

Aunt Ellen was the only person who called Tatty by her full name. She had been delighted when Maurice called his daughter after her grandmother. It seemed to reproduce for her Natalie, the little sister whom she had adored and spoilt from the day of her birth.

Maurice launched into an account of Tatty's latest sayings and doings, knowing very well that he had a sympathetic audience. His heart warmed to Aunt Ellen; he asked her to come to supper that night with the others. Marriage had improved Maurice so much, Aunt Ellen thought. As a young man he had been rather alarming to her; she felt that she had nothing to say to him that could interest him, and she had at first been afraid of his fashionable bride. But a baby had made all the difference, thought Aunt Ellen, who had been taught to believe that married life was happy if you had children, but almost wrong without them. A child was necessary, her mother had told her, to draw the parents together. It was in fact, Aunt Ellen had gathered, hardly respectable that they should be drawn together by anything else. She often thought happily of Evelyn and Maurice, now that they had Tatty, achieving their first real union. She waved to Maurice's departing car, and walked on up the drive.

Maurice was thinking about her as he drove through

the town. Poor Aunt Ellen ! What a life ! Grandmamma's
slave up to the day she died, and spending what spare time
she had doing odd jobs for the rest of the family. Hadn't
she always come to stay when they had measles, when his
mother was ill, or when they were getting ready for a
party ? He could not remember that she had ever had any
fun of her own, or that anyone had even suggested that
she should. So often there was someone like that in a
family, someone who was unselfish, and did all the dirty
work.

For the first time the thought occurred to him, Was
Rhoda's life going to be like Aunt Ellen's ? Oh, surely
not; Rhoda, who had had so much more education, who
was so much more intelligent, who went about and saw
people and did things, and lived in such a different world !
And yet in essentials it did look rather like it. Surely
Rhoda's life was going to be more than that ! Oh, it was
a mistake to be unselfish, thought Maurice, seeing for the
first time what her life might be.

His mind went to Tatty, who was so like Rhoda, who
was so ready to give away her toys. He said to himself
that he would teach Tatty to be selfish, yet he knew that
he was fonder of her for the ungrudging way in which she
gave her love and her small possessions. Her mother
always knew what she wanted, and went for it, and that,
Maurice said to himself, was admirable. The fact that it
sometimes gave him a cold turn was one of the many
things that he suppressed. Tatty must learn to be like her
mother. She must learn to take what she wanted from a
world that certainly would not give it to her on any other
terms.

It was damned difficult, he thought, this question of

giving up or helping yourself. What was his own business but a continual effort to get orders for steelwork from other people, cutting down prices, using friendship, influence, any weapon except bribery ? If you abolished private enterprise, could you prevent the ordinary man from pursuing his own advantage at the expense of other people ? Or would the strain upon the natural man be too great; would he fade and die, leaving a bloodless creature without essential juices ?

God knows ! thought Maurice. It seemed as though the natural man lived by fighting, and the whole object of civilisation was to abolish it. He felt in himself the tug of that conflict. Most people felt it, he thought, and, as the battle swayed this way and that in their very guts, it altered the course of their lives. Not many of them were whole. It was the thing that his generation yearned for, wholeness, but wholeness was difficult, the supreme achievement. I shall never be whole myself, Maurice thought in a moment of clear vision, but I wouldn't mind if I knew how to bring up Tatty whole ! He did not know, and the bringing up of Tatty was largely out of his hands. There remained the day's work. Maurice turned off the tramlines, drove into the yard outside his works, parked his car in a shed, and went into the office.

CHAPTER IX

"You might have told me that Maurice had come," Mrs. Powell complained.

A familiar nerve in Rhoda quivered. You can't bear to be left out of anything for a minute, can you? she thought. A quick pity succeeded. Her mother would be more and more left out as her generation thinned and vanished, the next one clinging together as generations do, the younger one rising, hardly aware of her.

"If you saw him go past, Mother darling, you knew," Delia replied cheerfully. "Poor old Maurice!" she added.

"I don't know why you should say that, Delia. Maurice is very lucky. He has a nice home and a good wife and a dear little girl, and his father's business, which was all ready for him to step into. I don't know what more he could want. If he isn't satisfied, he must be very hard to please."

"Like you."

"That's very rude, Delia," Mrs. Powell replied with dignity.

Yes, Delia reflected, it was. Her mother was the only person to whom she was ever rude nowadays. It was because, even after all these years away from home, she was not quite free where her mother was concerned; she could still revert for a moment to that devastating sixteen and seventeen-year-old rudeness with which she had fought for her liberty. She ought to have got over that by now !

" I'm sorry, Mother," she said.

" All right, dear."

When Natalie Powell smiled or was gentle, it was easy to see why Ellen had spoilt her, and why Tom had married her. The sweet and loving woman that she should have been appeared for a moment like a spirit taking possession of her body and ousting the changeling who had been foisted into it, the changeling who was a girl half grown up, querulous, exacting, unfair. So many people were changelings, Delia thought. Only at rare moments the true person filled the shell and shone through, brave or generous or tender, making you rage against whatever powers had bewitched them and impoverished the world.

" The first van is nearly full," Rhoda said. " Perhaps we ought to be getting over to the other house."

She felt impatient, eager to be settled in the other house, to draw the new life round her. Once they were in there, falling into the routine of even days, she would lose this feeling of being threatened by new demands. She wished that Delia had never made that proposal. She almost wished that Delia had never come home, making a break in her familiar life through which flowed in, like distant music, the sound and stir of a wider world.

" Let's go over now, Dell. We can come back here later on."

" All right. But there's somebody coming. Why, it's Aunt Ellen ! "

" I thought Ellen would come," Mrs. Powell observed, with the satisfaction of one receiving a due tribute.

Aunt Ellen came towards them over the grass. Her long grey tweed coat was flapping open, and the ends of a woollen scarf hung down across her greyish woollen dress. Her brown hat was of a curious round shape, like a school hat a little battered by weather. Whatever kind of new hat Aunt Ellen bought, it always became that shape by some mysterious process.

" Well, Nan, dear ! " she said, kissing her sister.

" Well, Nell ! "

Strange how Aunt Ellen, with her narrow, uneventful life, seemed the more experienced, had achieved a poise and certainty which the mother and grandmother had never known. Aunt Ellen, for all her odd ways, was dignified. She could put herself out of the picture. The fact that she made none of those little strivings and assertions by which so many people try to impress others gave her dignity.

She turned to kiss Rhoda and Delia. Rhoda felt her dry cheek against her lips. This was Aunt Ellen who had been so exciting. When she was a little girl of five or six, it had been so exciting that Aunt Ellen was coming to stay to-morrow that she had not slept. All visitors were an event. Aunt Ellen, driving up in a cab with her box on the roof, was a lovely visitor, a thrilling event ! Wonderful things that she had made came out of the box, dolls' hats of stiff yellow straw trimmed with ruches of ribbon, and sometimes paper dolls. Aunt Ellen had come to the nursery to cut out ladies from magazines and make them stand up on the table with cardboard stands. She had taught Rhoda to make pincushions with lace frills and rosettes of ribbon at the corners. She had a box full of bits, scraps of lace and coloured satin, lengths of narrow shaded ribbon with picot edges, fragments of embroidery, some threaded with gold, some studded with bright things that Rhoda called beetles' wings. To be allowed to dip in that box was like being offered the treasures of Aladdin's cave. When Aunt Ellen drove off again in the cab, Rhoda cried bitterly, hiding her face in the cushion of one of the hall chairs. Not till long afterwards did she remember that Aunt Ellen always arrived in old clothes, and went away in new ones, very often in new ones that her mother had bought for herself but did not like. Not until she was nearly grown up did she realise that Aunt Ellen had to ask Grandmamma for money every time she wanted a railway fare or a new pair of gloves. By that time Aunt Ellen was no longer exciting. Rhoda and Delia and Maurice had to be urged to write to her for her birthday, and to thank her for the Christmas presents which somehow were never anything they wanted. When she came to stay, they saw her at meals and rushed off in between to their own devices. They did not dislike her, but they had grown too old for rapture in her company, for pleasure in the little treats and toys that she could manage to give them, and they had not yet reached the age of consideration.

Was it so much better, the age of consideration? You learnt to think " Poor Aunt Ellen," because she had given up her life to Grandmamma, and was elderly and diffident and poor and lived alone. You very often thought, Aunt Ellen would do that for me, when you had a difficult bit of dressmaking, or wanted help with some tiresome voluntary work of which you had undertaken more than you could manage. But you never wanted Aunt Ellen for her own sake. You went to see her from habit, or kindness, or duty, not because you couldn't do without her company. I may be like that some day, thought Rhoda. She saw herself in the future receiving Tatty's dutiful visits; saw Tatty throwing down a tennis-racquet and saying, "Aunt Rhoda here? Oh, bother!"—Tatty, who now ran to the gate and stood on tiptoes watching, and called out, "Auntie! Auntie Rod!" and made an ecstatic plunge, all legs and short curls and clinging arms. Rhoda put her arms round Aunt Ellen and kissed her again more warmly than usual.

"It was kind of you to come and see how we were getting on!"

"You didn't suppose I should desert you all to-day," Aunt Ellen said. "Why, I'm longing to see you settled in the new house. I think it's going to be so nice and cosy! It feels a lucky house to me! I'm sure you are going to be very happy there."

Her tone had the automatic brightness and encouragement of someone who had lived with an elderly invalid for very many years, of someone who for very many years had begun two-thirds of her remarks with, "Never mind!"

"I can't imagine being anywhere else but here," Mrs. Powell complained. "We've had such happy years here, haven't we, Ellen, when the children were small? Do you remember?"

Ellen might have remembered that she had spent most of those years nursing her father in a long illness and consoling her mother in the intervals, but she only said, "Never mind! You'll have a lot more in the new house. Let's go in and get your things on. The van is just off and the girls want to be going. I've brought some lunch for a picnic in that basket. I thought we should want it soon after we got there, and it would save trouble. And I must say good-bye to cook."

They went into the house together, the tall grey figure of Aunt Ellen bending a little above the smaller black figure of Mrs. Powell, as though in protection. Rhoda watched them.

" Aunt Ellen is the only completely unselfish person I know. I shall never be like her."

" Oh, well, I should hope not ! Nobody ought to be completely unselfish ! "

" It's better if they can be, surely ? "

" No, I'm certain it isn't ! Unselfish people make selfish ones. It would be awfully demoralising to live with a completely unselfish person."

" It's pretty bad to live with a completely selfish one, as Maurice does. Evelyn has her own way about everything."

" Maurice shouldn't let her. Jim won't let me."

" You wouldn't want it, Dell, not all the time. You're fair-minded."

" Evelyn and Maurice don't often say what they think to one another," Delia mused. It was difficult to imagine not sharing her ideas and conclusions with Jim. Even to Hilary, during her first brief engagement, she had generally said what she thought; that had been part of the trouble. Surrounded by his own admiring circle, safely walled off by them from the outside world, Hilary had not expected anyone ever to think him wrong. It was a pity about Hilary, Delia reflected with detachment. That fine, keen, cutting brain, so clever and critical, but not quite clever enough to know itself balanced on the adolescent, shrinking emotions. It was Oliver who was the real trouble, of course. They probably didn't do what people thought they did—that lot so often thought it fashionably and unfairly—but the feeling between them tipped the balance of their ordinary lives.

" Do you remember Hilary staying here, Roddy ? "

Rhoda, deep in her own thoughts, jumped.

" Yes, of course. Why ? "

" I was just thinking about him. Do you remember how disappointed he was when he got here and found it didn't look like an industrial area, no moors or mills in front of the house ? He expected a grim, stark, literary Yorkshire, with chimneys smoking outside the front door and curlews crying outside the back, and all of us inside very Brontë. I really think it was when he found I belonged to an ordinary, bourgeois family that he began to discover that he couldn't do with me. It was too dull. And when I saw him up here, he didn't seem real. Maurice was only just polite to him ! I was furious with Maurice, but, all the same, I was annoyed with Hilary for thinking Daddy and Maurice stupid, and not seeing that they had a different kind of intelligence. Daddy had an intelligence of the feelings that was worth all Hilary's brain. I couldn't bear to see Hilary patronising him."

How lightly, thought Rhoda, how lightly she talks about him; he is something that happened, rather funny now, not like Barry, all that there has ever been of my real life !

" I was sorry for Hilary. I think he was shy, and couldn't get on terms with us. He didn't know what to make of ordinary people. I rather liked him."

" You'd have done much better for him than I should. I thought so at the time."

It was the first time, Rhoda reflected, that they had talked about Delia's broken engagement. She had gone straight to Germany after it, and on coming back had made it quite clear to her family that she had put it behind her. Involuntarily, she said:

" Dell ! Didn't you mind ? "

" Oh, of course I did ! It had been so lovely, and it went bad. We quarrelled and were wretched, and I felt as though I could never be sure of anything again. The whole world seemed flat and grey; nothing had any life in it."

" Yes. I know."

" But it doesn't last."

" I'm not sure."

" Not unless you sit down and hug it. When I was on the boat crossing to Germany, I thought I should feel like that for ever ! But soon after I got there I got interested in the people I was with, and it was all new and exciting. At first I was rather disgusted to find myself feeling better. I thought I'd been madly in love with Hilary and was broken-hearted, and it was annoying to find that I'd just been ordinarily in love with him and felt bad when it was over. But, after all, it has to be like that. You've got to get over things and go on to something else. You must. You've got to live."

" But you don't think all feelings are only temporary, do you ? "

" Yes, unless they're in action. I'm going to marry Jim, and live with him, so I expect I shall go on loving him, but if he died, or married someone else, I don't suppose I should be loving him very much in ten years' time."

" Oh, Dell, how can you ? "

" But it's true ! "

" You do make it an inexorable world ! "

" I didn't make it. If you hang on to a feeling after there's nothing for it to do, it would be rather inclined to go bad, wouldn't it ? I know it sounds romantic, but then such a lot of the things that people used to think romantic were a bit rotten in the middle. Besides, who wants to spend their whole life being sad about something they can't have ? "

Rhoda was tearing a leaf into thin strips. She tossed the fragments on to a flower-bed.

" Come on. I think we'd better go in and get our things."

As they walked across the grass together, she asked a question that had been in her mind. Half laughing, speaking nervously, she said :

" Dell, do you think that some day I shall be like Aunt Ellen ? A dull old woman, alone, who has missed everything, and who hadn't anything to do ? "

She waited for Delia to say, " Of course not, Roddy. Don't be absurd ! " She could not herself have given any other answer to such a question. She would have divined the need for reassurance, have felt a pang of sympathy, and given it promptly. Delia only said gravely, " I don't know, Roddy. You wouldn't be dull, and you'll never be quite alone unless I die first. But I'm afraid you may find you've missed everything if you don't take it in time."

CHAPTER X

IT HAD BEEN SO SMALL a thing that had spoilt that last visit of Barry's to which she had looked forward with such eager and hopeful anticipation. He had always come to stay with them in the long vac when he and Maurice were at Oxford together, and afterwards, when he was working in London, he still came every year for a week of his summer holiday. Of course, she saw him in between; she was often in London staying with Ursula. She had never written to him regularly until that year; he was still officially Maurice's friend rather than hers; but after an evening that they had spent together in February, dining and dancing, he had written to her, a long, gay, and casual letter. She had kept the letter in a private drawer, and read and re-read it, going up to her room a dozen times a day to shut herself up with it, and poring over the sentences that she already knew by heart. After restraining herself with difficulty for five days, she answered it. They began to write to one another every week.

Ever better than the visit itself, she remembered the last days of anticipation. She had rolled and rolled the tennis lawn, mended the netting, repainted the garden seats. She had gone round the garden watching all the flowers and hoarding their beauty. This will be out when Barry comes. I hope that won't be over ! If she could she would have had every flower in the garden out at the

same time for him. Looking back, she thought that her
condition must have been perfectly obvious to everyone
in the house, although then it had never occurred to her.
She had been an absurdly solemn and immature twenty-
five ! That came of being so " well brought up," and
leaving school just after the war, so that her first adventure
into the grown-up world had been too late for the war-
time forcing-house, and too early for the return of more
normal life. Or perhaps it had been something in herself,
a slowness of growth, a hanging back from each new
stage. Surely no girl of twenty-five nowadays would have
been so inexperienced, or have let her happiness be spoilt
so easily ! It was a pity, Rhoda thought, that I'd had no
practice ! Barry, coming into her life when she left school,
had blotted out all other young men for her. She just
had not bothered about them. There were not so many of
them about in those post-war days, and the remnants of
a generation expected to be bothered with, were so
valuable in their scarcity, and so sought after, that they
had no time to notice a girl, not strikingly pretty, rather
quiet and clever, who made no effort to attract their
notice. There was Barry, so they did not matter.

At the time it had been difficult to understand what
was going wrong. The change in herself had puzzled
Rhoda. Her rising wave of anticipation, coming to a crest,
had suddenly fallen flat. She lost her ease with Barry. She
found herself withdrawing from him, wanting to avoid
him. Underneath his gaiety, he was a sensitive person;
he felt the chill, and himself became uneasy. By common
consent they kept apart. They played tennis a good deal
with the Marshalls, and Barry laughed, flirted, and ragged
with Linda Marshall, whom Rhoda disliked. It had been

painful to see her saucy and triumphant airs. She knew
perfectly well that she was taking possession of Rhoda's
young man. Rhoda's own feelings shocked and disturbed
her. Sitting by the tennis court, watching the leaping
white figures and making polite conversation with Mrs.
Marshall, she thought just how much she would like to
kill Linda, and where she would put her thumbs on the
smooth, honey-brown throat. You did not think things
like that ! The remorseful Rhoda planted herself next to a
schoolgirl Marshall at tea, and left Linda and Barry
together. She fancied that he looked at her reproachfully,
but she would not let herself see. She talked laboriously
to Olive Marshall, who was bored, but stayed herself with
cream buns.

In the evening, while some of them were playing bridge,
Rhoda ran up to her room for a book. She looked out of
the window, and saw Barry alone, walking up and down
the garden path. She leaned on the window-sill watching
him, hoping that he might turn and look up. He walked
quickly, his head down, his hands in his pockets. He
looked as though he were thinking hard. Perhaps, like
Rhoda, he was wondering what was wrong. Her heart
melted out of her body towards him. She wanted to run
out and stand in front of him in the new frock that she had
bought for this visit. She wanted to tell him that he was
hers, and not Linda's; to show him beyond all doubt that
she loved him, that she wanted him to love her. She did not
go. She might have been held back by an enchantment.
She watched him for a long time, and then went downstairs and sat in the room where they were playing bridge.
She held her book open on her knee, but the print was only
blurred marks on a white page, and her body trembled.

Looking back in amazement at her young and foolish self, she thought that the trouble had begun on the evening before Barry arrived, the evening when she had been trying on her new dress, and had run downstairs to show it off. She had been shopping that afternoon, and had recklessly pledged all her next quarter's allowance. Her purchases were spread out on her bed: a new tennis frock of thick white silk, a yellow cardigan, two pairs of stockings, a straw hat, and the evening dress, deep cream lace with a belt of turquoise blue velvet. The dress suited her. Excitement and hope had made her really pretty; her cheeks were pink, and her dark hair sprang up from her forehead full of life. On an impulse she ran downstairs, fastening the last hook of the soft blue velvet as she ran. Through the open door of the room they called the library, the room where they all did everything, she saw her father getting an envelope out of his desk.

She ran in and said to him. " Do you like my new dress, Daddy ? "

He turned from the desk and looked at her, smiling. " Yes, I do," he said. " You look very nice ! "

The warmth stirring in her was all ready to overflow to anybody. She pulled his face down towards her and kissed him. She had not heard her mother until a voice from the doorway behind her said:

" Is that your new dress, Rhoda ? Let me see it."

Rhoda turned round at the sound of her mother's cool voice. She lost some of her new confidence as her mother's eyes travelled up and down her, appraising and criticising.

" It's quite nice. It suits you." She added with a little smile, " I suppose that's for Barry ? "

The blood rushed up Rhoda's neck, covering her face

and temples. She did not answer; she could think of nothing to say. She stood looking foolishly at her mother, her hands hanging down. Then she ran across the hall, up the stairs, and into her bedroom. She unhooked the belt, unfastened the dress, pulled it off and threw it on the bed. She knelt down and pressed her burning face against the cool silk cover of her eiderdown. She felt angry with her mother, ashamed and miserable. Everything was spoilt ! She had been so happy, but her mother's eyes and words and looks had condemned her happiness. She lifted her face, saw the dress, and pushed it away from her. She would never wear it ! She would put on her oldest and ugliest dress when Barry came, the green dress that her mother said was hardly fit to wear again.

Of course, she did nothing of the sort. Her life began to grow over the desperate moment half an hour later. She hung up the dress in the wardrobe, and wore it the next evening, recovering a good deal of her pleasure. But it was as though the green bracts had been pushed back from a bud not yet ready to open, and the bud had never been able to open properly. They were further from one another at the end of the visit than they had been before Barry came.

But the trouble didn't really begin that evening, Rhoda thought. It was only that her mother's look and remark about the dress touched something in her mind already there. How often had she heard her mother and other people say critically, " Molly [or Betty, or Peggy] is running after that young man," with an implication of intolerable condemnation ? How often had she been told not to show off, not to look at herself in the glass, not to attract people's attention ? Spoken and unspoken, her

upbringing had forbidden her to invite love; had been
based, she now saw, on her mother's unexpressed conviction that love was wrong. That was the damaging
thing in the roots of their home. Because of that she had
been frightened off love by a word, and Maurice, she
thought, had chosen a wife in whom something was dead;
who would want him as a husband, companion, and
father to her children, but never as a lover.

I've always despised Evelyn for not loving, thought
Rhoda. I said to myself that I had loved Barry more than
most people were capable of loving, but perhaps after all
I didn't. Perhaps I was only making that into a platform
for myself to stand on. All my friends were married and
having children, or working. Evelyn came here as a
bride, very pleased with herself. I had to find something
to stand on. I said to myself that I was really in love and
they weren't; that I had the real thing. But, if I had,
perhaps it would have been so strong that I shouldn't
have been afraid. I could have forgotten myself and
Mother and everything else, and gone to Barry that
evening. Perhaps it was as Dell just said: "I thought
I'd been madly in love and was broken-hearted. I found
I'd been ordinarily in love and felt bad after it." Perhaps
all these years I've been like one of those awful people
who don't treat a relation very well when he's alive, but
keep on putting flowers on his grave when he's dead.
Eugh !

Only, if it's like that, I haven't anything. I'm empty,
standing on the ground. At least that's better than a sham !
I've got Mother; she needs me. We clash, but I love her
and she loves me. I won't think about myself any more.
I'll make her happy. That's a real thing. It's the only real

thing Aunt Ellen's ever had, but it was so real to her that perhaps it was enough ! Thank goodness I've got my hundred a year and don't have to ask Mother for every penny ! All the same, I'm not sure Aunt Ellen hasn't had a happy life. When you stop wanting happiness for yourself, you get peace. I wish I could ! But I want it, really; I've always wanted it. Only I've never been brave or clever enough to get it. How did Aunt Ellen learn to do without it ? I can't ask her, and she couldn't tell me. These things happen deeper down in themselves than people know.

CHAPTER XI

SHE WAS IN HER BEDROOM, kneeling on the floor, stuffing the last of her possessions into a suitcase. The past slipped away from her, and the present came back as Delia knocked and thrust her head in.

"Roddy! Can you come down? Lucy Carter is here, and wants to see you for a minute. Shall I finish that for you?"

"It's ready; it only wants fastening. I'll come down."

She did not particularly want to see Lucy, one of those friends who are made by circumstances. Lucy's father and mother had danced with her own; her mother had been bridesmaid to Lucy's mother. She and Lucy had been to tea in one another's nurseries, danced at the same dancing-class in accordion-pleated silk frocks and bronze sandals, although in those days Lucy was one of the bigger girls, working away accurately if a trifle solidly in the top division, while Rhoda, grave, slender, and absent-minded, stood up with the little ones and was told to copy. The six years between them had narrowed from a wide gulf to a hardly noticeable division now that they were in their thirties, playing tennis at the same club, helping with the same bazaars and babies' welcomes. Lucy's mother had died some years ago, and she lived with her father in a house like Stone Hall, another of the big houses on the outskirts of the town built by her great-grandfather in the eighteen-forties. She played games with vigour, gave up a lot of her time to voluntary work of different kinds, and was always busy and cheerful, but could never leave home because of her father, who was old and ailing, and depended on her for company. Rhoda often wondered if Lucy were happy, but, in spite of the long acquaintance, they were not really on terms of intimacy; they did not discuss their personal feelings.

Lucy was standing on the front-door step, restraining her Sealyham, who was trying to get inside. She was a square-built young woman with healthy, ruddy cheeks and bright brown hair rolled into a rather untidy knot on the nape of her neck. Her bluish tweeds were well made and comfortably old.

She said, " Hulloa, Rhoda," and kissed her—an unusual display of affection. " I came to see how you were getting on, and if there was anything I could do."

" I don't think so, Lucy, thank you very much. We're just going over to the new house to see them get the first lot of things in."

" You won't come and have some lunch ? We can have it any time you like."

" I don't think so, thanks awfully. It's rather difficult to break off, you see, once we start at the other end."

" Yes, I suppose it must be ! It must be an awful business."

Lucy spoke seriously, as one contemplating a disaster.

" Anyhow, Jim is coming to us to-night, isn't he ? Would he like to come to dinner ? "

" We're all going over to Maurice's, so perhaps, if that would be all right, Delia could drive him over to you at bedtime ? "

" Of course. Whenever he likes to come."

" I expect you're busy." Lucy made a movement to go, and then hesitated. She looked round the garden at the smooth lawn, the border still bright with colour in the sunshine, the noble dignity of the copper beech trees. She broke out with sudden vehemence:

" I hate it ! It's a shame ! "

" What ? " asked Delia, joining them.

" Cutting up this place for a housing estate ! Cutting down those beautiful trees, and pulling down a house built by people who really could build, and made things to last ! They'll put up a row of nasty little jerry-built houses without one decent bit of work in them, and they'll all fall down in thirty years. They're covering the whole country with shoddy, temporary new things ! I wish they could leave the old ones alone ! "

" Slums, for instance ? "

Lucy looked at Delia with suspicion. She never had liked Delia as much as Rhoda.

" Of course they can't leave those, but they could pull them down and put up blocks of flats or decent houses in the same place. It would be much better for the people. They don't want to live so far away from their work," protested Lucy, quite unaware that she meant, I don't want them to come and live so near me.

She turned from Delia to Rhoda. " You're quite sure there's nothing I can do ? Could I take anything over in the car for you ? "

" No, really, thanks very much."

" I shall come and see you as soon as ever you are settled."

She doesn't really want to see me, Rhoda reflected ; she

never has, any more than I really want to see her. But
she feels that we ought to draw together, our sort of
people, the owners of property. Even if some of us fall
out of the ranks as Mother and I are doing, she feels she
must keep in touch with us, leave no gaps. She knows
she's threatened. Wasn't there some talk of the corporation
buying a piece of their land ? People like us are gradually
going; the whole industrial system that produced us is
changing. Lucy wouldn't admit that, but she feels it.
She wants to play Canute with the waves, and it's just
about as much good.

"Are you going to be at home for a bit, Delia ? "

"Only for two days. Then Jim and I go off walking
till the end of the week, and then I go back to work."

" I'm afraid I shan't see much of you, then." There was
little regret in Lucy's tone. Instinct warned her that
Delia was a traitor. Feeling cordial to Rhoda, she held
her hand for a moment.

" I shan't drive into town this way any more ! I
couldn't bear to come past and see the house pulled down
and the garden ruined, and horrid little houses springing
up everywhere ! I shall go in by the Avenue. Well, I
mustn't waste any more of your time now. Good-bye ! "

She walked off with the Sealyham. Her sturdy, well-
balanced figure disappeared among the trees round the
bend of the drive.

Rhoda and Delia looked at one another and smiled.

" She means to be kind, Dell ! "

" Do you see much of her nowadays ? "

" Well, yes, we do things together sometimes, but it
isn't a great success. I've never really got anything to say
to her."

" I shouldn't think you had ! She makes me feel as though I'd stepped back half a century ! "

" It's you and your friends who've stepped on half a century, I think ! "

" You don't think most of England's like Lucy Carter ? "

" Perhaps not, but most of it wouldn't agree with you, or the friends I've met when I've been staying with you. I don't know if it ever will. I think perhaps you and your friends are almost too logical for real life."

" Hilary always used to say that he couldn't understand why the country didn't follow the intellectuals."

" If Hilary was one of them, I should think the answer was pretty obvious ! "

They both laughed.

" All the same, Roddy, Hilary wasn't a fool. He had a real brain. He didn't swallow clichés; his mind bit. He knew a lot, and he knew the difference between knowing a thing and not knowing it, which is something nowadays. It would be better to have him leading the country than Lucy Carter."

" Well, would it ? She'd be stupid, she'd probably be unfair without knowing it, but she'd never give or crack. If she took anything on, she'd see it through."

" But she'd see all the wrong things through, and never, never believe that they could be wrong ! "

" Yes, I daresay she would, but what would worry me about Hilary would be the feeling that he'd give, suddenly, in unexpected places ! I don't know how it is that all the clever young men nowadays seem to be in the worst mess —in themselves, I mean. The husbands of Evelyn's friends aren't very interesting; they're just ordinary, nice

young people who think about what they're doing, but
they aren't badly jangled, and they can bring most of
themselves to bear on whatever they are doing. But
Hilary and his friends seem to me to have such terrible
divisions between their thoughts and their feelings ! You
can almost see them pulling against one another and
working different ways. It's as if you saw a pantomime
horse that hadn't been rehearsed properly, so that the
back legs could never go with the front ones."

" I suppose they're finer and more sensitive stuff, so
they get the strain worse—all the strains there are."

" It's not much use being clever if you can't make
yourself work in some sort of harmony."

" Sometimes I think their cleverness gets in their way."
Certainly, she thought, it had got in Hilary's. His knowledge of books and history was so accurate and com-
prehensive, his taste in art and letters so discerning, he
knew himself so often right, that it was natural to suppose
he would be right on the less frequent occasions when
instead of art and letters he thought about people. But
oh, thought Delia, what a mistake ! As though all the
art and letters in the world weren't less complicated,
easier to understand and know about, than the simplest,
stupidest person !

" Jim is intelligent and solid," Rhoda mused.

" Jim's partly Scotch, and he's a doctor. His cleverness
is used every day on real things."

They were leaning against the pillars of the porch, the
sun on their faces. You had expected to be so busy to-day,
and after all you had the feeling of a timeless interval,
sleepy and unreal in the golden morning. From inside the
house Mrs. Powell called:

" Rhoda, where are you, dear? I thought you'd be coming to help me."

Rhoda's movement was impatient, but the strings that bound her tightened.

" I'm here, Mother. I'll come. What is it ? "

" I've got one or two little things in my room that I want to take with us in the car. There's my dressing-case and my fur coat. Don't let Aunt Ellen carry them all ! Let Rhoda have that case, Ellen ! "

Her mother always ordered her about more peremptorily when Aunt Ellen was there ! It seemed that the presence of Aunt Ellen brought back her own home, revived the dead figure of her own mother, dominating, served by a willing daughter, and she had to reproduce her. That was how family life went—a ceaseless chain of reproductions.

" It's all right, dear," Aunt Ellen said briskly. " I can manage these little things easily ! "

CHAPTER XII

Cook and Ivy came downstairs in their things
ready to go. Ivy was going over by bus to the new house
to help to make up the beds and get the furniture straight,
but she was sleeping that night at her boy's home. His
mother had promised to give them rabbit for tea, and
then they meant to go to the pictures. Ivy had already
made friends with two of the removing men, and had
refused an invitation from one of them to go out with him
on Saturday evening. He was a daft lad, and since she'd
been with Wilfrid she'd never been out with another
young man, but there was no harm in being pleasant.

Cook was crying. Her round blue eyes swam with tears,
and one or two ran down her pale round cheeks. She
sniffed, and searched in her bag for a handkerchief.
Well, I never ! thought Ivy. Grumble, grumble, grumble
all these weeks because there was too much work in the
house, and the kitchen was so large, and She would have
everything just as She was used to have it, and now
crying ! There was no pleasing some people !

Rhoda came into the kitchen and stood just inside the
doorway, looking shy. She always felt shy when she penetrated to that downstairs world. The life lived so near to
them and so far apart from them was a dark continent,
full of unexplored mystery. It had distressed her lately to
think that cook and Ivy were managing somehow to do

the work of a house that had once been run by five maids. It had not really distressed her mother. Mrs. Powell would be very kind to a servant who was ill or in trouble, but she could never quite feel that they were independent human beings. It astonished her that they should be unwilling to sacrifice an afternoon out for her convenience. When they had birthdays and were given presents of bath salts, powder-puffs, and coloured beads, she commented on it to Rhoda with surprise. What did they want with things like that? Regarding them at the bottom of her heart as automata, she handled them with assurance and precision, while Rhoda was secretly afraid of asking too much, and got a far more unwilling and inefficient service.

As Rhoda came into the kitchen, the ease of cook's body changed to stiffness, and a mask fell over her face. She stopped crying. She did not dislike Rhoda—at the moment she was sorry to part from her—but Rhoda was on the other side. As soon as she came into the room Annie Hargreaves became cook. Rhoda knew it, and minded more than Annie Hargreaves. Here was a woman only a few years older than herself, living in the same house with her, full, no doubt, of hopes and fears and sorrows and wishes, and as far apart from her as a foreigner who did not speak English. It seemed absurd.

" We're just going now, cook, and Mother wants to say good-bye to you."

" I'm coming now, Miss Rhoda. I've cleared out the larder and left everything here ready. There's one bottle of milk and some eggs left that Ivy can take over with her to the new house."

Rhoda smiled at Ivy, who grinned back at her. In the

new house, Rhoda perceived, there would be no unexplored dark continent. There would be Ivy living at
close quarters with them, talking to them about her own
affairs because she would have no one else to talk to in
between her days out. When Ivy came in at ten o'clock
and bounced into the drawing-room to show them her new
Marks & Spencer jumper, Mrs. Powell said that she did
not know her place. Ivy was nineteen, and belonged to a
generation for whom this mysterious place hardly existed.
Her complete unconsciousness of it was defeating Mrs.
Powell, and would defeat her still more as time went on,
and, while deploring the old respectful servants, she would
find Ivy's affairs interesting. Ivy was good at telling them,
racy, sturdy, sardonic, a peasant living in a town, the
lineal descendant of the free-spoken, free-spirited girl of
English folk-songs.

Cook went out, and Rhoda and Ivy were left together.

" Are you looking forward to being on your own,
Ivy ? "

" I aren't worried," replied Ivy cheerfully.

Mrs. Robins padded across the table, and bent her
head for a moment to touch Rhoda's fingers, giving the
small caress that is all you have a right to expect from
a cat.

" Little soul of a lamb ! " exclaimed Ivy fondly, stroking
Mrs. Robins's fur with a square, red hand. She flashed into
sudden animation that made her round face pretty.

" Do you know what we're going to do, Miss Rhoda, me
and Wilf ? We're going to get a tandem bicycle, 'alf 'is and
'alf mine. His pal has a friend that's got one he wants to
sell. We'll soon learn to ride it, and we'll go away out into
the country. We'll have some good times ! "

It's absurd, thought Rhoda, to envy this child, but I believe I do. She's independent. She's a servant in our house, but she can go whenever she wants. She has her good times and enjoys them. She's out in the world, at grips with it, working and keeping herself, not just a parasite. I expect it would be better if I hadn't a penny in the world, and Mother couldn't afford to keep me. I've been caught in a trap because I've been brought up in a fairly prosperous family. People like Maurice and me ought to be born poor, and start earning our livings early ; it would be the best chance for us !

Ivy, looking at her across the sunlit floor of the kitchen, was moved by something that she did not know, and said in the warm, protecting tone she would one day use to her babies :

" When we get over to the new house, Miss Rhoda, I'll put the kettle on, and make you a nice cup of tea straight away."

Cook came back into the kitchen, wiping her eyes. Sometimes she had liked Mrs. Powell and sometimes she hadn't, but to say good-bye to anyone without crying would have been indecent. Besides, it made you think. She would have a bit of a rest now, but it couldn't be more than a week or two, because her people were all miners. They couldn't do without what she sent them. Shameful it was how bad things were for them ! She'd take care next time to get a smaller kitchen, modern, not these old-fashioned stone floors. You could pick and choose, that was one thing. You were always sure of good work, and people didn't go against you if they could help it ; too much afraid of losing you !

But I've had almost enough good work, thought Annie

Hargreaves. Forty next month, and in service since I was fourteen. Please may I slip out to post a letter? Would you like the chicken hashed or done a fricassay? Now then, young man, you were told we wanted that meat before twelve o'clock. You get tired of it! Changing over makes you think like. What I wanted, if Edith hadn't married that good-for-nothing fellow, we'd 'ave run a fried fish shop together, our own business and our own little shop, a nice machine for slicing up the potatoes, and everything very clean, not low class at all; regular customers coming in every day and knowing us. They say it's hard work, but we'd 'ave been working for ourselves, me and Edith. You get sick of other people's houses.

" Ivy, you get the cat basket out for Miss Rhoda, quick now! And go and catch Mickey! I saw 'im in the bushes outside, and if you get over to the new house without dropping those eggs and breaking them, I shall be surprised."

Ivy put out her tongue, unobserved, as she turned her back and went in search of Mickey. She paused in the scullery to watch the china packer, who was standing by the loaded table wrapping cups and saucers separately in paper and straw. An oldish man with bent shoulders, his big hands were grained with dirt, and looked like the hands of a labourer, yet they were handling the delicate china with gentle certainty.

" By shots! " Ivy remarked, interested. " Don't you never break none? "

" We've to report anything we break. I ain't had a piece broken since April."

" It's a good thing it's your job and not mine."

The packer smiled, a superior and kindly smile.

"You'll learn to be more careful when you've a house of your own."

"I aren't in a hurry," Ivy said. Suddenly she saw herself no longer going out with Wilf on Sundays and Wednesdays, when it was a holiday for both of them, but living with him and his mother all day and every day, not having them for treats and being a treat herself, but cooking and cleaning for them, looking after his mother as she got older, perhaps being scolded for her untidy ways that they laughed at now, perhaps having several children, growing fat and tired, buying no pretty clothes nor lipsticks nor powder, because she would be a girl no longer. She could not have put her vision into words, but she paused half-way between the scullery table and the back door as though the future had risen up before her. The next minute she was outside, chasing Mickey. He ran up a tree and crouched lionwise on a low branch, defying her. Her beret fell off as she tried to reach him, and her rough, bright hair caught the sunlight and sprang out from her round cheeks. She forgot the clean print dress under her coat, and began to swarm up the tree-trunk, reaching out till her hand could close firmly on the warm, vibrating black-and-white body.

"You bad cat, you!" she said tenderly. "I'll cut your tail off!" She had forgotten all about the future.

Cook, putting flannel in the cat basket, was thinking more about the past. Little Annie Hargreaves was walking home from school on a winter afternoon, her satchel slapping her back, her nose so cold that she pressed her hand in its woollen glove against her face to warm it. The sun was a red ball behind the chapel roof. The village rang with the noise of boots, tackety boots ringing on cobbles.

as the men came home from their shift in the mines.
They had black faces like chimney-sweeps, in which the
whites of their eyes and their teeth showed beautiful and
clean. Her own father would be among them, coming
home for his bath and his tea. At the thought of tea, Annie
Hargreaves began to run, wanting to get in out of the raw
air and the slush that chilled through her boots, wanting
the rough taste of bread and the sweet taste of jam, and
the comfort of hot strong tea, and yet curiously happy in
this very moment, in the sullen yellow daylight between
the houses and the dusky red sun above; in it being
Friday afternoon, no school to-morrow; in herself,
Annie Hargreaves, alive and running down the street.
The mature Annie Hargreaves smoothed the piece of
flannel in the bottom of the cat basket, and unpacked
from somewhere inside herself that little Annie coming
home from school, that moment so causelessly happy that
it had become permanent, and lived yet in the sun-
splashed kitchen on a September morning thirty years
later.

" Now then, Ivy, don't stand there playing with those
cats ! You've no time to waste ! Put them in the basket
and have done with it."

CHAPTER XIII

R H O D A stood in her bare room looking round it. The bed had gone, the wardrobe and dressing-table and wash-hand stand had gone. The bookshelves built into the wall beside her bed remained, the only thing that had really been hers. She had borrowed the room from the house and given it back to it. The house had received it again, taking no notice of her. She stood there, a stranger.

It was very silly to mind. She heard the car below in the drive, Delia bringing it round from the garage and grinding the gears because it was so long since she had driven it. It was an old wreck, and ought to be scrapped, but somehow it held together and was very useful. Her mother would be lost without it. How could she possibly go away and leave her with no one to drive her? She could have done it ten years ago when they had a chauffeur; then it might have been natural and not unkind. It was the time at which you did things that was important! They say there is only one half-hour when a pear is really at its best for eating. There is one time in your life when you can do a thing best for yourself and everyone else. If you don't do it then, you don't do it at all, or you do it with loss and damage! Hilary had always said that the difference between an actor and an amateur actor was in the timing.

She picked up her bag and gloves and ran downstairs.

It seemed odd to be leaving in this way, just as if you were going for a drive in the morning and coming back for lunch. You could not help feeling that the end of thirty years ought to be more dramatic. That was expecting life to be like a book or a play instead of the inconsequent business that it was, with flat places in the middle of excitement, and peaks of excitement in the middle of ordinary things. Rhoda looked at her mother, feeling sharply for her the pain of parting, but Mrs. Powell was bending over the cat basket on the hall table, listening to the stirrings and plaintive mewings. The lid lifted a trifle at one side, pushed upward by the heads that were so hard and yet so soft, and a broad white paw appeared between the lid and the basket. " Poor pussies ! " Mrs. Powell said, tightening the fastening. Rhoda loved her when she was like that, gentle and forgetting herself; it made it easy to do things for her.

" Now we're off," she said. She picked up the basket.

" Do you want to drive, Roddy ? "

" No, you go on. I'll get in behind. But where's Aunt Ellen ? "

" She wouldn't wait. She said there wouldn't be room in the car with all the things in it, and she'd slip into a bus and get there as soon as we did."

" Why, we could easily have made room ! "

" Yes, I know, but she would have it that way."

Those were the things that made you impatient with Aunt Ellen, when she would sit in the draughty chair, and eat the burnt piece of toast, thrusting selfishness upon you against your will.

" Ellen is used to buses," Mrs. Powell said complacently, settling herself beside Delia.

A swift indignation surged in Rhoda. How odd to think that there was one order of life for you and one for your sister ! She could remember now little things that she had not noticed at the time, how it had seemed natural to her mother to buy three new hats and give Aunt Ellen her old ones; how she had said, " Ellen won't mind," when they went out to dinner and Aunt Ellen, staying with them, was not asked. The feeling that she had at the moment was more than a feeling for Aunt Ellen; it went back to the time when she was a little girl, watching her mother dress to go down to dinner. She remembered the pattern of a biscuit-coloured lace blouse, and the tur-quoise brooch fastened in it, herself playing with a scent-bottle on the dressing-table, pushing the stopper in and out and thinking that soon she would be in bed, alone in the dark and her mother and father would be downstairs having dinner. Her feeling for people left out of things was still half the feeling of that little girl imagining them at the table, with the lamp lit under the pink frilled shade, and sometimes with the little dishes of crystallised fruit that she had seen put ready in the morning.

" I don't think I've ever seen the garden look more beautiful ! " Mrs. Powell said mournfully.

" Like the seaside on the last morning of your holiday."

Delia's tone, sympathetic but cheerful, annoyed her mother. She drew her mind away from her, turning her head to speak to Rhoda in the back seat.

" You know how people always say when they come here that it seems miles away from a town. I can't bear to think of the grass all broken up, and the trees cut down, and rows of horrid little houses, with the washing hanging out all day."

We ought to have been able to stay here, her mind ran on. Had not things always been arranged so that she could do and have what she wanted? Her feeling while Maurice and Rhoda and Delia were being born had been a sense of outrage that this unpreventable pain should happen to her, and no one should stop it. It seemed to her now that Providence ought to interfere to stay the movement of the tide that was sweeping over the city; to keep her alone in the large house with the quiet garden round her, and to stem the rush of red bricks and gimcrack-looking pink wooden windows and doors; to keep behind a barrier the harassed women in cretonne aprons, the screaming children with toy cars and cycles, dashing into the road. She had never been into a slum nor seen the houses that they came from; she had lived within the circle of her own life, the smallest possible world in a very large one.

Rhoda looked back as the car went down the drive and saw the house standing square and dignified among the trees. They rounded the curve, and it was no longer visible; the big beech at the corner hid the greyish-yellow stone. That was that! She was surprisingly aware of freedom. A rope that tethered her had perhaps been cut. It was absurd to spend so much of your time in one place when there was all the world to be seen! There was a sparkle in her blood not yet extinguished.

After all, change meant new things and possible adventure. She would have expected to feel sad at this moment, but, suddenly, being sad seemed untrue, like words set to the wrong music. How people exaggerated their own existences, writing them into a novel to read to themselves! Rhoda laughed. Delia heard her, and was surprised but pleased. Mrs. Powell heard her, and was annoyed because she did not know what she was laughing at, and felt that her behaviour was not appropriate to the occasion. It reminded her of Tom, very easy, genial, and hungry at lunch after her father's funeral, when everyone else had correct faces. She still thought sometimes that it was an odd family into which she had married, and which she had borne and brought up. She was not sufficiently interested in other people to know that everyone marries into an odd family, since all families are odd except your own, and remain so to the end. She did not even know that Evelyn often thought it, and would have resented it very much if she had, becoming one with her husband and children at any suggestion of criticism.

She turned round and saw Rhoda nursing the cat basket on her knee, and looking out of the window. She warmed to her, not only her daughter, but her husband and son, her parents and sister, all that now belonged to her going with her from the old home to the new one. She was not pleased because Rhoda was smiling absently and did not respond to her eyes. She could not bear a closed door in anyone she lived with. She wanted a latch-key to every room in their person. She was just going to say, " What are you thinking about, dear ? " when Delia spoke to her, and recalled her attention. The car turned out of the drive into the road.

PART II

AFTERNOON

"Who is't that hinders you?"
" A foolish heart that I leave here behind."
MIDSUMMER NIGHT'S DREAM

CHAPTER XIV

Evelyn always disliked altering her arrangements. She had planned the day beforehand, and a family party in the evening was not going to make her change her plans. She did her housekeeping, rang up the shops, and then went up to her bedroom to get ready to go into the town. She must have an autumn hat before taking Tatty to the birthday party this afternoon. One of the secrets of being well dressed, her mother had often said, was to have a new winter hat at the very beginning of the autumn, and a new summer hat very early in the spring. You stole a march on your friends that way. They noticed your new hat more while they were still wearing their old ones. Mrs. Amber would have agreed with Hilary's views on timing if she had heard them, but she had only met him once, and had disliked him. She said that he was not manly, stumbling upon a truth for the wrong reasons in the way that irritated Maurice. Her reason for saying it was that Hilary wrote, which seemed to her an odd profession for a man. Men should, if possible, be in the services; they could be doctors or lawyers or architects, or even clergymen, and it would be interesting, though not very probable, that they should be actors. If they were in business it was a pity, although useful if they made a lot of money. This was Evelyn's most fundamental reason for wanting Maurice to get on and make more money; it would justify her choice in her mother's eyes. Her sister, Daphne, had married a soldier.

Evelyn was thinking about her mother and Daphne, as she put on her hat. She pulled out the close waves of hair, and arranged them carefully on her temples and behind her ears, slipping in tiny hairpins to hold them. Mother was clever to give us such good times ! It wasn't easy in Gillans Cross, where most of the people we knew were so much better off. It wasn't easy to manage tickets for the dances and shows they went to, and to go to all their parties when we couldn't have them back to anything much. It was difficult sometimes scraping up the clothes. Lots of little things were difficult going about with rich people. When you were shopping in London with them, they would suddenly decide to stay up for dinner and a show, and you had to pretend you were meeting someone, or had asked someone to dinner at home and must get back. All the time you were with them you hoped they wouldn't want to take taxis, because, of course, you must pay your share.

Evelyn sighed, remembering a prolonged and exhausting struggle. Her grown-up years in Gillans Cross had been a fight, with Daphne as ally, and her mother in command, a fight to live on equal terms with people who would drop you and forget you if you didn't do everything that they did, who would leave you out for good if you refused a few invitations. It was a queer, strenuous life, going about with a crowd of gay, spoilt young people whom you called your friends, and knowing all the time that your friends were the enemy.

The enemy had not won. There had been no flaw which they could find in the weddings of Evelyn and Daphne.

Daphne's Gervase was in a good regiment; he was tall, brown, blue-eyed; his family had plenty of money. He produced handsome parents, a sister married to a baronet's brother, and a pretty little niece to stumble up the aisle with Daphne's train. Evelyn's Maurice, if not quite so unexceptional, was good-looking. His family had a quality which Evelyn felt, even while she resented their indifference to certain standards of her own. Rhoda made a nice-looking bridesmaid, Delia a very pretty one. It was all as it should be.

She had not had time at her wedding to notice whether the two groups coalesced or not. It was later on that she discovered that her new relations had used their quick eyes and ears, and come to their own conclusions about her friends. They were never rude enough to say so, but she perceived, to her surprise, that they were scornful of Gillans Cross, and thought its standards vulgar. " Edwardians gone to seed," Maurice called them, after a party, during their engagement, which he had not enjoyed. Evelyn thought that absurd. Her friends wore the latest clothes, saw the latest films, had the newest drinks, and went to the newest places. They were nothing if not up to date, she protested. " So were the Edwardians, darling," Maurice said, and began to talk about something else. Evelyn and Daphne had often resented the standards that made life so difficult for them, but they had absorbed them. Evelyn did not like them to be mocked at and disregarded. What right had these people, living up here in a dirty northern town, to think themselves superior to people living in touch with London, people much smarter, more travelled, more worldly wise, more successful? Evelyn had not really been so fond of any of her acquaintances at Gillans Cross as to resent criticism of them, but she knew that Maurice's criticism, anyhow, was a translation from the particular to the general. She said to herself now, with sudden bitterness, it's Mother he doesn't like !

As she knotted a scarf under her chin she found that her fingers were trembling with anger. What right had Maurice to despise Mother ? What right ? Could he have done what she had done if he had been left with two baby girls to bring up on almost nothing ? He had never done anything so difficult in his life ! He thought it was vulgar to have money standards, to think of people in terms of money. If you had much less than you wanted, you damn well had to ! His people were hard up now, but they had had plenty when he was growing up. They hadn't done so well for their children, either. Delia was all right in a way, she had looked after herself, but her Jim wasn't much, and Rhoda was going to be an old maid like Aunt Ellen.

She was ready and she turned to go. She looked round the room for her purse. She had taken it out of her bag to pay the window-cleaners. It was lying on the end of the mantelpiece, next to their wedding photograph. She paused with her hand on it, looking at the photograph. Not too good of her—the light made her hair look darker than it was, and her smile was stiff; she never did take well—but very, very good of Maurice. He looked proud, young, happy and hopeful, a gay bridegroom who had got the girl he wanted.

Her mood swung over and softened to tenderness. There had been something between them, then, that ought not to be spoiled. There was something now, a closeness even when they were apart in feeling. Looking at the young

face of her bridegroom, Evelyn turned to him from her
mother, putting her mother outside the small, innermost
circle of her life that held Maurice and herself—and
Tatty ? She had, just for the moment, forgotten Tatty,
going back in her mind to those early days before she was
thought of. She had not planned for a baby at the very
beginning, nor been in a desperate hurry to have her.
Of course she was pleased when she came along—and
Maurice ! Maurice had behaved as though she were the
only baby ever born ! He was crazy about her ! A feeling
that she could not define nor accept flooded Evelyn for
a moment like black poison, and faded. It was not one of
the things that she could consider, the possibility of being
jealous of your own child.

The telephone bell rang sharply and then stopped, cut
off in the middle. Footsteps came upstairs, and there was
a knock at the door.

" Mr. Powell on the telephone."

Evelyn ran down, and picked up the receiver.

" Hulloa, Maurice ? "

" Hulloa, darling ! I just wanted to tell you that I went
round by home this morning, and Aunt Ellen was there,
so I asked her to come to supper, too, with the others.
I thought I'd better let you know there'll be one extra.
That's all right, isn't it ? "

Maurice's tone was conciliatory, and faintly apologetic,
as it often was nowadays when he was not cross. Evelyn
unconsciously despised anyone who tried to conciliate her.
When anyone gave before her, she pushed harder. Her
voice was cool and indifferent as she replied.

" Of course. I've ordered a meal for them."

" That's all right, then." Maurice, feeling himself

repulsed, hardened as though he had made an apology which had not been accepted, and the balance was now in his favour. His feeling reached her over the wires, and she said more pleasantly.

" I'm just off to town. I'm going to take the bus across to the new house on the way, and look in and see how they are getting on."

She was offering him her interest in his family as a friendly advance, and he accepted it. He said more cordially:

" Having lunch in town ? "

" No, I don't think so. I expect I shall come home."

" Well, I've got a Rotary lunch, so we couldn't have it together."

" No, never mind. I've got to get back in good time. Tatty's party begins quite early."

" What's Tatty doing now ? "

That was not the voice in which he had asked her where she was having lunch, it was a different tone altogether, deeper, with warmth and colour in it. All at once she remembered the first morning after their honeymoon, when she was alone, unpacking glass in their new house, and Maurice had rung up, " What are you doing now, darling ? "

The telephone is a betraying instrument, conveying shades of thought and feeling all too accurately. Evelyn stood for an instant remembering that morning, a glass bowl on the table like a bubble of light, herself in a green overall scrambling up from the floor, the little glow of warmth that spread through her at the sound of Maurice's voice.

She said coldly: " Tatty's in the garden."

She knew that Maurice at the other end of the telephone was smiling.

" I must be off, now, Maurice ! I shall miss my bus ! "

" All right, darling. Good-bye ! "

" Good-bye ! "

Tatty was playing on the lawn in front of the house, where Mary could keep an eye on her as she turned out the dining-room. She saw her mother come out of the front door, and ran to her.

" *Look* how high I can jump, Mother ! *Look !* "

" I see. Well done ! "

" I can jump off the top step with my feet together. Would you like to see me ? "

" I haven't time now, darling. I want to catch the bus."

" The red bus ? "

" No, the blue one. I'm going to see Grannie in her new house, on my way to the town."

" Are you going to have lunch with Daddy ? "

" No, not to-day. I'm going to buy a hat."

She hurried down the path, Tatty skipping on the grass at the side.

" When you die," said Tatty cheerfully, " shall I have all your hats for a hat shop ? "

Callous little brutes children are, thought Evelyn.

" I dare say I shan't die for years and years."

Tatty considered.

" When you do, I shall live here with Daddy, shan't I ? "

" Don't swing on the gates," Evelyn said, in a sharp voice. " You'll break the hinge, where it joins at the side. I've told you before. Run back and play ; and play on the grass in front of the window. Be quick ! You're making me late ! "

She looked down at Tatty, and Tatty looked up at her

without moving. Something flashed between them that was not only the feeling of a mother and a disobedient small child. It was the stuff in Evelyn's mind of an October evening, London shops lighting up, and a green sky above Regent Street. She was going home, but the others were going on to a theatre, and to supper afterwards. The gay plan had flowered out of an unexpected meeting. She stood aside, feeling out of it, but her heart lifted suddenly when Mark said that he would come back with her. It was Olga, looking at him through her eyelashes, who cried, " Oh, Mark ! Stay and be matey ! Evelyn doesn't mind ! " She had said, " Of course not ! You stay, Mark. I wish we hadn't got those stupid people coming ! " Holding her head high and making a cheerful, casual gesture of farewell, she had walked off alone. Mark was in India now, married; and Olga was married too, and had gone to Kenya. So far as her life was concerned, they were no longer vital figures; colour had faded out of them. Only this moment by the garden gate touched and revived that moment when she walked off and left Mark with Olga, the moment when she stood looking in at a jeweller's window, and saw the brilliant display suddenly blurred like lights seen through rain, and heard the taxis hooting behind her in the street.

Time came back again between that moment and this. It was Tatty, her precious little daughter, looking at her with large eyes over the rail of the gate.

" Run along and be good, darling ! I want to get back in time to take you to Bobby's party."

Tatty nodded, climbed down from the gate, and skipped away across the grass. Evelyn saw the big blue bus turning the corner ahead of her, and hurried towards the stop.

CHAPTER XV

M_{AURICE}, in his office, put down the telephone, disappointed. He did not know what of, nor what he had rung up for, but it was not really to tell Evelyn about Aunt Ellen, which he could perfectly well have done when he got back. He sat staring at the calendar on his desk. He would have liked to ring the number again, and say to Evelyn, " You don't love me ! Everything is different now. It was so lovely at first, but everything is spoiled ! You hold me off; you don't want me to come close to you or touch you. I'm just the husband that you have to have for the kind of life you want to lead ! "

He recalled a dozen incidents of the last year, refusals and withdrawals that had humiliated him. He remembered small things, times when he had asked Evelyn to come for a stroll after dinner, and she had turned the wireless on and let him go by himself. He had wanted to spend the evening with her alone on his birthday, and she had asked the Barbours in to bridge. On their summer holiday she had been glad to let him take Tatty on the sands while she went about with her mother. All these details piled up in his mind into one great accusation which he longed to hurl at her, to hurt her, to make her angry and ashamed, to make her different.

But could he make her different ? He could startle her, perhaps, into behaving differently, but the thing that he would really be asking for was something that you couldn't get by asking, something that flowed free and unforced or not at all. There flashed across his mind his mother in the months of his engagement. From inside the circle of enchantment in which he was living, he had been aware of her; she had been able to penetrate to his happiness with her complaints and appeals. " I can't expect Maurice to think of me first, now." " You'll be taking Evelyn out in the car this afternoon, I suppose? I don't get my nice drives now at the week-ends." Those appeals had made Maurice ashamed for his mother; they had hurt his sense of her dignity and embarrassed him, because he could not give her what she was asking for. He could take her for drives in the car, but he could not love her more than Evelyn, and the futility of her wanting it was painful. He saw that he himself would be just as futile if he tackled Evelyn. A relationship is spoiled as soon as you begin to demand more than the other person wants to give.

For one sombre moment Maurice looked this truth in the face. Then he began the usual human game of covering it up. I mustn't let myself get morbid. I daresay I'm exaggerating all sorts of little things. Evelyn's reserved, undemonstrative. She and her family don't say things as freely as we do. Their mother brought them up not to waste their energies, to do everything *ad hoc*. They weren't brought up in a house where people were interested and curious about things for their own sake, or talked nonsense, or went to see their friends just for fun. They were in training, those two, from the time they left school, and years before, probably. I think our casual ways bother Evelyn sometimes. Her mother's an old Tartar; and

Daphne's a tough little nut, not the gay flibbertygibbet she looks. I ought to remember that because Evelyn's different about little things she doesn't necessarily feel different. I expect I've been selfish. After all, it can't be quite the same when you've been married four years, and have children.

Children, thought Maurice, and sat up straighter and smiled. What luck to have the very dearest little girl ! His mind turned happily from the relationship that was complicated and difficult to the relationship that was easy and natural. He remembered that hour in the early morning when he had first seen Tatty, lying on her side in the blue frilled cot which Evelyn had prepared for her son. She was a neat baby with a lot of dark hair. Her two small mottled hands were curled against her mouth as though she were playing a trumpet. Her dark blue eyes were open, grave and considering. She made faint sucking noises. The sight of her released a spring of tenderness in his heart such as he had never known, for she was some-thing that he could love without the smallest fear of rebuff, without those shynesses and difficulties and outside interferences that beset the relationships of grown-up people. There was nothing to worry about in loving Tatty, and in her warm, ungrudging response. It was a revival of his own happy times as a little boy, loving and trusting his father and mother, being given treats by them. Tatty had brought back to him the life that had ended when he first went off to his prep school, small, round, and tearful, at nine years old.

He was still thinking about Tatty when he was told that Mr. Parkinson wanted to see him. Mr. Parkinson, whom his mother called " that nasty common man," was the builder and contractor who had bought their house and land, and proposed to develop it. Maurice liked him, finding him a shrewd bargainer for his own advantage, but reasonable, prompt, and good-tempered in his dealings. He was grateful to Parkinson for taking the white elephant off his hands. The place had been mortgaged some time ago to raise money to tide the business over an awkward corner, and the annual payment would have been an impossible drain on his mother's small income and on his, apart from the fact that she could not afford to live in the house. Parkinson, as Maurice had often pointed out to his mother, was a benefactor to the family. She persisted in regarding him as a vulgar and presumptuous person who was taking away her house and garden from her. This morning, for the first time, Maurice had a twinge of the same feeling. He knew that it was absurd, and suppressed it, rising to greet Mr. Parkinson.

"Well, well," Parkinson said. "They've got a fine day for the move. A tiresome business. Your mother will be glad when it's over. I've just come down about one or two details in the agreement. We'll get it signed to-morrow ! "

He explained his points to Maurice, sitting square and solid in the oak chair which had been bought for the office by Maurice's grandfather. He looked very prosperous, Maurice thought, ruddy and confident in a well-cut suit of good cloth, with a late autumn rosebud in his buttonhole in a silver holder. The small alterations and additions to the lease that he wanted were reasonable and clear. Over one of them, he gave way to Maurice at once. He was too able a man to be fussy about small points.

Maurice's childish feeling of anger faded. He had a reaction towards geniality.

"I'm glad it's all settled," he said. "You'll begin to build at once, I suppose? Are you going to pull the house down straight away?"

"I haven't made up my mind about that yet. We might use it for a club. I'd have turned it into a block of service flats, but I don't think it would be an easy house to convert."

"No. They didn't build with any idea of change. Will you have a cigar?"

"Thank you."

Maurice watched Mr. Parkinson neatly cutting the end of the cigar—thick, ugly fingers, square, competent hands.

"No, they didn't know much in those times about what these times were going to be like! You won't remember your grandfather, I dare say?"

"Oh, yes. Quite well. I was fourteen when he died."

"I remember him coming down once to a sale of work at the church here when I was a lad. He was up on the platform making a speech, and then he came round afterwards to the sweet stall, and bought sticks of chocolate for all of us. Very jolly, he was. I was at the Church school there, and my mother kept a little shop. It's queer how things happen. I never thought I should be buying his house."

"I'm sure he would have liked you to have it," Maurice said. It was quite true, he thought. His grandfather, like his father, sat loose to property, admired character in any walk of life, grudged no man his rise. Their Liberal spirit had clashed with the stubborn Conservative temper of his mother's people. Old grandfather Lister had hated his

son-in-law's easy, democratic ways, grumbled at what he
called his weak-kneed views and fancy notions. His
mother disliked them too. " How can you want to know
them ? They're not ' our sort of people.' " But his father
had gone on wanting to know anybody who was interesting, and had thought himself no more privileged and important than the rest of the human race. There was the
same rift, Maurice thought, between himself and Evelyn.
He was less sociably inclined than his father, but he could
not feel that he and others who had had the same opportunity were set apart, entitled to any more fortune or consideration. Evelyn did feel it. He remembered her saying
about something, " It seems extraordinary when it
happens to our sort of people." In his family, thought
Maurice, they never married wives of the same mind as
themselves ! A swift yearning possessed him for a complete
union, for Rhoda's mind, or his father's, in Evelyn's
beloved body. He jerked himself out of his thoughts with
an effort to listen to Parkinson.

" Yes," Parkinson was saying, " I've made my way !
When I was a lad I've run about barefoot in the streets
behind here. You don't see barefoot children now, for all
these bad times."

" Oh, no. Things are a lot better in some ways."

" They may be, Mr. Powell. I dare say they are, but
people are softer. There wasn't so much given away when
I was young ! I knew damn' well that I'd got to work for
anything I wanted. I knew it when I was a little nipper
still at school. When I was an office-boy first, at Blacketts,
I went to night-school every evening. We'd to wait four
years, my wife and I, to get married. They weren't giving
away houses in those days ! You'd to look after your own

children, and get milk and medicine for 'em. There weren't any babies' welcomes."

" Didn't you feel it was all very unfair ? "

" I never thought owt about it. I hadn't time. I've not much patience with the people that go about whining about a hard world. It is a hard nut to crack, but you can crack it. I've proved that. And I'll tell you another thing, Mr. Powell. It's been the cracking it that I've enjoyed most. I've got a good house and a nice garden and a good car, and my wife and I, we entertain our friends, and my boy's going to Cambridge next year, and the two girls are at a fine school in the south. We've just had a holiday, all of us, in Sweden and Norway. I won't pretend I don't enjoy all that, because I do; but I can tell you this: what I've enjoyed most in my life was working for it. You can put food into a man's mouth and give him a house to live in and doctor his children free and educate them for him, and he thinks he'll be all right, but I think the poor devil might as well be dead ! I'd do anything I could to help cure unemployment; I'm as sorry as anyone for a man that can't get work; but when they talk about the State doing this for everyone, or the State being responsible for that, I say, ' Let the State keep out of it, and give a man a chance to sweat for what he wants, and know what it's like to be really alive ! ' I'll tell you the one thing that troubles me, Mr. Powell: I'm afraid that'll never happen to my son."

No, thought Maurice, my great-grandfather and grandfather, working together, built up this business. They were out and about all day getting orders and over-seeing jobs, and working up a connection; and then they came into the office here about five o'clock to write all their letters by hand and make copies of them, with only a boy, in the early days, to stick them in envelopes. I've never done a day's work like that in my life !

Mr. Parkinson leaned back in his chair, puffing at his cigar. He thought with an affectionate pride of his son who would be going back in a few days to his Public School, of his voice and his casual manners and his small lordlinesses, his friends and his clothes and all that he was learning. It was a fine thing to be able to give him all that, and yet sometimes he wondered. Perhaps the one thing that he couldn't give him was the best thing of all, and that was the fight for it.

" It's all right for you, Mr. Parkinson," Maurice said. " You had much more than the ordinary pluck and ability. What about the average people who started when you started ? They didn't have much chance to get enough of anything."

Parkinson shrugged his shoulders.

" A man's entitled to what he's worth, and that's what he can get for himself."

" Don't you think he's entitled to a fair start ? "

" I didn't 'ave any start, Mr. Powell. I didn't complain, and I didn't ask for any. It's nature's way, isn't it ? When you sow seeds, some come up and some don't; and, of the ones that come up, the strong ones push their way above the others. The weaklings get thinned out. It's the same all through."

" It ought not to be like that ! "

" I don't say it ought to be, Mr. Powell. I say it is. Neither you nor I can alter it. A sensible man makes the best of things."

Mr. Parkinson put the stub of his cigar in the ashtray, and rose.

"Well, I'm not going to keep you any longer. If you want to go over the place at any time, or if there's anything your mother wants later on out of the garden, a plant or anything like that, just do as you like, and let me know if there's any little thing that I can do for you."

I suppose, Maurice thought, that my grandfather must have felt like that. It was his grandfather Lister, his mother's father, of whom he was thinking. He and his widowed mother had been left nearly penniless when he was ten years old. At twenty-five, he was driving his carriage. When Maurice remembered him, he had called his workmen lazy rascals for wanting an eight-hour day, had resented every advance of the trade unions as an unwarrantable impertinence, and had sacked his gardener for arriving late one morning.

It was a queer business ! The whole of life at the bottom was, as Mr. Parkinson saw it, a fight in which the fittest survived. The whole of civilisation was an attempt to alter that, to make life possible for the weak and the unfit, to prevent his grandfather and Mr. Parkinson from encroaching on them too far. Whatever struggles they had, it was all so much easier for his grandfather and Mr. Parkinson, working with nature instead of against it; they were like people swimming with the current, not divided in themselves.

Damn it all, thought Maurice. They're lucky ! I do admire them ! There rose in him for a moment something which had risen in the whole of over-civilised, bewildered, harassed Europe, an admiration for the barbarian. The danger that presses on the baffled is the danger of acting their own fantasies. At the elbow of nearly every baffled man is a fantasy of himself, a creature of rampant and fantastic maleness, mistaking force for strength, and self-assertion for power. Maurice thought, I'm sick of worrying about other people and what things ought to be like ! I don't know why I ever give it a thought. What's the use ? The only sensible thing is to do what Parkinson has done, take everything you can get for yourself, and never give anyone else a thought. That's what I'll do in future ! I'll look out for myself, and shove everyone else out of my way if I can. I'll take hold of Evelyn and shake her ! If I can't make her want me, I'll find someone else that will ! I'm sick of being so half-and-half about everything ! I'll get down to reality !

For a minute or two he glowed with the warmth of this new impulse. Then the blustering adolescent retreated from his mind. Decency was his reality. It was in his blood and in his training to try and be fair. The small Maurice, grabbing the chocolate or the toys, had been told by his father, " No, no, half for Rhoda. You must be fair ! " His father had scolded and interfered so little, had been so blissfully free from that love of interference for its own sake that appeared to the young Maurice to beset grown-up people ! Looking back, it seemed to him that when his father had scolded, or interfered, it had always been something of the same sort. " You've had your innings, old boy. Out you go. Someone else's turn to bat." " I can't take you to-day. It's Rhoda's turn. Must be fair." He had said very little more ; he had not lectured or argued, but he had made Maurice for ever more ashamed of unfairness.

No, it wouldn't do, Maurice decided, for the world to

be run by people like Parkinson. Even going against the current, one must try for fairness. It was silly to call one lot of things nature and the others civilisation, since, after all, civilisation itself was a natural growth. Some natural thing in humanity had driven it to struggle towards fairness. God and the devil was more like it, Maurice thought, oh, much more like it ! Sometimes you felt that only religious people, however deluded they might be, really understood mankind and the universe.

If Evelyn doesn't want me, he reflected, I can't force her. And I know I don't really want anyone else. I wish I thought it was only that she wants to be careful about the baby. She's so dead against the idea of contraceptives. But it isn't that, really, it's me she doesn't want. No use thinking about it now ! I must look into those costs again ! Perhaps I'd better go and see Rushworth directly after lunch. I ought to get round some of those architects in Bardon Buildings. I haven't been for a long time, but Rushworth's secretary said he'd be going home early, and I don't want to miss him. We want that Haveford job badly ; it's a nice piece of work, and they'll have some more coming along. I'd better send for the file.

Maurice picked up the telephone and forced himself back to the morning's work.

CHAPTER XVI

THE NEW HOUSE was not really new, a great relief to
Rhoda, who had been depressed by the inspection of a
series of bright, ornamental villas. It had once been the
lodge of a big house, built just outside the town on the
other side of it from Stone Hall. The owner of the house
had added to the lodge to make it into a small house for
a widowed sister who came back to live there. He had
built on a good-sized sitting-room, a tiny hall, a new front
door, and had added two bedrooms and a bathroom
above. The result was without symmetry, and conformed
to no known rules of architecture, but had a certain
individuality, and, inside, could easily be made charming. It had half an acre of garden enclosed by a wooden
fence. On three sides the view over the fence was of grass
and trees, for the big house had become a convalescent
home, and the field in front of the garden was left untouched for air and space. It was the fourth side that had
made it difficult to persuade Mrs. Powell into the house,
which, as the harassed Maurice explained to her daily,
was better and cheaper than anything she was likely to
get. The fourth wall of the house flanked the pavement,
and across the road a raw, new housing estate covered
what had lately been farm land.

Delia drove through this carefully, slowing down, every
few yards, for small children with toy cars. Rhoda looked

out and saw a traveller with a suitcase full of samples
coming away from the door of a house, walking down
the short garden path and opening the gate. He was a
grey-haired man who looked dejected and tired. He
walked up the next path and rang the bell. The woman
who opened the door to him had a mob cap over her
hair and a rubber apron covering her dress. She said
something and the door slammed smartly. Annoying for
her to have to go to the door every five minutes to somebody who was selling something, but sickening for them,
up and down those little paths, clicking those neat gates,
so seldom ever getting a hearing !

"We shall see their washing from our windows ! "
Mrs. Powell said mournfully.

Good Lord, thought Delia, what a generation they were
to expect to live so separate ! So long as they were all
right, they didn't give a damn ! There were two worlds:
one for them, comfortable and easy and well mannered,
and one for everyone else, where they could do what they
liked so long as they didn't come out. It was like having
a tidy room and shoving all the mess into the cupboard.
Well, there was a removal going on all over England that
was turning out that cupboard, and a good job too, even
if it spoilt the tidy room. Get the dirt out ! Say the things
that hadn't been said, hear the people who hadn't been
heard, look at the things that had been shoved out of the
way, spread what was in the cupboard all over the room,
and sort the mess somehow ! That was the job for her
and Jim and her generation.

And Rhoda ? Rhoda was leaning forward from the
back of the car, saying gently:

"You won't notice it, Mother, and it will only be

Mondays, probably. Besides, we shall want to hang ours out, and it's only fair ! "

That was waste of Rhoda, who ought to be a part of the new vigorous world, not soothing the old one. You loved her for being gentle, but were afraid, knowing that it takes a certain amount of ruthlessness to live.

Mrs. Powell sat still in the car while Rhoda and Delia carried her small possessions into the house. She was in no hurry to get out. She huddled her knees under the rug, feeling old. What was there to look forward to ? Tom gone, who had always loved her and been patient with her; Maurice, her son, had gone to a home of his own; Delia was going. If it wasn't for Rhoda, thought Mrs. Powell, I might as well be dead. She is the only one who needs me, all I have to live for. The thought of living for Rhoda encouraged her, but she looked out of the window at the new house and hastily withdrew her head. Horrid little place ! Not nearly as good a house as Evelyn's. She could not bear to think that Evelyn was now the wife of the head of the family, thrusting her out of the position that had been hers for so many years. That rather badly brought up girl with the dreadful mother ! To be pushed out of the centre of the family picture by that girl was nearly as bad as being driven out of her house by circumstances. Natalie Powell trembled with indignation, a childish rage against forces too strong for her. She had had her own way so much and so long, she felt surprise and mutiny in her very bones. Like a child, she looked round for something to kick or smash. Rhoda, coming back to the car, saw her face, and her own heart sank. It was absurd to mind when her mother was cross, to feel her nerves quiver away from the impact of her displeasure.

" I thought you'd forgotten me," Mrs. Powell said. " You've been such a long time ! It's cold waiting here in the car, and those children are staring at me ! "

Why can't I just laugh and say, " Don't be silly, of course we hadn't forgotten you ! " and not worry any more ? Relationships are so easy when carefulness doesn't get into them ! It's like walking on a slippery road : so long as you don't think, you're all right. When you think, you stiffen, and rhythm is broken. How badly we're beginning, coming into the new house like this !

" It all looks so nice and clean, Mother. Come in and see it. They've got the carpet down in your bedroom; it fits very well."

" I don't know how we shall ever get the furniture in."

Rhoda was not sure about that either, the heavy, handsome bedroom furniture was an encumbrance that her mother would not be persuaded to part from.

" Never mind ! " Rhoda began, and stopped herself. Delia had said, laughing, that morning that half Aunt Ellen's sentences still began with " Never mind ! " She heard in her own voice the shallow, bright tone that she had heard so often in her grandmother's drawing-room when Aunt Ellen poked the fire, or picked up a dropped stitch, or closed the window. Something like panic seized Rhoda, so that she felt trapped in the tiny hall among their bags and bundles. She murmured something and ran upstairs, leaving her mother to Delia.

Her own bedroom was empty and peaceful, already a refuge. She looked round it, catching the newness that was like the bloom on a grape, so quickly brushed off. It

was the newness of the seaside when you went out after
tea the first evening; the newness of your bedroom in a
friend's house, on a first visit, when you were shown into
it, your bag there, just brought up, and the jug of hot
water covered with a towel; the newness of your first
foreign journey, walking from the boat to the train
through strange voices, thinking, I'm in France ! It was
precious because it went so soon. Other things succeeded,
but never that peculiar enchantment. This fragile bloom
was on the whole house, the rooms they had not slept
nor eaten in, the garden where they had picked nothing,
and the tangle of neglected flowers not of their growing.

My yellow room is like Ursula's, Rhoda thought. The
walls, that had seemed to be closing her in, retreated, as
though Ursula had made a breach in them. She would
never be altogether cut off while Ursula was her friend.
There were some people so much alive that life reached
you through them. As though she were drawing close to
a fire for warmth, she drew closer to the buttercup-yellow
room in the Hampstead flat; to the dear, casual household, and Ursula welcoming her at the door, always so
glad to see her; to the free air of the young household,
and the liberation of their unhampered talk, yes, and
even more, of unhampered feeling. They were so soundly
in love with one another, Ursula and Giles, that you felt
a secret, vital current in their house, so that everything
flowed the right way. Lucky babies, lucky Prudence and
David absorbing that essential rhythm, not growing up in
a house where feeling, turned back upon itself, went
widdershins ! Delia would have children like Prudence
and David, sturdy little things growing up unafraid. Or
perhaps she wouldn't, for two and two never made four

with human beings, some incalculable element always made it three or five. That moment, turning to Ursula, recalling her life outside her home, had restored Rhoda's courage. She heard her mother and Delia on the stairs, and went out to meet them.

CHAPTER XVII

AUNT ELLEN AND IVY came on the same bus, and arrived at the new house together, talking agreeably about Ivy's boy and his mother, and a party that they were going to have for Ivy's birthday. Aunt Ellen was very much interested. She rarely wanted to talk about her own affairs. Having very few to talk about, she had developed early in life a capacity for being interested in other people's. She's a nice one is Miss Lister, thought Ivy. Moved to confidence, she told Miss Lister how glad she was that Annie was going. Annie was always on at her about this and that, and wouldn't believe she could do anything, but she could, by shots ! " I've seen you can," Aunt Ellen said gently. That anyone should want to talk to her was something that she requited with an eager sympathy. And Annie, Ivy went on, was always wanting her to wear her clothes different; said you couldn't go out on Sunday in a beret, and didn't like her earrings that she won at the fair, but you was only young once, wasn't you ? Yes, said Aunt Ellen, who had hardly even been that. But she did not, like Annie, want to suppress the exuberant youth in this round-faced creature. She felt a tender pleasure in it. She did not even blink when Ivy told her that, as soon as they got the tandem bicycle, she was going to have a pair of shorts. They arrived at the new house on very good terms with one another. Ivy threw herself on the cat basket in the hall, and bore it off to the kitchen with cries of pity and welcome.

Aunt Ellen stood in the tiny hall. She could hear them moving about upstairs, the voices of Rhoda and Delia calling to each other and to their mother through the empty rooms. I wish, she thought, that this was my little house! Such a wish had not stirred in her for many years, not since that summer long ago when she had a tussore coat and skirt, and a straw hat trimmed with violets, and played croquet in them with Bernard.

Ellen was looking at a smooth green lawn, and at the bent head and shoulders of a young man in a clerical coat who had just put his ball into position, and was aiming at a hoop. Her lips curved tenderly. It touched her that Bernard, who was so good, so serious and clever, should play croquet with such solemn purpose, even kneeling down to remove a small dandelion that might obstruct his shot. It delighted and astonished her to find that he wanted to play with her, and did not mind her uncertain judgment, and her fatal habit of sticking at the third hoop. That summer, people told Ellen that she was looking well, and that the violet hat suited her. They went to the sea, and she had a cambric dress with a rose-red belt, and a rose-coloured parasol. Bernard came over for the day, on an excursion train. It was a hot, bright day, very still, the sea hardly moving. Somehow she and he left the others behind, and found themselves walking along the beach alone, away from the bathing-huts and the chairs. They sat on a rock, and looked at the sea anemones in a pool, and talked in short, breathless sentences. They came back late for tea, at which Nan was cross and complained of a headache, but for once Ellen had no sympathy for her. She felt as though all her mind and body had melted into a haze of swimming gold.

It was very soon after they came back from the sea that Nan announced her engagement to Tom, making up her mind in the end suddenly, and flinging the news at them on their first Sunday evening at home with a kind of excited defiance. Ellen's affairs had to fall into the background. The house hummed with the preparations for Natalie's wedding. Her trousseau, her wedding dress, her house, absorbed Ellen's attention. She withdrew a little from Bernard, and there was no time for croquet. Besides, the summer was over. Ellen had hardly finished packing up the wedding presents before her mother was taken ill with typhoid. She nearly died, and, after her slow recovery the terrified Ellen told Bernard that she could not leave her.

Back came that wet April afternoon, the two of them in mackintoshes walking along the road by the gravel pit, the cold rain sluicing down upon them, and on the green buds just breaking into " bread and cheese."

" I can't," Ellen kept on saying. " I can't leave Mother. It would be wrong ! "

Bernard protested gently.

" I wouldn't ask you to do anything wrong."

His young, fresh-coloured face above the turned up collar of his coat was puzzled and distressed, but Ellen would not look at it. She would only plod by his side, repeating :

" I can't do it. You know she nearly died."

" But she's quite well again, now," he pleaded. " I wouldn't have bothered you until she was. I didn't ask you before, on purpose. I've waited a long time. But she

really is better, and, of course, if she was ill again, you
could always come back to her."

Something had happened to Ellen when her mother
nearly died. The world had cracked, and she must sit on
the crack for ever for fear that it should open and let her
through. She shook her head and looked straight in front
of her, trying not to cry.

" You can't really love me ! "

" I do. Oh, Bernard, I do ! " The tears ran down her
cheeks, mixed with the cold raindrops.

" You can't ! If you did, you'd marry me and leave
your mother. It can't be that really. What is it, Nellie ?
Are you frightened ? Don't you trust me ? "

" Yes. Oh, yes ! "

Of course she trusted him : he was so good, and so kind !
She was so fond of him. Why couldn't he understand ? He
put his hand in the crook of her wet elbow.

" Well then, Nellie, dearest . . ."

He was smiling down at her, drawing her towards him.
She pushed him away, and said stubbornly : " I can't.
It would be wrong ! "

The exasperated young man dropped her elbow and
called her a prig, which seemed to her dreadful from a
clergyman. He went away to a London parish, and later
they heard about his wedding to a nice girl, the daughter
of a schoolmaster, pretty and very musical. Ellen cried
secretly in her bedroom, but was sure that she had done
right. It was all over years ago, and she had never
questioned her own decision. Only this morning, as she
stood just inside the front door, smelling the smell of
new paint, watching the light strike across the clean wall,
an old wish came back to her for a little house of her own

to arrange as she liked. She had lived most of her life in her mother's house, and later at Lyndoch, in what Miss Russell called her Private Residential Hotel. Miss Russell was very kind; the cooking was good, the chairs comfortable, and often you had pleasant company.

If it was the other sort, well, you couldn't expect everything in this world to be just as you liked it.

Aunt Ellen was practised in resignation. She had been brought up to think it a virtue not to expect much. The virtue had been instilled into her by parents who had not envisaged the inevitable result, that she wouldn't get much; or, if they had, they had perhaps concluded that for their daughter virtue should be its own reward. It never occurred to Ellen, recalling those god-like parents out of the past, that they themselves had pursued and enjoyed a lot of other rewards besides virtue. She had accepted their serene conviction that they were always right, just as she had accepted their view that it was a pity when " the lower classes " became discontented or tried to do or have things " above their station." Ellen's father and mother had laid great stress on the duty of being satisfied, one which they were well able to perform themselves, and which suited them in their children, dependants, and employees. I'm sure, Ellen thought, I ought to be very thankful. Such a happy home with Mamma for so many years !

A door banged above, and startled her back into the moment. She reproached herself vigorously. Good gracious, here am I dreaming and wasting time, when there's such a lot to do ! What am I thinking of ? She let go of her own life. She had always let go of it easily. She ran upstairs into the bedroom on the first floor where Nan and the girls stood looking out of the window. Sunlight spilled over them; the fresh, empty room was cheerful.

"Well!" Aunt Ellen said briskly. "Here we are! Ivy and I got here in the bus in no time! Nan, dear, I'm delighted with the house now it's all ready! I think it's going to be charming!"

CHAPTER XVIII

THE BIG VAN rolled up and stopped opposite to the back door of the house. A woman wheeling a perambulator on the other side of the road paused to have a good look. A few small children collected on the pavement. Even so much publicity was distressing to Natalie Powell. As she saw her bedroom furniture carried in, she felt as though she herself were being exposed in the street to curious eyes. She went upstairs to her own room, and looked out of the window, across the little garden, to the grass and trees of what had once been the Burtons' private park. The trees shut off the house, and she could see no building from her window except a glimpse of red brick mellowed by sun, a corner of the high wall round the walled garden.

I wonder what sort of state that garden is in now, she thought. Lucy Burton had been a friend of hers, a long time ago before they all married, and Lucy went away south with her husband, and old Mr. Burton died, and the house was sold. Natalie remembered going to tea there one afternoon in the summer, walking round with Lucy afterwards to the walled garden. It was like opening a door and walking into a bath of sun and sweetness. She put her hand on the wall between the leaves of the espalier pear, behind the ripening fruit, and the red brick was warm with an almost living warmth, as though it had not only

been steeped in the day's sunshine, but had soaked in the
sun of many summers. She and Lucy had walked between
the low, trimly-cut box hedges that divided the flower
borders, and Lucy had picked her a great armful of
lavender. She remembered the scent of it shaken in the
air, and the silvery stalks and mauve spiked heads against
Lucy's blue dress. They had talked about next winter's
dances, and about Lucy's brother's wedding. It had been
one of those afternoons when she had been very happy and
nothing much had happened. To think of the walled
garden, perhaps neglected or used only to grow vegetables
for the Convalescent Home, appalled her. The things
of her old world seemed like a row of sand castles beset by
an incoming tide of the ugly and utilitarian. She admitted
rebelliously and honestly in her own heart that she was
sorry when beautiful things were turned into useful ones.
She felt outraged that anything which had been a part of
her own life should become public property. I suppose
I'm very selfish, she thought ruefully, but the feeling
persisted against conscience and reason.

Rhoda and Delia stood outside the door as the men
carried in the furniture, saying: " The green bedroom,
that one; the yellow room; the maid's room." Familiar
pieces of furniture looked strange and disconcerted as
they were lifted down from the van and carried over the
threshold.

" It's like watching the sack of a city the other way
round," Delia remarked.

" You'll be moving into your own flat soon. How will
you like housekeeping, Dell ? "

" I think I shall love it. I do like that sort of thing."

" I don't really, very much. I make myself do it."

" Wouldn't you like it if you were on your own, and doing things your own way ? It's so difficult to work with the last generation. That goes in the bathroom, doesn't it ? "

" Don't you suppose they felt the same about the one before them ? "

" The crack's wider this time than ever before."

" How can you tell ? They're all wide when you're near them."

" There is such a change, though. There's no goodness now for its own sake. Goodness has become what's useful."

" Nothing more than expediency ? "

" Well, why is there need for any more ? Expediency's a bad word; it's got to have rather a low meaning. But surely, when you get down to it, being good is only being sensible, and anything more than that is a private hobby ? Is all that furniture really going in Mother's bedroom ? "

" I hope so. We've measured it, and it really does go in on the plan. I don't think she'll have much room in the middle of it."

" There you are ! Furniture goes with ways of living ! They cluttered up their rooms and their lives with things that weren't any use."

" Dell, you're too cocksure ! How can you tell what's any use to anyone else ? Don't you see there are other kinds of use besides the actual ones ? Mother wants the things because she's always had them, they're part of her life with Daddy, and she loves them. That sort of need may be just as urgent as the need for a washstand to wash in. Don't be too hygienic for other people ! "

Delia laughed. " I expect you're right. You're much

more patient with people than I am. Is that the old nursery high chair ? "

" Yes. We used to put Tatty in it when she came to lunch, and Mother wanted to bring it, ready for when they have another one."

" Lunch ! " murmured Delia. " I'm awfully hungry. I feel as though we'd had breakfast before the flood. There's no proper time in a day like this, is there ? It's just a sort of interlude, quite elastic. I wish I'd thought of bringing some chocolate."

" I believe Aunt Ellen's unpacking the picnic-basket. Would you like to go and see ! Oh, here's somebody coming ! "

" It's Evelyn."

" Damn ! "

Evelyn came towards them, stepping lightly, between furniture and packing, on her long slim legs. Her cheeks were flushed from hurrying and from the fresh air. Beneath her dark blue straw hat her silvery pale hair caught the light. Pretty ! thought Rhoda unwillingly, with a reluctant pleasure which she pushed away from her. It was somehow necessary for her to dislike Evelyn, it was a defence against a surrender of which she was afraid; and yet it was an unnatural thing, foisted upon her natural geniality. She had lapses into cordiality that were not insincere. What you see is so seldom the other person. It is a character in your own novel, in the story of your life that you have foisted upon them, made of the things in your own mind. It is a novelist's character that you have made out of the person, stressing the outlines, omitting inconsistencies, giving coherence, adding emphasis. Rhoda thought that Evelyn was a hard girl, with no ideas beyond food, clothes, and possessions, who had grabbed at Maurice because she wanted a husband. Waiting in the church porch with the cool striking through the thin stuff of her bridesmaid's frock, walking between the shining rows of presents, she had thought this unhappily, and it was true like a caricature in outline, but just as untrue. For the injustice that it did Evelyn, Rhoda was sometimes sorry.

" It was nice of you to come. We're really getting on very well," she said.

" How's Jim, Dell ? " Evelyn asked.

Evelyn, who knew where she was with Rhoda—poor Rhoda, nice but dull—did not quite know where she was with Delia. Delia was very pretty, and she admired good looks, but Delia worked at strange, unfeminine jobs, and Evelyn distrusted women who did things like that. She and Daphne had cooked and washed, scraped and contrived, but had never seriously considered getting a job. Gillans Cross, with its cocktail parties and scarlet finger-nails, its week-end flights to Cologne and Le Touquet, had been very Victorian. Evelyn, whose own mind walked firmly down turnpike roads, smelled and distrusted the free range of Delia's mind. She thought that anyone so pretty might have done better than the undistinguished Jim, and a hole-and-corner wedding; and yet she would have been glad to talk to Delia about the wedding and the flat, she was interested in anybody's engagement, or wedding, especially in the arrangements, the buying and spending.

" Tell me all about the flat," she said. " I should like to see it ! Maurice has to go up to Town in October, and I'm hoping to go up with him, and spend a week with Mother. I must come and see it."

" The people don't get out till the end of October, but that doesn't matter, we can go round any time."

" What would you like from Maurice and me ? "

" Oh, would you give us some things for the lab ? We want a lot ! "

" Things for the lab ? "

" We're going to have a lab in the basement, where Jim can go on experimenting in his spare time. And he's going to work on specimens for Miles—Dr. Crowe, you know, his great friend ; in practice just near. Some day they're going to have the ideal combination, a G.P., a psycho-analyst, and a bacteriologist working together, all in one house. The patient comes to the G.P. first, you see, and gets sent on to whichever he needs, perhaps both. The psycho-analyst is training now, a friend of theirs who's been in general practice in Liverpool."

" Jim isn't going to leave his job at the hospital, is he ? "

" Oh, no, not yet. Not till we get the whole thing worked up. But it's what they've all three wanted since they were students."

Evelyn shook her head.

" I don't know about these things ! I think I'd rather give you a tea-set ! "

She turned to Rhoda.

" I mustn't stop. I've got to dash into town and get back again to take Tatty to her party. Is Grannie up-stairs ? Can I just go in and say ' good morning ' to her ? "

" Yes, do. Come in and look round.'

" Dell's full of schemes," Evelyn said, as they went upstairs. There was a faint note of resentment in her voice. She had thought about her furniture and clothes throughout the twelve months of her engagement. She did not like anyone to be different from herself, especially any of Maurice's family. It disturbed and annoyed her when they mocked an accepted view or inquired into a convention. Safety and success, as Evelyn had known them, lay in being exactly like other people.

" She makes an awfully good job of life."

Evelyn could not see that it was such a good job as all that. Jim was quite poor, not particularly good-looking, and had queer ideas. It was going to be a small wedding —no white for the bride, and Jim hadn't even got a top hat; and Delia was only going to have a woman in part of the day. As soon as they had a baby, she would be hopelessly tied. Nobody in Gillans Cross would have thought anything of such prospects. What really pricked Evelyn was the consciousness that Delia would not have cared twopence for the opinion of Gillans Cross. Reaction from this knowledge made her very friendly to Rhoda.

" I do hope you're going to like it here, Roddy. It's a dear little house. Let me see your room now it's finished. That yellow's nice, isn't it; it holds all the light. You'll be very comfortable in here, I should think."

She meant to be kind, but to Rhoda it sounded like the tone of someone finding a good place to put that piece of china or those pictures that had been hanging about rather in the way, and now we can put them in the cupboard and they'll be all right, we needn't bother about them any more.

Rhoda said suddenly : " Well, I may not be here much. I'm thinking of going to London and taking on Delia's job at the lab, when she leaves to get married."

" You are ! " Evelyn looked at her in astonishment.

" I've been thinking about it."

" But, what about Grannie ? "

Rhoda was silent. She thought, you left your mother, and nobody exclaimed, everybody petted and praised you.

" You couldn't leave her to live alone, could you ? "

Why should she matter more than I do ? Why do I think these things and not say them to Evelyn ? Because I never disagree with her; it would be letting her come too near me.

" It's only an idea, Evelyn. I don't suppose I shall really go. Delia suggested it, and I was just wondering what it would be like. Don't say anything about it."

" All right, my dear."

Evelyn went over to the window and stood looking out at the strip of garden. Fancy Rhoda even thinking of it ! Of course she couldn't go. She couldn't leave her mother to live alone now, and what would people think if she did ? It would look most unkind ! And she wouldn't really like the sort of jobs that Delia did, and living on her own in London, after being at home all this time. She wasn't that sort of person. For Evelyn she was hardly any kind of person. She was someone who had failed to pass the crucial test and could be counted out. All the same, Evelyn was sorry for her, wondered if she was dull and bored and felt out of things. She said quickly :

" I'm going to have one or two people to play bridge in the afternoon on Friday week. Could you come ? I'd love to have you."

" You know what my bridge is like. Wouldn't you rather I came some other time ? "

" No, I wouldn't. I want you at my party very much."

There are days when a small kindness, even from someone you dislike, can sting almost to tears. It is disconcerting that people will not be all of one piece, that hard
people will suddenly be tender and gentle people hurt
you. It breaks into that novelist's tale that you are making
of your own life and theirs, and makes you ashamed.

" Thanks awfully, Evelyn. I'd love to come."

" Is that Evelyn ? " said Mrs. Powell's voice in the
passage. " I didn't know you were here, dear ! How kind
of you to come ! How nice you look in that hat ! "

Childish and absurd, thought Rhoda, to feel a stab of
jealousy because her mother never said things like that to
her, but said, when she was ready dressed to go out,
" You want a new hat, don't you ? " or, " I don't know
how it is that you never seem to have the right things,
like other people." How often she had been feeling nice-
looking and a word like that had put the sparkle out and
made her a plain, quiet girl. Her mother never tried to
impose her will on Evelyn. Perhaps she did not fight when
she knew she would be beaten. Evelyn was tougher. For
a moment Rhoda saw her mother differently. She looked
at the two of them, standing together, smiling and talking
in the doorway of her room. Her mother was a little,
pretty, elderly lady whose face was lifted by animation
out of its peevish lines, not formidable. We make people
formidable to ourselves, it is part of that novelist's tale.
We make them into policemen and park-keepers for fear
we should pick pockets or walk on the grass. If only I
could keep on seeing Mother as I do now, a little, pretty,
elderly lady, not formidable !

Rhoda was a little girl again, and had been naughty.
She had run amuck in her mother's bedroom for no reason

that she could remember. She had twitched the counterpane off the big bed, and thrown her mother's brushes out of the window and scattered her powder all over the floor. She had been smacked and put in the corner. Her face was very near the wallpaper; she put out her tongue and licked the pink petal of a wild rose that peeped round a brown trellis. She licked the blue ribbon that tied its stalk. There were two little wet patches making the colours darker, but the taste, dull and powdery, added to her misery. She was alone in the room, and she said aloud: "I hate Mother." Her heart thumped, and she waited for God to punish her. God did nothing at all, and the dark patch dried. Just for one second she nearly laughed; she was nearly safe in a world where everything was much less alarming. Then she heard her father's step outside; he knocked and put his head in. Shame at being found in the corner drowned the glimpse of a new freedom. She cried, damping the wallpaper with her tears. Her father went downstairs to intercede for her, and the evening ended in forgiveness and a feeling of new-washed virtue like the morning after a rainy night.

Her mother and Evelyn were saying good-bye. They did not really like one another very much, but they were friendly and smiling, talking about Tatty. A small child in a family was an island where belligerent powers could meet.

"I shall see you all to-night," Evelyn said, and walked away to her bus, conscious of duty done.

"It was nice of her to come," Mrs. Powell remarked. She added, with more conviction in her voice: "I always wonder how she manages to leave her house and go out so much in the mornings."

"Her house is always all right, Mother, whenever you go there. I think she does everything that's necessary first."

"I suppose so." Doing what was necessary seemed to Mrs. Powell to be less than right. A house to her had always been something to fuss over and slave for, a thing which should be encouraged to demand sacrifices, and, by so doing, increase your sense of virtue.

"Well, what's the sense of doing any more?" They had argued about this so often, and it was no use, no use at all, Rhoda knew. You could not argue with someone who was so entirely conscious of being right that she ruled out reason. It would be the same in the new house as it had been in the old. You changed nothing by changing places. She would want to go for a long walk, and her mother would want the curtains taken down and washed that afternoon. Either she would go out and feel guilty, or she would wash the curtains and feel rebellious. The new house was a trap like the old one, and she was caught in it. She exclaimed suddenly and childishly:

"I hate houses!"

All at once she felt near tears.

Her mother looked at her, and said gently:

"You've had such a lot of bother with them lately, and you're tired. I hate houses too, sometimes! Come along and have some lunch. Aunt Ellen's got a lovely picnic lunch all ready in the sitting-room. Call Dell, will you? The men have finished unloading that van. They're having some tea before they go back."

She slipped her hand through Rhoda's arm.

"Cheer up, little girl! It won't be so bad when all this is over and we settle down here together. I'll make it nice for you."

Sometimes you were ashamed, suddenly seeing yourself the difficult one. Rhoda kissed her mother's cheek, and ran downstairs to call Delia. In the sitting-room Aunt Ellen was spreading paper napkins on packing-cases of books, and putting sandwiches and hard-boiled eggs on cardboard plates. She was flushed with the happiness of being useful, of being able to offer kindness instead of to receive it. It was a pleasure to have things to do. As soon as she had time she would ask Nan if she might use the telephone, and would ring up Miss Russell and say that she would not be back for supper. She felt necessary, wanted, and a little proud that Miss Russell should know it. There were so many evenings when she sat in the lounge drawing-room with her sewing and saw other people go out, or have friends in. Sometimes she was all alone, and Miss Russell put her head in to look at the fire, and said: " All alone, Miss Lister ? Well, now ! Would you like the evening paper ? " Aunt Ellen would be glad to tell her that she would be back late. She would enjoy being driven back in the car by Maurice, the little fuss of arriving, calling good night to him from the doorstep, seeing the lights sweep round over the trees in the garden as Miss Russell opened the door. It would be dreadful, Aunt Ellen thought, to be alone in the world and to have no relations ! It would be dreadful to be like that old Miss Garden, whose only brother lived at Torquay, so that she only saw him once a year. She was very lucky to live so near her family ! Taught to be thankful for what she had, Aunt Ellen congratulated herself on her good fortune as she set out the lunch, arranging sandwiches neatly, and opening a tin of chocolate biscuits.

CHAPTER XIX

As soon as she had finished her lunch, Rhoda slipped
out into the garden. It had been neglected during the last
eighteen months while the house had been empty. There
were plenty of roses and sturdy, herbaceous plants in the
long bed that ran down the side by the fence, but the
roses, unpruned for two summers, had thrown out a
shower of smallish blooms, and sprouted here and there
into briars. Nasturtiums had sown themselves all over,
covering carnations, pansies, and the edge of the grass
with their green umbrellas, and with a generous profusion
of gold and tangerine trumpets. Insidious strands of convolvulus wound their green coils up the stout stalks of the
hollyhocks. The garden, Rhoda reflected, would take a
lot of cleaning, but there was plenty of stuff in it. It was
easier to feel at home here. No place out of doors was
ever so strange as the inside of a strange house. Going
out to tea as a little girl, she had felt shy as soon as she
crossed the threshold, subdued by unfamiliar rooms and
furniture, but it had been all right in the garden.

She strolled down to the far end, where a row of
currant bushes hid her from the house. A broken stone
vase had rolled on its side, and provided a convenient
seat. She sat down and lit a cigarette. It was an exquisite
relief to be alone for a few minutes, to know that it did not
matter, because her mother had Delia and Aunt Ellen,

and wouldn't be feeling deserted or wanting something done for her. In a few minutes she must go in and help to unpack the bedding and make up the beds. Another van would arrive, and unload furniture and possessions into a house that already seemed full; books and china, knives and plates would all have to have places found for them. For the moment Rhoda was aware of a more urgent need than any practical demand on her. She tilted her head, and watched the thread of smoke go up between the leaves of the chestnut-tree that stretched its boughs over the fence.

To-day, she thought, is like a crack in my life. Things are coming up through the crack, and, if I don't look at them, perhaps I shall never see them again. Ordinary life in the new house will begin to-morrow and grow over the crack and seal it up.

Queer that when the present cracks it is not so much that the past is behind you as that it is all there inside you, part of you. It's odd to think what each one of us carries about: that man driving the van this morning, the one with the grizzled moustache and bright eyes, who was whistling " Jockey to the Fair," carrying with him his little boyhood, and school, and his father and mother and brothers and sisters; and his first going to work and growing up; the war; and getting married, having children— all that in the outside shape of one man sitting on the driving-seat of the van. We're like snails, really. We do carry our house on our backs wherever we remove to. It's all there with us, packed in layers of pleasure and pain. How much of what we do is trying to repeat the pleasure and avoid the pain ? The sharpest pain I've known, that day when Maurice had a letter from Barry telling him that he was engaged, telling him about Phœbe. I had seen the writing on the envelope, and knew there was a letter for Maurice from Barry. It was there on the table when we came in from Christmas shopping. I thought that he might have written to ask if he could come for Christmas. All the evening I was wrapping up parcels in the hall; it was frosty and the fire wasn't lit, but I didn't feel cold. Maurice came in and stood by the hall table, reading the letter; he exclaimed and looked up, smiling, and suddenly I knew what he was going to say. This had happened before ; all my life I had been afraid of it; it was a moment waiting for me. When the world began to go on again like something just able to move, we were sitting at dinner. I was putting food into my mouth, but it didn't taste at all. I told them who I had met in the shops, and we talked about Barry's wedding: it would be in London, where the girl lived, and, of course, we should all go up for it; we wondered what she was like, and laughed because Barry's letter had said the things they do say, she was lovely and marvellous. I knew that Daddy knew, but I daren't look at him. If anyone had been kind to me I couldn't have managed.

After that I suppose what I wanted most was to be safe. It was safe to stay at home and be a good daughter, to be unselfish. When you give up your life to other people you think you do it for their sake. I'm beginning to wonder whether you don't often do it to reduce your own risks. When you are like Aunt Ellen, old and alone with nothing to do, and no one needing you, people despise you or pity you, kindly, perhaps, but they do. I've always thought less of them for doing it, but perhaps there's something right at the bottom of it. When the small children at Tatty's dancing class cry and won't try to dance, their mothers are ashamed of them. You must join in or not count.

She leaned her head back against the trunk, and stared up at the tower of green leaves above her. When you really look at it, everything has hard edges, inexorable. Life says, Take it or leave it. Delia knew that in time; she takes it. I didn't know; I waited for it to be given to me. I can remember that party now when I wouldn't go and dip in the bran-tub. A little boy in a sailor suit came running to fetch me, and I got behind mother and cried. They brought me my present, wrapped up, with the bran still in the crinkles of the paper, but they shouldn't have done that, even at a party. It doesn't happen! I can't stand Evelyn's mother—every time I see her, I admire my own parents more for their delicacy and integrity—but she did teach her children to go for what they wanted and get it; and Evelyn does. The children of this world being wiser in their generation than the children of light. I shall be sorry if Tatty grows up like Evelyn, not even seeing that there is anything except what she wants herself; but I shall be afraid for her if she grows up like Aunt Ellen, always giving up her own way. I hope she'll manage fifty-fifty!

Delia came running down the garden path.

"Roddy! Where are you? There's another van arriving. Have you been having a few minutes' peace?"

"Yes, I've been thinking."

"About going to London?"

"No, not exactly." Like a wave, feeling deeper than thought rose against Delia's suggestion. "I can't go, Dell."

"You could really, if you want to."

" Well, perhaps I don't want to. Oh, Dell, leave me alone ! "

" All right."

Rhoda went into the house. Delia stood for a moment on the small square of grass.

The difficulties that people make for themselves, compelled by the pressure in their own minds ! She was in the drawing-room of Sally's house, just back from the theatre, eating sandwiches. Sally lay in the big chair with her fur coat thrown over the back; she and Hilary were talking. Delia listened while the two of them discussed the play they had all been to; Sally and Hilary like two fine sharp knives dissecting a body. She herself was very hungry, eating a lot of sandwiches, drinking lager, thinking that Hilary would have been a good husband for Sally. She admired them; they had both seen so much more in the play than she had. Every sentence, every movement, had held more for them than for her. " She shouldn't have looked at him there." " It was wrong to finish with that line." " He didn't move like a Frenchman; the French don't . . ." Backwards and forward the two sharp knives went, cutting up and probing all the tiny nerves and ligaments that had bound the play together.

And then Hilary, getting up to refill his glass, exclaimed irritably :

" But, really, the whole thing was out of date ! Things like that don't stand in our way nowadays. We know where we are about them." It was that evening, Delia thought afterwards, that she began to fall out of love with Hilary, began to want to throw up her job with Sally and do something that was some use. For they didn't know at all where they were, Hilary and Sally, about anything on the ground floor. They lived elegantly and agreeably in the first-floor drawing-room of their minds, and never went downstairs. They talked a good deal of psychological talk about unconscious minds and repressions; they fashionably called things Freudian. That kind of talk, nowadays, was part of the furniture of an intelligent drawing-room. You put everybody in their place by saying, She had a complex, of course; or, It was his inhibitions. But when the inhabitants of their own ground floor knocked on the ceiling, Hilary and Sally played the piano or talked brilliantly, or read a book, until the interruption, disregarded, was over. It was one way of doing it, and sometimes seemed to work. But when they heard of anyone, like Rhoda, who had an open path before her and could not go down it, who had made a five-barred gate out of some secret inner prohibition to prevent herself, they said that really things like that don't stand in our way nowadays. We know where we are about them.

CHAPTER XX

E VELYN got off her bus in the centre of the town, strolled along, looking at the shop windows, and finally turned in at the big doors of Varleys. It was like coming back into her own familiar world. The warm air, scented with cosmetics, lapped her round. The bright lights shone on counters of expensive oddments, fantastic gloves, fragile stockings, handkerchiefs like bright flowers, handsome heavy bags. There were a lot of well-dressed people about, shopping or looking. The women behind the counters served them with skill and deference. Once you got inside those big doors, you were in a world which, provided that you had money to spend, existed for your convenience. It offered its best for your choice, was pleased if you accepted it and apologetic if it was not quite right for you. It existed to help you to give yourself pleasure, to wrap you in soft furs, dress you in rich or delicate colours. It saw to it that the small doings of your everyday life, smoking a cigarette or powdering your face, were surrounded with luxury and grace. The shop was always full of women who spent far more time than was necessary for their actual shopping.

Evelyn felt different as soon as she got inside. She held herself a little more easily, walked more lightly, and breathed more deeply. She was back in what was, to her, the civilised world. She looked at a case of gloves, evening

gloves with ruffles of net up to the elbow. Not my style, but
just right for Daphne. She had always kept to trim,
tailored clothes, leaving frills and flowery stuffs to
Daphne, who had a rounder face and looser hair.
Daphne's prettiness, rather like the prettiness of a smart
kitten, had been an asset at Gillans Cross. She had not
looked as though she could cook and wash, and had to
worry and scheme over getting a new evening dress, or
joining a theatre-party. She had looked as though all the
good things of life ought to fall into her lap quite naturally
without her having to bother about them. A lot of them
had. People took her out a little more than they took
Evelyn. They offered her spare seats for a show, they asked
her to come abroad with them. She was amusing, saying
outrageous things with a demure recklessness. She had
really enjoyed the parties, dances, and tennis more than
Evelyn, had not made quite so much a business of them.
She had even found a certain spice in their shifts and
contrivances.

People liked her more than me, Evelyn thought, looking
at the ruffled gloves, and seeing them on Daphne's round
arms. She wondered whether anyone but Maurice had
really liked her very much, and perhaps Maurice didn't
now. If I could have married Mark! But it had not
seemed, then, as though Mark would be able to afford to
marry for years, and, if he could have, he might have
asked Daphne; he went about as much with her. A nice
boy, her mother said, but no use to either of them. It had
been painful wanting him with such fierce intensity, a
queer emotion that sometimes seemed almost more like
hating than loving. It had been a sort of holiday after he
had gone, being fond of Maurice, and having Maurice in

love with her; enjoying the atmosphere of success, the clothes, and the presents. The fact that Maurice was different from all her friends gave Evelyn an unconscious reassurance which she needed. Trying once to express it, she said to herself that Maurice didn't want anything, except that she should love him and let him love her. He was the first disinterested person she had ever really known.

Nowadays she thought that he was altogether too disinterested. She missed in him that capacity for marshalling all his forces against the world which had been so notable in her mother. Evelyn had learnt one lesson from her very early: you fought to get on. Maurice didn't seem to want to get on—not, at least, as Evelyn understood it: making more money, becoming more successful, having a better house, better clothes, holidays, and parties. He did not seem to understand the difference between being rich and successful, or being poor and making things do. Evelyn knew all about that difference, the taste of the knowledge was bitter in her mouth, but, when she tried to make Maurice understand, he laughed and said, " What does it matter ? " Once, when she pointed out to him that people treated you differently when you were doing well, he said, " But who cares about that sort of people ? " She saw that he was on some platform of his own, despising them. He remarked that things were divided unfairly enough, anyhow, without going all out to make them worse. Evelyn wanted to shake him. Unfortunately, she refrained, and began instead to feel a faint contempt for him. It was rising in her now as she walked through the shop and thought of all the things she would like to buy but could not afford.

It was not her only feeling. She stood in front of a case looking at a model dress of sea-green taffeta. She had had a dress that colour when they were engaged, and Maurice had liked it so much that, although it was quite old, he would not let her discard it when she bought her trousseau. She had taken it away on their honeymoon, and worn it the first night to please him, although it was a real deprivation not to put on one of her new ones. But then, just for a short time, she had felt like that: pleasing Maurice had been more important than doing what she wanted. Looking back, she thought it had been restful. Being out of herself had meant an incredible peace, but she was back inside herself now, and Maurice inside himself, two separate people speaking to one another from opposite houses, and finding, now that they were so far apart as to need words, that they did not speak the same language. Evelyn sighed, and went on to the hat department.

Buying her hat she felt more cheerful. She looked so pretty in all of them. The saleswomen were relieved; there was no need to persuade her that she looked nice in something that did not really suit her. The oddest little shapes alighted like birds on her trim, pale gold hair. She bought one which was odd enough to be new, but not odd enough to be absurd, and put it on, leaving her old one to be sent home.

Now that she was here, she thought that after all she might as well have lunch. An obscure desire to comfort herself made her decide to stay here as long as possible in the middle of the colours and lights and luxuries. She telephoned to Mary to give Tatty her fish and milk pudding, and went into the restaurant.

She would really have liked to lunch alone, looking at people's clothes, and indulging in a little private greed. You got so tired of nursery food for lunch. She was going to a table in the far corner when she saw someone waving to her, and recognised Marjorie Shovel, the mother of a small boy who played with Tatty. To Marjorie, who had an open nature, that constituted friendship. She pulled back a chair, and beckoned joyfully to Evelyn, glad that she need not have lunch alone. Evelyn was not naturally sociable, but she had learnt sociability as a duty, and she was conscientious on Tatty's behalf, exchanging invitations with every mother of a suitable three- or four-year-old; beginning already, though she did not realise it, to follow her own mother's example. Tatty must have nice friends, she said to Maurice, who laughed and agreed, wondering why he felt oddly disconcerted by the statement. He was not aware that in Evelyn's social life, as in other things, it was spontaneity that he missed.

Marjorie burst into eager conversation.

" I haven't seen you since we came back from our holiday. Do you know I'm having another baby in February ? I'm awfully pleased about it. I want a little girl this time, or I might have twins. My great-grandmother had them—Ann and Deborah. I'm going to call her Ann Deborah, or Ann and Deborah if it is twins."

She paused, smiling widely and confident of sympathy, to receive Evelyn's congratulations.

" I shan't go into a nursing-home this time. I shall have her at home, and send Fips to his Grannie. What do you think I ought to do about telling him ? Of course, he's only two; I don't think he'd understand much. But it's supposed to give them awful complexes if they don't know, isn't it ? "

" He's so small, I don't think he'd take it in, would he ? "

Evelyn was not really thinking about Francis and his possible complexes. She was wondering how on earth the Shovels were going to afford another baby, and how Marjorie was going to manage two small children with one little maid, part nurse, part cook, and not much good at either. Marjorie answered her thought.

" I expect Deborah will bring us to the workhouse. I'm sure Doris will leave when she arrives if she doesn't leave before. I can't think how we're going to manage." She added with unforced cheerfulness, " We're both delighted about it, though. I *do* want Deborah."

She did not look as though she were worrying. She was pale and rather spotty, already losing the lines of her figure, and almost shabby in a two-piece suit that had been part of her trousseau, and a hat of last year's shape, but she was enclosed in serenity, as though nothing could disturb her very much, as though she was doing something so fundamentally right that no drawbacks were of any importance. Doris might leave, they might all arrive at the workhouse, but Deborah was coming, Deborah coming like sap pushing up in spring; make way for Deborah.

Evelyn felt a pang of envy. Such instinctive, casual living was beyond her. She could not have borne to look forward to the birth of a baby unless every detail was arranged and every contingency provided for. She did not like to go out for a day without knowing what time she was coming back.

"Of course," Marjorie remarked, "Deborah is an accident, really. We meant to wait a bit longer; Ronald thought we ought. But then, when we were away, we thought we wouldn't worry; we'd chance it. After all, it's worth while, isn't it? It spoils it all so, being careful."

Evelyn broke off to order her pudding. She felt herself closing like a sea-anemone at a touch. She could not talk about her private affairs except to her mother and Daphne. She did not trust the rest of the world. Besides, she could not say to the easy Marjorie that she did not think it was worth it. She did not even know that that was how she felt. She only knew that she had made up her mind not to have another one, anyhow, till the end of next year. It isn't having the baby, she said to herself, it's feeling so ugly before it comes, and feeding it all that time afterwards; getting so tired, and all that washing and changing its clothes, being so tied to it. Her mind was hard and tight about this business of having another baby. She pushed it away from her. Sometimes, when she dreamed about it, it was Maurice whom she pushed away. She did not want to talk about it, nor to hear Marjorie talk about Deborah any more.

"Are you taking Fips to Bobby Wilson's party this afternoon?" she asked.

Marjorie, feeling, without knowing, that she was being held off, followed the talk readily into the new channel. They talked about Fips and Tatty until the end of lunch.

CHAPTER XXI

Maurice had become a Rotarian partly because he was pleased to be asked and could think of no good reason for refusing, partly because of a continual hankering to get into other worlds than his own. He was a new member, not yet acclimatised and not sure that he ever would be. The whole thing amazed him. It was one of the modern substitutes for religion, he thought, with its insistence on virtue and unselfishness, its small rituals and ceremonies, the bond of fellowship between its members. It was a religion that had a strong flavour of Nonconformity, a certain heartiness and flatness that Maurice associated with chapels, but the fellowship was real. A good deal of the virtue and kindliness seemed genuine, if a little over-stressed. You got sick of hearing about them, but they were there. Your fellow-Rotarians might irritate you by talking about fellowship, but if you wanted help they really would help you. After all, to talk about things or not talk about them was only a convention, Maurice reminded himself. His own education had tended too much the other way, making him often hold back self-consciously from some spontaneous outburst, some genuine remark that would be better said than swallowed. At a Public School you learned to suppress too many sides of yourself. Maurice was convinced of this, but retained a desire to suppress one side of his fellow-Rotarians when they stood up and bleated too often about goodwill and service.

The speaker after lunch that day was a member of a neighbouring Rotary Club, a young clergyman who had been for a holiday to Russia. If I were a dictator, thought Maurice, the first thing I'd do would be to lock up all these people who go to a country for three weeks and then come back and tell you all about it ! He didn't approve of dictators, but he couldn't help wondering whether there was anyone in the world who hadn't at some time or another, if only for a few minutes wanted to be one ! Russia was an odd sort of holiday for a clergyman to choose, thought Maurice, and wondered what impulse had taken him there—curiosity, the attraction of the opposite, willingness to see the other side ? It showed at least a certain capacity for adventure. Maurice leaned forward to look at him. The face which he saw looked nervous, but that might be the prospect of facing an audience, although clergymen as a rule were used to it. People who came back from Russia often looked exhausted and strung-up. It was an attractive face, Maurice decided ; not too much set in a clerical mould, but it was the face of someone unsure of himself. Maurice felt a pang of sympathy ; he would have liked to sit near the man, who was about his own age, and talk to him.

He listened to the speech with close attention. It was more commonplace than he expected—the usual hotchpotch of tourists' impressions, collective farms, nursery schools, theatres, journeys, the naïve surprise of the ordinary visitor at finding himself treated with courtesy and returning in safety. Maurice got no more than his usual impression of vigour and constructive energy, oppressive regimentation and supreme intolerance, hope and dirt and poverty. He had a growing impression that the speaker had been both fascinated and frightened. A single sentence stuck in Maurice's mind. " I can't tell you," the young man said, " how ruthless it all is. Ruthlessly good and ruthlessly bad ! "

He sat down amid rather unenthusiastic applause. Maurice's neighbour, the manager of a big hardware store, summed up the feelings of the audience in a line from a popular song. He drank off his glass of port, stubbed the end of his cigarette in the saucer of his coffee-cup, and remarked finally:

" *You can't do that there 'ere.*"

No, Maurice thought, I don't think you can. Not in that way. The last quality you'd ever get from English people is ruthlessness, either for good or bad. Thank heaven we can't manage the bad ruthlessness, but I wish we were a bit better at the good ! I wish we saw things sharper; got on with them quicker; didn't feel so damned comfortable about it all ! You've got to be a certain amount ruthless to get anything done ! The question is, how much ? After all, it's always proportion that matters. The devil of it is that it so often seems to be a choice nowadays between liberty and equality. If you can't have both, I think liberty's more valuable. Perhaps they're always incompatible, and there'd never be equality if people had liberty. It's proportion again, I suppose; the best balance you can manage between the two. I'd like to know what that young man really thought and felt out there, and what difference it made to him, but I don't suppose he'll be able to let himself think. Queer how you come across people like that and just touch their minds; never speak to them or know them and never see them again.

Thinking that it was still too early after lunch to go and see Rushworth, Maurice turned into his club for a cup of coffee. It was the oldest club in the city, had been established nearly a hundred years before, and drew its members from the county and from those families in the town whose great-grandfathers and grandfathers had made fortunes, and had established a kind of industrial aristocracy. To the last two generations membership had been a coveted privilege. Maurice's contemporaries were less impressed, and Maurice himself found the place dull. He did not breathe easily in the sombre Victorian dining-room. The weight of tradition hung heavy upon him; he was still sometimes oppressed by the timidity of the new boy, and struggled against the new boy's passionate desire to conform to the standards around him. Sometimes, in a rebellious mood, he wanted to tell these elderly men, friends, a good many of them, of his father's, that their world was over. Their enclosed security, their provincial prestige, their steady resistance to ideas, belonged to the last century. They still felt themselves to be a segregated and privileged class, as they had felt when they were undergraduates or young dancing men at the assemblies or the Bachelors' Ball. This unshakable conviction annoyed Maurice, and with the annoyance was a tinge of envy. It seemed to him, generalising unsafely, that they were all so sure of themselves and of the universe.

To-day, however, he had a reaction towards the club. There was a certain dignity and indifference about it

which soothed him. It let him alone. He ordered some
coffee and sat down near the fire at one end of the hall.
He was a little late. A few people were playing a midday
game of bridge upstairs; one or two were having a
belated lunch in the dining-room; but most had gone
back to their work. Occasionally a member passed and
nodded to him, but no one came to disturb him. The
interval of peace was grateful.

All the same, Maurice thought, I don't know why I go
on belonging to this place. The subscription is more than
I can really afford. I could get just as good a lunch anywhere else, and I don't enjoy coming here much. But I
don't want to give it up. He came to the conclusion that
he didn't want to give it up, especially now that the old
house had gone, because it was one of the places that held
for him the image of his father. As a schoolboy and an
undergraduate he had come here occasionally as his
father's guest; as a young member he had sat with his
contemporaries at the long table just inside the door, and
had been aware of his father among the older members, a
little easier than they were, a little warmer, because a
little less afraid. His father had never been paralysed by
the cramping fear of doing the wrong thing or knowing
the wrong people; had smiled at new members instead of
ignoring them; had known, somehow, which football
team the waiter followed, and which church the hall
porter attended; had listened with a twinkle to his fellows,
realising, as most of them did not, that importance in a
northern provincial city was not importance in the world.

I suppose, Maurice thought, there is no personal
immortality ! All that remained of his father was this
vivid image in his own mind, in Rhoda's, in his mother's;

less vivid in the minds of others, but alive still in an incident, a word, a gesture that had left its print. Here on the end of the club fender his father had sat twelve months ago, intervening in a dispute that was growing heated, laughing at the two disputants, making them laugh unwillingly. Once he had looked across at Maurice, and smiled, sharing the absurdity. Maurice had loved him at that moment, because he was never pompous, did not take offence, never stood upon his own dignity, saw clear. And all that remained of that living, breathing figure on the end of the club fender was the memory growing fainter, like a ripple of sound spreading out in widening rings through the air.

I wish I could see him again !

For the first time there rose in Maurice a strong desire for a son. He had always wanted a daughter, and Tatty was dearer than any daughter he could have imagined. He had thought that he did not mind whether they had any more children or not ; it was Evelyn herself he wanted ; children were of secondary importance. But a son might be like his own father. If he had a son, something missing in his life would be filled, a relationship that had been wiped out would return to him. To be a father with a son would revive the lost companionship, fill up a constant need now that he was no longer a son with a father.

He had finished his cigarette, and was just going, when someone who had come out of the smoking-room stopped, and then turned and came towards him. He saw that it was Legard, and was pleased. Legard was one of the members most congenial to him, a man of his own age and in very much the same position—a constructional engineer, running a small family business with difficulty.

They had not known one another very long, for Legard had been with a London firm until the death of his father two years ago had brought him back to the North. He and Maurice had lately been discovering that they had more in common than circumstances and the fact that they were competitors. They shared the feeling that they were, as Legard once said, fighting with bows and arrows against cannon-balls. Legard was more definite than Maurice; he voted Labour, was eager for State control of the major industries, and admitted that he wanted to sell his business and find some means of livelihood that was more in line with his convictions. In the meantime, he had a young wife and two children to keep, and had to supplement his mother's income. Maurice liked his wife, a dark, candid girl who had been at Somerville and shared most of her husband's views, but a meeting of the two families had not been a success. Evelyn thought Judy Legard " odd and intellectual," and looked critically at her clothes, while Legard dried up in Evelyn's presence; but at the club he and Maurice discussed practical difficulties and more general problems with a growing pleasure in each other's company.

Legard came across and stood by Maurice's chair.

" Hulloa," he said. " I didn't see you at lunch."

" I wasn't here. I've been at a Rotary lunch. I only came in for five minutes."

" Back to the old round ? " Legard said sympathetically.

" I suppose so."

Legard sat down on the club fender and lit a cigarette. He smoked for a minute in silence. He was a long-limbed, loose-jointed young man who would have looked like an undergraduate but for the deep lines in his face. He said:

" Why do we go on with it ? "

" Well, what else can we do ? "

" Chuck it ! Get an ordinary workman's job and live in a cottage."

" And our families ? Suppose we didn't manage to get an ordinary workman's job ? Plenty of people don't. It wouldn't be a case of living in a cottage. It would be living in two rooms in a house on Public Assistance."

" We'd be no worse off than a lot of other people. The children would get free education, and I believe they'd be a lot better knocking about in elementary schools than being taught to be devitalised little snobs in expensive boarding-schools."

" It doesn't seem fair not to give them every chance we can. Our parents gave us the best education they could, and I think we owe it to our children to do the same."

" But I'm not sure whether giving them the cream off the top when they're young is the best chance. Judy's not sure either."

Thinking to himself that Evelyn would be quite sure, Maurice felt a pang of envy of the Legards, of their free exchange of ideas and shared experiments with life. He remembered the first evening that he had spent in their house, when Evelyn was away for a week-end with her mother. He had been happy, unfolding his ideas and queries in sympathetic company, knowing that it did not matter what he said. He had stayed very late, and gone away with a feeling of refreshment, seeing things anew with the dust rubbed off them. He had been so eager to ask the Legards back and repeat the pleasure. Evelyn had agreed at once, had arranged dinner for them and bought flowers, and welcomed them pleasantly, but the evening had been flat, difficult, and lifeless. The evening in their house and the evening in his passed like a film through Maurice's mind: two ways of living, two kinds of people. He did not know that he sighed. His mind circled back to Legard's last remark. He said feebly:

" Yours are boys."

" It doesn't make much difference, do you think ? You don't want Tatty to grow up into a nice girl thinking about tennis and her next permanent wave ? "

" I want her to be happy." But it was true, he wanted a richer and more vital happiness for her than that. He had sometimes got as far as saying to himself that he would not have liked Tatty to grow up in Gillans Cross. His mind, pursuing this train of thought, came upon something that he did not care to contemplate. He recoiled from it, and swung over into irritation. He saw Legard for a moment as Evelyn had seen him: rather untidy, rather unpractical, lacking in worldly poise and assurance.

" Talk sense ! " he said. " After all, what do you think we can really do ? Things are changing by degrees, but I don't see how we can hurry them. What do you think we personally can do about it ? "

" I don't know. But I do know that I'm not going on very much longer drawing £1,000 a year profits out of a business that pays its workmen 50s. 0d. a week. Oh, I know it's made into a company now, and that's called my salary, but it's the same thing. I don't work any harder for it than the men do."

" You've more responsibility."

" Well, I'd sooner have responsibility than work a riveting machine all day. What I think I ought to do is to take a living wage, and then pool the rest of my salary among us all, the men in the works, and me, and the people in the office.

" It seems to me," Legard went on, " that some people have got to start doing that, to look like fools and perhaps be fools, and then after a time the rest of the world will follow them, and then it will look like common sense. Because really, you know, very often common sense is what fools and cranks thought yesterday. Look what everyone thinks now about war and what they thought twenty years ago about conscientious objectors ! I don't believe Governments can start this sort of thing. I believe it's got to be done by willing people; a few first, and then a lot. Do you read your D. H. Lawrence, Maurice ? ' The world is waiting for a new great movement of generosity, or a new great wave of death.' "

" I think you may be right, but I know I shan't do it." I shan't do it, Maurice thought, because of Evelyn. But was that fair ? He was not at all sure that he would have done it without her. He might have been able to face altering his way of life, doing without a lot of the things that he was accustomed to, but he did not think he could face the plunge over into absurdity, the departure from the normal. That was what really took courage, to live by the common sense of the future instead of the common sense of the present. He felt himself to be unequal to it. He was an ordinary person. But ordinariness, he perceived, was a question of time. The ordinary post-war person would have been a pre-war crank. In the great world of space and time, to be ordinary was the poise of a moment, like a figure in action arrested in a snapshot, or a bee hanging for a second on a flower.

Legard got up.

" I don't suppose I shall do it either." He grinned ruefully down at Maurice. " I'm lazy, and greedy like everyone else, but I wish I could do it, and some day I might.
In the meantime I must go back to the office and try and
make some more money. See you later in the week, I
expect."

" Yes, I'm sure to be in."

Legard hesitated, wanting to suggest that they should
come in one evening, but remembering that he could not
talk to Maurice's wife, and Judy had said that she was
sure Evelyn didn't like " Maurice's queer friends."
Better leave it, perhaps. He nodded, and strolled out of
the club.

CHAPTER XXII

THINKING that he had put off going to see Rushworth as late as he possibly could, and would like to put it off altogether, Maurice turned in at the stone doorway of the big corner block of offices and rang for the lift. As he was carried up through the echoing building, he tried to shake himself out of an insistent distaste for this part of his work. He envied the doctor, not allowed to invite patients to come to him; the architect, forbidden to go and ask to be employed. Not that some of them don't, he thought, in their own way. Rushworth would always be very careful not to do anything against professional etiquette, but he'd always know the right people. He would never mention a job to them, but, when there was one going, he'd just happen to be playing golf with them or to ask them to dinner if they were up here, or he'd run across them in London somehow. I oughtn't to think less of him for it, I suppose. It's the way things are done. He's good at his job, none of his work's shoddy, and he wouldn't take a bribe. He doesn't do anything dishonourable ; he knows his world and gets what he wants from it. It's not fair to criticise him, but he's so infernally successful and on the spot, he gives you the feeling that he picks all his acquaintances because they'll be some use to him. The minute they seem unlikely to be any use, you feel he'd just stop bothering about them. He only bothers about us because his wife likes Evelyn.

The Rushworths were older than the Powells and had no children. They played golf and bridge well, went abroad a good deal on their holidays, gave admirable little dinner-parties, and spent much time and thought on their garden. Before her marriage Thelma Rushworth had run a very successful hat shop in London. She put up with the industrial North good-humouredly, but did not pretend to like it. A common distaste for it, and a liking for good clothes, good food, theatres, and anything competent and successful, united her to Evelyn, who really enjoyed her company very much more than that of her contemporaries, the mothers of Tatty's small friends. From their fresh and ingenuous goodwill she turned with relief to a cynical and hardy experience that reminded her unconsciously of her own mother. The husbands had less in common. Maurice chafed against Dick Rushworth's placid acceptance of established conditions; he resented his way of damning all opinions except his own as " sentimental," and of brushing aside so many things as " highbrow." Rushworth admired Evelyn, but thought Maurice a dull, quiet fellow, not likely to get on. Still, they often met, played bridge and golf together, and considered themselves friends.

" Hulloa, Maurice," Rushworth said. " I suppose you've looked in about that Haverford job ? I'm glad you have, because I was going to ring you up this afternoon and ask you to come and have a word with me. How are you all at home ? All right ! Thelma's been up in Town for a fortnight, but she's coming back on Thursday, and we must fix up an evening for some bridge. It's quite a long time since we've seen anything of you."

" I've been rather busy. My people have been removing, and I've had a lot to see about. We're selling the place, you know."

" For building, I suppose ? It's about the next bit of land, isn't it ? They're spreading out very quickly that way."

" Yes. Parkinson's going to make a housing estate of it."

" It's a pity when a good house like that has to go, but nobody wants one that size nowadays. Those big, old-fashioned places are awfully inconvenient to run, and they swallow a pot of money."

Maurice felt a twinge of anger at the dismissing tone. For an instant he wanted to tell Dick Rushworth exactly what he thought of the expensive white sun-trap villa which he had built just outside the town. Evelyn's envy and admiration of the Rushworth house had always annoyed him, and he did not realise that he irritated her by his own unconscious habit of comparing all houses with Stone Hall.

" It's the Haverford job I wanted to see you about." Rushworth pulled a paper towards him. " We've got all the prices in now, but I haven't sent them through yet. I don't mind letting you know your tender's not the lowest."

It so often wasn't, Maurice thought bitterly. A small firm couldn't do things as cheaply as a large firm, and he never felt that they were keeping their costs down as low as they ought, but it was difficult ! To buy large quantities of steel meant getting in a big bill long before they could hope to be paid for their work, and that would mean passing the limit of their overdraft.

" That's the lowest figure," Rushworth said. He

scribbled on a bit of paper and tossed it over the table.
" There's not much difference."

" No, not much."

We could have done it for that, Maurice thought, if
we'd cut our profit a bit. Not that we put on any more
than was reasonable; in fact, rather less; but still, I'd be
glad to do it at that price. It's a big job; it would keep
the works going just now while we're rather slack, and
we should get paid at once. Besides, they've got branches
everywhere. This isn't the only job they'll have to give.
It's a pity ! Disappointing to have been so near ! Whose
quotation is it, I wonder ? Well, it doesn't matter; it's
not ours, anyway !

" Look here ! " Rushworth said. " I'm not putting the
prices in for a couple of days. Would you like to quote
again ? "

It was a development which Maurice had not expected.
He had supposed that Rushworth wanted him to explain
as between friends that he could not accept his tender.
He looked up, surprised.

" Do you mean that ? It's very good of you ! "

" That's all right. All things being equal, I'd like you
to have it. There's a lot of nice work in it, and of course
you know they're extending all over, so it might lead to
more. Naturally I've got to accept the lowest offer, but if
you can quote as low as that, or a bit lower, I'll see you
get it."

Maurice felt grateful, and tried not to mind the feeling.

" Thanks awfully, Dick. It's very good of you, and I'm
really very much obliged. I want the job badly. We're
short just now. I'll look into it, and send you another
quotation to-morrow."

" Yes, do ! You've got the figure there, haven't you ? You'll keep that to yourself, of course. Between ourselves, that was John Legard's quotation, and I don't particularly want to give them the job. I don't find Legard an easy fellow to get on with. He's a bit of a crank, and he's got rather an annoying manner. I don't care for him. What's the matter ? "

" Nothing," Maurice said slowly. " At least, he's rather a friend of mine."

" I'm not saying anything against him. He's not much in my line, that's all. I don't know him well. I haven't seen him for a month or two except in the distance. I've no particular prejudice against him, but I'd much rather give the job to you, Maurice, if you want it, and if you can do it at the price. Look into it and see what you can do." The shrewd, light eyes shot a quick glance at Maurice's doubtful face. " Don't worry about Legard. You've got to look after yourself first in business."

" I suppose so."

" Well, of course you have. Or else," said Rushworth reasonably and truthfully, " you won't be in business long." He smiled at Maurice, but there was a faint hint of contempt in his good nature, and he glanced unobtrusively at his wrist-watch.

" Well, do you want to have another shot ? "

" Yes. Thank you very much."

" All right. Don't post it later than to-morrow evening."

Maurice said good-bye and got out of the room. He would not wait for the lift, but walked downstairs. Distaste for himself and for the whole of the business world possessed him. He was going to filch a job from Legard, whom he liked. He had been given an unfair advantage because Evelyn and Thelma Rushworth played bridge together. Of course he would send in another quotation. He had to appease the bank and make a profit if he could. He had to keep the works going, pay the men's wages, and the salaries of the general office and drawing office, as well as his own managing director's salary. He could not afford to offend Rushworth and lose all chance of work from him in the future. But he hated it. He felt like a traitor to Legard, although he realised that Legard would probably have to do the same to him. He longed for a world where people were not always cutting one another's throats. If only, he thought, it wasn't such a smash-and-grab business ! If things could be divided up fairly ! If only it could be arranged that everything you got didn't mean taking something from other people !

The worst of it was that in Rushworth, who didn't mind that, Maurice perceived an adjustment that was lacking in himself, some maturity to which he had not attained. Rushworth accepts things as they are. He's whole; he knows what he's driving at. If he'd heard that fellow at lunch, or listened to Legard, he'd just dismiss it all as nonsense. He'd say, " You can't alter human nature." His kind of person does say that, and it sounds sensible and convincing; it gives you that comfortable feeling of getting back to brass tacks. Like, when everybody's being high-falutin, somebody says, " Well, what about a drink ? " You think to yourself, " Well, that's something real, anyway," but what you mean is, " Well, that's one of the easy, real things, not one of the difficult ones." Rushworth's way of looking at things, that sounds so real, is only half real. It's too easy. After all, the one thing that's ever made any difference in the world is that you can alter almost anything, inch by inch and taking years over it, by intelligence.

He swung himself on to his tram, and climbed upstairs. It's all really, he thought, a question of pace, of timing. Trying to alter things too slowly is letting them rip and missing the bus; trying to alter them too quickly is tyranny and interference. Sometimes I think we concentrate so much on what to do that we never think enough about when to do it. He looked down at the part of the town through which he was passing. A thick pall of smoke lay over it, shutting off the afternoon sunlight. Between the high walls of factories and warehouses, side streets opened off the main street, huddled rows of mean houses. They were moving people out of those houses into better quarters, into clearer air, and clean houses with bathrooms and lavatories. Families gaining air and light and cleanliness, losing perhaps some shred of independence, the feeling of having only themselves to look to which had been a stimulus to such men as Parkinson. Gaining and losing, growing better, growing worse, the whole world swung to and fro in a perpetual state of removal, and it would take a wiser man than Maurice to see whether at the end of all it was creeping forward to the millennium, or rushing on to destruction.

Besides, he thought, we never really see the world ! When he was engaged, and in the first months of his marriage, it had appeared to him, if he thought about it at all, to be going on very well, and now, because he was unhappy and unsatisfied, it seemed a place where everything wanted altering. Really to see the world meant an almost unattainable personal freedom, an honesty too rare for most of fettered humanity.

Rushworth meant to be kind, thought Maurice. He was kind, and I wasn't too grateful. Evelyn will be pleased that he's done me a good turn; she's always wanted me to be friendly with him. I think I could get on with him better if he wasn't quite so smug ! I don't mind her if I don't see her too often; she can be quite amusing. I'll get Evelyn to ask them to dinner again soon, and I'll try and like them ! Of this effort he was not hopeful, for if you don't find people congenial you can't, and feeling is apt to leak through manners. They were congenial to Evelyn. They were like various friends of hers from Gillans Cross who had stayed a night with them on their way North to Scotland and the Lakes, causing Maurice to say, after they had left, how nice it was to be alone again. I hope to God, he thought, that Tatty won't marry some-one like that ! Oh, she won't; she's not that sort. But did you always marry your own sort ? He did not want to pursue that reflection. He pulled out of his pocket the slip of paper that Rushworth had given him, and began to make calculations.

CHAPTER XXIII

THE AFTERNOON was so warm that the children were able to play out of doors in Bobby Wilson's sand-heap at the far end of the narrow strip of garden. The revolving shelter on the lawn had been moved round to catch the sun. Evelyn and the other young mothers sat gossiping together, with a watchful eye on the fair and dark heads that bobbed up and down above the sand.

They talked mostly about their children, their achievements, temperaments, and ailments. It was their shop, as varied and inexhaustible as the shop of authors or barristers or engineers. Untaught except by such years as they had lived, they were tackling the living material for whose sake engines are made to run, books are written, and laws are made.

" I don't know what I can do when I smack Bobby and he does the same thing again ! " Carol Wilson complained. " I told him if he pulled the clean clothes off the rack again I should smack him, and he did, and I smacked him quite hard. He just looked at me and smiled, and went and pulled them off again ! "

" What did you do ? "

" I smacked him harder." Carol looked ashamed of her want of originality, and added sadly, " Even then I don't think he minded ! "

Mrs. Richards, an older woman who had no child at the party, clicked her tongue.

" I wouldn't do that ! It's so much better if you can try an appeal to their reason."

Marjorie Shovel laughed.

" Fips hasn't any reason when he really wants something ! "

" Oh, yes, he has, my dear, if you train him to use it. I always found it worked with Erica and Stephen. I used to explain the whole position to them clearly and calmly. ' If you pull the clothes off,' I should have said, ' they will get dirty and crumpled and have to be washed again, and that's very hard work, and wastes a lot of time and soap, so it's not a sensible thing to do.' When I explained anything to them, clearly and reasonably like that, they always saw it."

There was a silence heavy with unbelief.

" Perhaps they were older ? " Evelyn inquired.

" No, no ! They were quite tinies. I took that line with them from the very beginning, as soon as Stephen could walk."

A growing distaste for Mrs. Richards and for her Erica and Stephen pervaded and united the young mothers, depressed by the secret conviction that there were times when no amount of reason would deter an impish Fips, or a scarlet, yelling Bobby.

" I'm not clever," Marjorie Shovel said regretfully. " I'm sure I make awful mistakes over Fips. He really is a little devil sometimes ! "

Several voices assured her, with an emphasis not meant for her alone, that Fips was a dear little boy, and that you didn't expect small children to be good all the time.

Mrs. Richards listened with a carefully good-humoured smile.

" Of course, you don't want to suppress them. It's so bad for them, always to be saying ' Don't.' "

" It's rather difficult to manage without ! " It was a world, Carol Wilson was thinking, where so many things could burn and cut, where so many unsuitable objects could go into a small mouth in half an hour !

What nonsense, Evelyn thought; as though Mother didn't say " Don't " to me a dozen times a day ! She was ingenuously sure that anything that had been part of her own bringing-up must be right. She would have admitted at once that she was not as clever as Rhoda, not as unselfish and good-tempered as Marjorie Shovel, not as gentle and uncritical as Carol Wilson, but she retained the common human belief that what she was was something supremely right to be. How could she do better for Tatty than try and make her the same ?

" And then about sex," pursued Mrs. Richards, flinging the word at them inexorably. " I've always been perfectly frank and open with them about that. Erica and Stephen were given a full answer to every question they asked. I remember when Erica was just as old as Tatty, Mrs. Powell——"

" Tatty isn't interested in anything like that," Evelyn said in a cold voice. She hated any public discussion of intimate subjects, and she thought that Mrs. Richards was insulting Tatty by connecting her with improper curiosities.

Mrs. Richards *wants* to talk about it, Evelyn thought. She and all the young mothers felt that something indecent had just been mentioned. It was a rooted conviction in all of them, although they had lately been, or were still, in love, and the cherished fruits of their love were playing in the sand-heap.

" Let's go and see how they're getting on," Carol Wilson said to Evelyn. They got up and went across the lawn together.

" Mrs. Richards is a friend of my sister's," Carol explained apologetically. " She asked me to ask her to tea, so I did." She added in a burst of natural spite, " It's all very well talking, but we haven't seen her beastly little Erica and Stephen ! They may be horrid ! "

" They're at school, I suppose ? "

" Yes. Some special, cranky kind of school."

They stood together surveying the children.

" I wish I'd got a film in my camera," Carol sighed.

The children were playing gravely and separately, taking very little notice of one another, each one intent on his or her own game in the sand. Their mothers would have felt it rude if they had all been occupied within arm's reach of one another and had not kept up a constant exchange of talk, but the children ignored one another, except for a few necessary remarks : " You're stepping on my bridge." " Can I have your spade ? " Aloof and alone they played, and Carol, watching them, suddenly realised how mysterious they were. What did she know about Bobby after all ? She knew his solid little body, and sometimes for a second she was in touch with his hidden mind, but only for a second. Filled to the brim with wishes, fears, thoughts, imaginings beyond her reach, he spoke to her, and smiled or cried, he tried to make her understand what he wanted or what dismayed him, and then retreated again into himself. He was an explorer in a strange world, a primitive person making dubious experiments in a civil-ised country which did not speak his language. She loved him more than her life, but very often she could not speak to him without an interpreter, and there was no interpreter. Wanting to get close to him, she knelt down by him in the sand and pulled him towards her, putting her arm round him. He looked at her like a cat interrupted when washing, pushed her arm away, and resumed his operations on a sand castle.

Evelyn was watching Tatty and another little girl near, thinking that the child's yellow frock would have suited Tatty better. She would get some buttercup yellow wool and knit Tatty a frock for the winter. Tatty was too dark, really, for little-girl pinks and blues; the gypsy colours suited her. If I ever have another girl, thought Evelyn, I'd like her to have very fair hair, like mine—that is, if I didn't drown her ! If she had another baby, it must be a boy, it must, it must ! She felt that a boy, a child for herself, was badly needed to restore the balance of the household. The thought was hardly articulate. I'm odd man out now, but Maurice can have Tatty when I have my son !

" It's lovely for them having this sand to play in," she said politely to Carol. " Tatty always looks forward to it."

" It's so good for Bobby having visitors to share it," Carol replied with equal politeness.

She and the other young mothers were always a little more polite and formal with Evelyn than with one another. Without knowing that they did it, they tidied the nursery more carefully before she brought Tatty, and were more exacting in their choice of cakes and flowers. They were always particularly anxious that their children should wipe their shoes on Evelyn's front-door mat, and should not be sick nor break anything at her tea-parties.

Tatty was shovelling sand into a wheelbarrow with a small spade. Bobby had been making a castle and trying to add turrets by shaping them with a bucket, but the sand was too dry to stick together, and the turrets were only heaps rounded like beehives. Bobby grew bored with them, and looked across at Tatty. That was his wheelbarrow! It was his birthday present, given to him that morning, green, lined with scarlet. He seized the handles and turned it over, upsetting the load of sand.

" I want the wheelbarrow," he said. He added kindly, " You can have the bucket."

Tatty accepted the bucket. She was a good-tempered little girl, and perhaps she was getting tired of filling the wheelbarrow. She would build a sandhill, and put the bucket on top. She began to dig busily, the tip of her pink tongue sticking out of the corner of her mouth.

Bobby shovelled a little sand into the wheelbarrow, but perceived at once that to fill it was going to be a long and arduous business, and stopped. He pushed the wheelbarrow backwards and forwards for a bit, but found that tedious. He did not really know what to do with it, unless he had something to wheel in it. He was a little *blasé* this afternoon, slightly flushed and swollen with birthday pride. He looked at Tatty, who was just planting the bucket on top of her hill. He sprawled across, knocking down part of the hill, grabbed the bucket, and put it in the wheelbarrow. There are limits to the patience of even a good little girl of three. Tatty yelled, and hit him with her spade.

The two mothers swooped down upon them.

" Bobby! You naughty little boy! Let Tatty have that bucket at once! Look, you've spoilt her castle! You must help her to build it up again."

" Don't be so silly, Tatty! You've had the bucket for

a long time, and it's Bobby's turn ! Remember it's his
birthday. It was very naughty of you to hit him ! Tell him
you're sorry."

The two small creatures stared at one another, Tatty
grasping her spade, Bobby grasping the bucket.

A swift impulse rose in Evelyn, looking from Tatty to
Bobby's square little shoulders and stubborn face. She
wanted to smack him, to snatch the bucket from him and
give it to her daughter, to pick Tatty up in her arms and
comfort her.

" Bobby ! " Carol protested gently. " Give Tatty that
bucket ! "

Evelyn's cool tones were firm.

" No, Tatty's had the bucket for quite a long time. You
must let Bobby have it now, Tatty."

" But Bobby's got the wheelbarrow ! " Tatty cried
indignantly.

" Well, you've got a spade. Dig a nice castle."

That was off the point, as Tatty knew. Every one of
them had a spade. Besides, she had dug a nice castle and
Bobby had fallen on it. And she had let him have the
wheelbarrow. A sense of injustice overwhelmed her. Her
small face grew red and puckered for tears.

Evelyn was not thinking about justice ; she was pursuing
with determination her own idea of social behaviour.
Whatever you might really think, you blamed your own
child, and made her give in.

" He must give her the bucket," Carol said. " It was all
his fault."

Evelyn's will was stronger.

" No, she doesn't want the bucket. Tatty ! If you're
silly, I shall take you home—now—before tea."

Tatty knew that her mother meant what she said. She knew that there was a birthday cake with four candles; Bobby had taken her to peep through the window. She swallowed her tears, and began to dig a hole in the sand. Evelyn was satisfied, but Carol shook her head at Bobby. Her mood this afternoon was thoughtful; she had a glimpse of the small creatures so entirely at the mercy of alien standards. Half apologetically, she touched Tatty's dark head.

" We'll go in to tea soon."

She added to Evelyn in a quick whisper:

" Here's Mrs. Richards coming to appeal to their reason. Let's take her to see my new rock plants at the other end of the garden."

CHAPTER XXIV

Rʜᴏᴅᴀ ᴀɴᴅ Aᴜɴᴛ Eʟʟᴇɴ between them dragged
the big hamper of linen into the spare room, and began
to unpack sheets and pillow-cases and lay them in the
cupboard. Aunt Ellen patted the solid white folds.

" Your mother has some very nice things," she said. She
had always taken a vicarious pride in Nan's possessions.

" Some of these are almost worn out." Rhoda fingered
a darn.

" Yes; but they are so very good, you can use them
right up to the end. Mamma always said: ' Nan knows
quality when she sees it. You can always be sure that she
will buy the very best of everything.' Mamma was like
that herself. I was in Culver's the other day, buying two
guest towels to work, and old Mr. Culver came up, when
the girl was serving me, and said: ' Don't show those to
Miss Lister. They're poor quality; not the sort of thing
she would like.' And he sent her for some others, and,
while I was waiting, he was saying how very well he
remembered Mamma, and how he never dared to show
her anything but the very best he had in the shop. Mrs.
Lister liked the best of everything, he said."

Yes, Rhoda thought, the best of everything for Grandmamma, and no allowance for Aunt Ellen. If that wasn't
like them ! They lived at Stone Hall, and their workpeople lived in slums ! Her grandparents emerged out of

the past, the big, square, jolly old man with the silvery, well-brushed hair, and the bunch of seals hanging from his watch-chain; the stately old lady in her handsome silk gowns, with the diamond rings on her fine hands. Behind those two figures whom she remembered well were the younger grandparents, whom she had never known, but who lived in her mind from photographs, from old letters and a newspaper or two, from her own parents' talk. She felt that she knew them quite well—her grandmother, a young matron, dominating her children, spending freely on her house and clothes; ruling with a firm hand the servants of her day, who slept in attics lit by small sky-lights, and went out one evening a week. She could see her grandmother, in rich, stiff silk, going to church in her carriage, entertaining her callers at midday with madeira cake and glasses of port, sailing in brocade and diamonds into a ballroom. Her grandfather was no less vivid, a young man with curling hair and bright eyes, prosperous and sturdy, pushing his business with success, speaking with authority on Conservative platforms, taking his top hat to church, giving his friends good wine and a good cigar. They came back, those two, with an aroma of prosperity, outward and inward. You realised that they had not only known how to choose good linen and good port, and been able to pay for it; they had known their own minds, begotten and borne children with satisfaction, been sure of themselves and of the universe.

What had gone wrong? Rhoda wondered. Why were their children so much lesser personalities than them-selves, their grandchildren of divided mind, reaping a harvest of doubts and hesitations? They had been full of life, its pride and joy; and Aunt Ellen, this thin, dry, withered woman who had never had anything of her own, was their daughter. Their vigorous life should have begotten life. But their successful commercial enterprise had left a world of bad housing and unemployment. Anger stirred in her against those lusty, unheeding figures out of an undisturbed past.

" Aunt Ellen ! Do you think anybody ought always to have the best of everything ? "

Something in her tone startled Aunt Ellen, who looked round from the cupboard.

" No, dear, I suppose not. I often feel ashamed of sitting down to a good meal when other people are going without—the wives of the men with no work, and the poor little children ! "

" Oh, Aunt Ellen ! I don't think you've had more than your share ! "

" I've never gone really hungry, Rhoda, or short of warmth and clothes. I have a great deal to be thankful for."

" But you can have food and warmth and clothes and yet be miserable ! "

" Mamma always said that if you had a good home and good health and were miserable, it must be your own fault."

Mamma had said it, and so it was. So it was for Aunt Ellen, even though Mamma had been dead for eight years. At least, thought Rhoda, I'm free of that ! I think my own thoughts. Mamma had said it was wrong to be miserable, so Aunt Ellen had not been miserable. She had controlled herself, stopped thinking about herself, got something to do, said her prayers. Her strong sense of duty had sustained her. The trouble is, thought Rhoda, that mine isn't strong enough. Besides, we're all doubtful nowadays about that sort of duty. It's gone out of fashion, and, even if you stick to it, you can't help feeling doubtful about it. Perhaps the next generation won't have any doubts. Perhaps I shall see Tatty not troubled at all by the things that trouble me. As it is, we're a watery copy. Grandmamma assumed divine right, and Aunt Ellen gave her willing obedience. Mother wants to assume it, but can't quite, so she frets and struggles for it, and I obey unwillingly. Dell's fought clear of it, only not quite clear, because she is on the defensive with Mother; she isn't free and candid and happy as she is with everyone else; it's another broken rhythm.

Rhoda picked up a pile of linen from the basket. The sunlight from the window splashed across it; it was like a snowfield in her arms. She and Maurice were running across a snowfield, the snow creaking under their small heavy boots, the wind blowing a powdery scurry of snow against their cold cheeks, the soft flakes getting in their eyes and brushing their lips. The sun came out suddenly, lighting up the field and the heavy rounded shapes of the trees, the shape of a barn, an enlarged image of itself, one bare wall black, the straight lines of the roof made clumsy by snow. Ecstasy trembled all through her ten-year-old body, the world so beautiful ! But it was those moments that made you disinherited ; you were homesick in life because there were so few of them.

" Dreaming, Rhoda ? " Aunt Ellen said.

Rhoda handed up the pile of sheets to Aunt Ellen, who was standing on a chair to reach the top shelf. What secret joys and moments had Aunt Ellen known ? You saw her plain elderly body, and heard her kind voice with the deliberate lift in it of one cheerful for duty, but that was almost all you knew of her, that outline of a person which you made for yourself, carelessly and autocratically. Sometimes that outline prevented you from seeing things, got between you and the person. It had become important to Rhoda, to-day, to know more about Aunt Ellen.

" Why did Grandmamma say that to you, Aunt Ellen, about it being your own fault ? Were you miserable ? "

" I was foolish sometimes when I was young. Just after your mother was married, I went through a time when I was very ungrateful and discontented. I missed her very much, and there were other things. But then Mamma was very ill indeed, and I thought that I might have lost her, and that I should always have to remember that I had been tiresome and complaining in the last weeks of her life, and that cured me. After that illness, Mamma used to say sometimes, ' I may not be here another Christmas,' or, ' I may not see the trees come out again,' so that I never forgot."

" Oh," exclaimed Delia from the doorway, " How wicked of her ! "

Aunt Ellen's face flushed. A dull pink spread under the sallow skin, and made two unbecoming patches of red on her neck.

" How can you say such a thing, Delia ! Your Grandmother was one of the best women who ever lived ! "

" I'm sorry, Aunt Ellen ! But I don't think it was fair to keep on upsetting you like that ! "

" It didn't upset me. It helped me a great deal. When I was going to grumble, or perhaps if I had some little thing to do for Mamma, and was doing it carelessly or

hurriedly, I used to think, ' But I shouldn't like to remember that if anything happened to Mamma.' "

" When I'm dying, I'd rather you'd all quarrel with
me up to the last minute than feel like that about it !
If you are going to die, I think it's awfully mean to take
an unfair advantage of it ! "

" My dear," Aunt Ellen said gently, " it's natural you
shouldn't know much about it at your age." She looked
kindly at Delia standing in the doorway, so pretty, with
her cheeks flushed, and the dark hair ruffling back from
her square, white forehead. Aunt Ellen felt a pang of
pity for her, so young and happy, expecting her Jim that
evening. It was natural that she should not understand.
You don't know very much about life, reflected Aunt
Ellen, until you have loved someone more than your life
and lost them, but had to go on with it ! Delia, in her
turn, looking at her dry, elderly aunt, felt pity, and
thought, in the glow of her confident youth, Aunt Ellen
doesn't know much about life !

Supposing I went to London, Rhoda thought, and
Mother died ? But Dell's right, surely, only I wish I hadn't
thought of it. I want to get away ! For the first time the
wish was definite and clear in her mind. It was Aunt
Ellen she wanted to get away from, from being like her.
so unselfish and good and devoted, thinking of people's
latter ends. You ought to be selfish ! Being selfish kept
you alive ! But Grandmamma had been selfish, using
up Aunt Ellen, absorbing her life, sitting there, the stately
old lady in her handsome gowns, sipping the gruel Aunt
Ellen had made, and saying, if there were lumps in it, " I
may not be here next Christmas." Her selfishness had taken
life from Aunt Ellen. The selfishness of her generation

growing rich while their workmen stayed poor, that had made an industrial world in a mess that it hadn't yet got out of. It ought to be fifty-fifty, I suppose. Half selfishness and half not. In fact, love thy neighbour as thyself, thought Rhoda, was probably right after all. Not more, like Aunt Ellen, not less like Grandmamma, because one did for yourself, and the other for other people.

"Where's Mother?" she asked Delia. She was often faintly uneasy if she was in the house with her mother and had not seen her for a long time. You can bring your mind to reason in half an hour, and your feelings not at all, or perhaps, by great courage and skill, in ten years.

"She's in her bedroom," Delia answered, in a tone that said firmly, "I don't care where she is." She saw the cord that tied Rhoda, and wanted to cut it.

"Come and help me to get things straight in the sitting-room, Roddy. Then we shall have somewhere to sit down in between times."

CHAPTER XXV

" RHODA ! " her mother called. " Rhoda ! Where are you, dear ? Come along ! If you'd help me now, I think I could get things straight in my bedroom."

She stood in the doorway of her room, frowning, a faint pink colour flushing her cheek-bones. To have her bed-room in disorder was always something that she could not bear. She felt as people do when they have a limb dislocated; every nerve was on a stretch until things were restored to their proper place. All her life she had never gone to bed, even when she came in late after a dance, without hanging her dress in the wardrobe, and folding her underclothes across a chair. She looked round now at the stray pieces of furniture, the drawers from the wardrobe lying on the bed, a waste-paper basket on her dressing-table, stuffed full of odds and ends wrapped in newspaper. A pulse beat in her cheek, and her voice rose higher with nervous exasperation :

" Rhoda ! Where are you, dear ? I want you."

Aunt Ellen came up the stairs carrying an armful of blankets. Her narrow plain face above them was full of eager and cheerful importance. She put down the blankets on a chair, and straightened her long back, pushing the wisps of hair out of her eyes.

" Rhoda's busy downstairs with Delia. Wait a minute, Nan dear. I'll just pop these into the airing cupboard, and then I'll come and help you."

Natalie went back into her bedroom, not very pleased. It was Rhoda she wanted, not Ellen. Ellen didn't know just where everything went. You didn't want people outside the family interfering with your bedroom. Even your sister, if she didn't live with you, was outside your family; your own family was always the people in the house with you. Natalie's sense of privacy was fastidious. She could not bear anyone to get her coat out of her wardrobe for her, nor to handle any of her belongings. She stood by the dressing-table, unwrapping the odds and ends in the waste-paper basket. Her expression was peevish and discontented. She had been up here alone for half an hour, and Rhoda had not come up to see how she was getting on. It was not like her to be so inconsiderate. Natalie's closed lips made a tight line. It was because Delia was at home, and the two of them were together, laughing and talking. Of course they were young. They did not realise what it meant to their mother to leave her home. But it was not like Rhoda to be selfish.

The discontent grew in Natalie's mind. All day she had felt herself left outside that close alliance of Rhoda and Delia. She had seen their eyes meet, laughing at something which had not amused her. She had always resented any combination in her family apart from her; she had hated it when Tom and the children talked about things which did not interest her, or when Maurice and Rhoda, playing in the garden, obviously wanted to get away from the grown-up people. She felt angry now with Delia, an old antagonist. Delia at sixteen and seventeen had been rude, intractable, stubborn. Going through a difficult age, Natalie had said to Tom, and he, poor man, distracted between the pair of them, had sighed and smiled, and said gently to Delia, when he was alone with her, " Can't you behave better to your Mother, Dell ? " She had flashed back at him, " It's no use, Daddy. I can't ! You've always behaved too well to her, that's the trouble ! I'm sorry if I'm making the house hell, but if I knock under to her like you and Roddy and Maurice, I shan't be able to call my soul my own. So long as I live here, I've got to fight her." Natalie did not know of that conversation, but the feeling of it was in the air. It had been an uncomfortable period, lasting till Delia left school and went off to London, to come home for a holiday six months later, independent and well-mannered, almost a visitor.

I hope, thought Natalie, that Delia isn't making Rhoda feel unsettled ! A breath of fear touched her, chilling her heart. Perhaps it was only her fancy that Rhoda had grown different as the day went on, had answered her more casually, and shown her less sympathy. Natalie did not say to herself that she would be glad when Delia went away again and left them in peace. Of course, she was devoted to all her children. In theory Maurice was her favourite; it was traditional to like your son best. Actually Maurice, having transferred his allegiance to Evelyn, was far less dear to her now than Rhoda, although she would have expected Rhoda to put herself out any day for his convenience.

She had unpacked all the small things in the waste-paper basket, and there were the drawers on the bed, full of her things, waiting to be put into the wardrobe, and no one had come. The afternoon was getting on; she was tired; she longed to sit down to tea in an undisturbed house. What could Rhoda be doing? She was really being very selfish! This room would never be straight, and she could not bear the thought of sleeping in it unless it was. She seized the drawer by its handles and pulled it impatiently off the bed, but her wrists were not strong enough to hold it. It turned over, and emptied its contents on to the floor.

Aunt Ellen came running in at the noise.

" Look ! " Natalie burst out. " I was trying to get that drawer off the bed, and everything's upset ! It was too heavy for me. I ought not to lift things like that ! But there was no one to help me ! I don't know where Rhoda is; she seems to have lost her head entirely. It's not like her to be so inconsiderate. I really don't believe we shall ever get straight at all."

There were tears in her voice, and she knelt down and fumbled inefficiently with the untidy muddle on the floor.

" Never mind ! " Aunt Ellen said soothingly. " We'll soon pick them up again ! The girls are getting the furniture straight in the sitting-room, so there will be one room comfortable for you to rest in. Look, there's no harm done ! We can put a lot of these things back just as they are without unfolding them."

She began to sort the heap with capable fingers, humming a little tune as she worked. It was all so natural. Long before her life had consisted of doing things for Mamma she had been accustomed to doing things for Nan. She had darned all their stockings because touching wool set Nan's teeth on edge; she had patiently made all the buttonholes on two dresses, or on two sets of cambric knickers, because Nan couldn't make buttonholes. It

had been an understood thing in the family that Nan
couldn't do any tiresome jobs as well as Ellen.

The lid had come off an old chocolate box with a bunch
of flowers worked in shaded ribbon on the top. A hoard
of small treasures were scattered on the carpet: a broken
fan, a bunch of dance programmes with dangling pencils,
scraps of material, a spray of imitation orange-blossom,
a child's curl in a bit of paper, a plaster baby in a cradle
off the top of a christening cake. Ellen picked this up,
exclaiming, "Why that was on Maurice's cake, wasn't
it? I remember it quite well. There were silver birds
on it, too, and Mamma took one home with her. He was
such a dear little baby! Mamma was so proud of him!
Her first grandchild! She talked about him to everyone;
she thought the world of him."

Natalie was not listening to her. She was stretching
a small piece of pink silk over her fingers.

"Do you remember this, Nell? It was the dress I wore
at the Assembly the first time Tom took me in to supper.
I was so terrified that Bertie Hodgson would ask me for
the supper dance first! I didn't know if Tom would ask
me at all, and I thought if I told Bertie I was engaged,
I might be left without a partner."

Ellen said, in the teasing voice of forty years ago:

"*You* left without a partner!"

Back came all her triumphant pride in her pretty
sister's successes—pride that had made endurable the
gaps in her own programme between duty dances with
polite young men. When she could catch Nan's eye, or
watch the admiring glances that followed her, she could
bear the painful knowledge that they were duty dances.
The best part of the ball for Ellen had been the half

hour after they got home, when they brushed their hair together by their bedroom fire. Then it had been fun to look at the names on Nan's full programme, and to hear what they had all said, and discuss the dresses.

" Do you remember Carol Jackson's coming-out dance, Nell ? "

Their minds travelled back together to that past evening.

" Poor Bertie ! " Ellen said.

Natalie smiled, and made a pretty, conscious movement of her head. But Bertie had got over it long ago, and had married a girl from Edinburgh, and their daughter had been with Maurice to dinner dances.

" It was a lovely pink," Natalie said, pleating the scrap of silk into a rosette. " Mamma wanted me to have it dyed afterwards, but I never would. I had a new black net instead. Do you remember it, Nell ? It came back just in time for the Fentons' dance, and it was all wrong. We had to alter the fasteners."

Ellen remembered well. Back again in their own bedroom, she stitched on the tiny hooks and eyes for dear life, the flounces of black net billowing over her knee, and rising crisply from the floor, while Nan, dabbing her tear-stained face with cold water, leaned forward to look anxiously at her reflection in the glass.

" Oh, Nell ! Will my eyes get right in time ? I'll never, never let that idiot Miss Birch make me another thing ! "

Her eyes had got right; she always cried easily and recovered easily. She had looked so pretty in the crisp black flounces that Miss Birch was forgiven, much to Ellen's relief, for if Nan said they were not to let her make for them any more, then they wouldn't. Miss Birch's face, her anxious cow's eyes and her pale mouth perilously filled with pins, haunted Ellen through the evening.

Natalie lifted the broken fan.

" I've always kept that. It was the first present Tom ever gave me. I dropped mine and he trod on it and broke it, and then he sent me this one instead. Hand painted ! He bought it in London. I thought it was lovely ! I wish I hadn't broken one stick."

She spread it out, touching the painted, *poudrée* ladies with her fingers, feeling the roughness of the paint on the smooth surface of stretched silk. She had broken it one evening after they were married, after Maurice was born, when they had been going to a dance, and she had been in a temper. Her hair would not go right, her dress did not please her, and she had scolded Tom for it until he went downstairs, and then she had jerked the fan out of a drawer and caught it against the top. That had seemed to her to be Tom's fault too, and she had not spoken to him on the way to the dance, but had sat in the corner, filling the cab with her silent displeasure. She had never been taught to use her mind, and it did not occur to her to wonder how it was that after they were married everything seemed to be Tom's fault. It could not be hers, because she was now a wife and mother like her own mother, and the mother of a family was always right. Natalie had called Tom selfish and clumsy, had said to herself that men were like children, that they did not understand. Never once had she seen a puzzled young husband, wanting more love than she had to give, eager to give more love than she could do with, checked and dismayed by a wife who turned away from his caresses and began to nag. She had been brought up to believe her parents infallible, and she assumed infallibility as soon as she was in a house of her own, and on the way to becoming a parent.

Dear Tom, poor fellow ! Ellen was thinking. She was too religious to think " poor fellow " because he was dead, and far too loyal to her sister to ask herself why she had sometimes thought it when he was alive. She had felt sorry for him when Nan snapped at him or ran out of the room in tears; he looked like a dog that had been scolded for something he had not done. Nan had always been delicate and highly strung; the babies upset her, it was her nerves. All the same, Ellen was sorry for Tom, and glad that he was so fond of the children, especially Rhoda, his pet, so devoted to him. She always remembered Tom working in the garden with Rhoda helping him, or coming up to see the grandparents with a little girl in a blue skirt and red jersey trotting beside him. Seeing Maurice and Tatty together reminded her of Tom with Rhoda. Poor Rhoda, Aunt Ellen thought; how she must miss her father !

Natalie picked up the bundle of programmes.

" I might as well throw these away. Why, I can't even read half the names on them. It's silly to keep them after all these years."

Knowing that she wanted to keep them, Ellen answered :

" No, don't throw them away. It's nice to keep them."

She had never kept her own. The worst part of the whole thing had been showing them to her mother at breakfast the next morning. " George Armitage ought to have asked you ! " her mother said sharply; or, " Didn't Jerry Baines

ask you for a dance ? After dining here twice ? Very rude
of him."

Her spoken condemnation was for George and Jerry,
but her unspoken scorn was for Ellen. There had been one
evening before Nan was out when Ellen, home from the
Assembly, had thrust her nearly blank programme into
her bedroom fire, and had told Mamma next morning
that she must have dropped it in the cab, a sin which for
months lay heavy on her conscience.

Natalie was turning the bits of cardboard, and trying
to read the scrawled names.

" The girls never had as good a time as we had, Nell.
Not even Delia, although she is so pretty."

Her tone was complacent. It pleased her to think that
her daughters had never equalled her ballroom successes.
Ellen, who had not resented that complacency on her own
account, felt a desire to defend her nieces, and replied :

" Everything is so different now. It's better, I believe."
She was thinking that if she were young now she could go
out and be a nurse, instead of wishing for it, and being
told that she should be thankful she was not one of those
poor girls who had to earn their own living.

" I don't think it's better."

" Girls have so much more freedom."

" Yes. But "—Natalie, looking back into her past youth,
searched for words to express the difference—" we didn't
worry about anything," she said lamely. That was not
true in a way, for she had always worried, had thought
that her dress did not suit her, or that she would not have
the partners she wanted ; but she had not worried about
anything except her own affairs. Tucked into a warm
little private existence, she had neither known nor cared

that some people were too poor while others were too rich, that wars might break out, and social orders might be turned upside down, and perhaps ought to be. She had never felt the smallest responsibility towards the world. She knew that Rhoda, Maurice, and Delia, each in their different way, did feel responsible. A vague pity troubled her as though she had seen a small girl carrying a baby much too large for her.

" No," she said firmly. " They don't have as much fun as we did. Everything's so complicated ! "

The shade of an old dimple appeared in her still smooth cheek.

" Do you remember Mamma would make us come away before the end ? And sometimes I slipped upstairs again with my cloak on, and took it off in the room, and had another dance. Once it was the lancers, and it took so long that Mamma found out. She was ready, and there was the cab waiting. She was angry with me ! "

Ellen laughed.

" Yes, and it was snowing, do you remember ? And old Mr. Hobhouse couldn't come with the cab, and sent a young man who wasn't quite sober, and he nearly drove us all into a ditch on the way home ! "

Delia, running upstairs and opening the door, saw the two elderly women kneeling on the floor, her aunt smoothing a scrap of pink brocade, her mother fingering a bunch of old programmes. They looked up at her as though she were irrelevant.

" The room's all ready, and Ivy's made us some tea. Aren't you coming down ? "

" Yes. Go on, dear. We're coming."

They scrambled up stiffly, smiling at one another. They

had shared so much that these young things had never known !

" There's nothing like old times, is there, Nell ? "

Natalie put her arm through Ellen's, thinking that Ellen now was all that was left to her of the old times. They went out of the room together, and downstairs.

PART III

EVENING

"What pleasure, Sir, find we in life to lock it
From action and adventure?"

CYMBELINE

CHAPTER XXVI

A REMOVAL, Rhoda perceived, is like a slow journey across difficult country, full of halts and pauses, interspersed with odd meals and cups of tea consumed hurriedly, like meals and drinks in a station waiting-room. She left the others in the sitting-room, and rummaged among the unpacked glass and china on the hall table until she found a cup-shaped bowl of clouded glass. Arranging bowls of flowers was her passion. By choosing strange colours and putting them together, combining the vivid discords in a brilliant harmony, she expressed and satisfied a deep, unsatisfied longing for charm and colour. She ran out into the garden and picked, apparently at random, but really with design, a dark red rose, the scarlet flowers of a geum, a handful of flame and gold nasturtiums, a spray of early Michaelmas daisy, shafts of golden rod, a cluster of wine-coloured pansies, grown small in the flower and branching in the stalk with neglect and want of cutting. She carried the flowers in and put them one by one in the clouded bowl, lifted them and shook them gently, setting free their airy grace with a light touch, as though she shook loose a flock of butterflies into the air. She carried the bowl into the sitting-room.

"Oh, Roddy!" Delia exclaimed. "How lovely!"

"You are a funny girl!" her mother said, half fretfully.

" Fancy bothering to arrange flowers with all the house
in such a mess ! "

" I think it was very clever of Rhoda to find them,"
Aunt Ellen soothed in her flat, kind voice. " Flowers make
a room look like home. I always say that nothing else
makes so much difference. And you know, Nan dear,
we're really getting on very well. We shall be straight in
no time. There's no need for you to do any more. You
just sit here and have a rest. The girls and I will finish it."

Natalie shook her head.

" I must see that everything goes in the right places."
She picked up the teapot. " I think we ought to make
some fresh tea for Jim. He'll be here in a minute, won't
he, Delia ? "

Delia put down her cup.

" I'll walk along to the end of the road and meet him.
There's nothing particular to do just at the moment, is
there ? I won't be long."

Rhoda saw her face as she turned away; it was soft,
happy, and excited. Delia was different because Jim was
so near; she had forgotten all of them, moved away from
them to meet him. They saw her move past the window,
bareheaded, in her jumper and skirt.

" She ought to put a hat on if she's going past all those
houses," Natalie fretted. " I daresay Jim's train will be
late, and she'll waste half an hour standing about waiting
for him."

" It's nice to see her so happy," Aunt Ellen said gently.

Mrs. Powell would have kept Delia back if she could.
One of her children running from her to someone else,
to a young man that she did not really like. She would
have preferred Hilary as a son-in-law; he had distinction,

and good manners; she had quite liked introducing him
to her friends. They had not often seen his plays, which
were not the kind of play they selected when they were up
in Town for a week's fun, but they could see that he was
something out of the ordinary. Hilary had not seemed to
Natalie Powell like an intruder taking her daughter from
her, perhaps because she had been shrewd enough to
realise from the beginning that the relationship was
insecure, and not likely to be permanent. No such reassuring thought had helped her to put up with Delia's
engagement to Jim. Natalie was always clever enough to
see when a fight was lost. It was clear that the square,
tenacious young man meant business. And he had red
hair, and had not even been to a good Public School !
In the opinion of his future mother-in-law, he combined
the defects of Sir Robert Peel and the Duke of Wellington,
having no manners and no small talk. He disagreed with
her on a good many subjects, and sometimes made the
fatal mistake of saying so.

" Delia will be very busy now, getting ready for her
wedding," Ellen said.

" Of course, I think it would be so much better if they
put it off for another year. You see, Jim is only changing
over to this other part of the hospital, the Pathological
Lab, or whatever they call it, at Christmas. I think it
would be much better for him to have a year at the new
work first, and be able to give his mind to that without
having to think about getting married at the same time.
And he might get more money at the end of a year. I
think they'll find it very difficult to manage on his salary.
It's all very well for Delia to talk about going back to
her lab to give extra help, and do odd jobs two or three

afternoons a week, but she won't find it so easy when she's
got the flat on her hands, and all their meals and shopping
and everything. She's only going to have a woman in to
clean one morning a week."

" I'm afraid it will be very hard work for her," Aunt
Ellen agreed anxiously.

" She's never done very much housework or cooking.
I can't think how she'll manage."

" I hope they will get proper meals, and not live on
tinned food, as I believe young people often do nowadays."

Rhoda stirred impatiently. How frightened they were,
how anxious about what might happen ! How their minds
picked out the difficulties, the things that could go wrong,
and missed the central core of joy and adventure ! It had
always been like that; a network of her mother's fears had
surrounded her all her life. " Be careful, dear, don't
fall ! " " It's too late for you to come back alone." " You
must never speak to strangers." " I don't think you would
really enjoy that as much as you expect." Hedged in by
fears, you began to live negatively. Delia from the first
had been brave, had fought her way clear of them.

" And if children come, I can't think how they will
ever manage ! " Mrs. Powell said.

Rhoda got up and went out. She did not want to stay
in the room with these two elderly women and their misgivings; she might become like them. If you were brave
yourself, cautions did not matter. It was when they
touched hidden springs of diffidence and fear in your own
mind that they paralysed you. She went along to the
kitchen, where a rich confusion prevailed. Most of the
loose property of the family seemed to be on the floor.
In an empty case that had held china, Mickey played

joyfully among the discarded wrappings, plunging and pouncing. His face, with its absurd black nose, light eyes, and broad, soft cheeks, appeared for a moment above the edge of the packing-case, then vanished, and there was a flump and a scurry, a joyous rustle of paper. Ivy, with Mrs. Robins asleep on her knee, sat on the coal-box, drinking tea out of a mug. Her thick, waved hair was ruffled, there was a smear of dust across her rosy cheeks, but she looked settled and at home. After all, thought Rhoda, she had been making herself at home in other people's houses since she was fourteen. She had the experience and the temperament of a soldier of fortune; she adapted herself to life as she found it.

" Are you getting on all right in here, Ivy ? "

Ivy nodded.

" That lad that come with the vans, the one with ginger 'air, asked me to go to the all-in wrestling with 'im on Saturday evening."

" You wouldn't like that, would you ? "

Ivy smiled. " I went once, and it was grand ! Everybody shouting and laughing and singing, and there was a man put his shoulder out." She added, " I'm not going, of course, because Wilf wouldn't like me going with another boy, and 'e goes out with 'is mother on Saturday evenings, so 'e can't take me." She added wistfully, " There was a man killed one week ! "

" Oh, Ivy, you wouldn't like to see that ! "

" That was only one week," Ivy explained. " They often get hurt, of course, but then, as that lad says, they get paid for it." Her Elizabethan indifference was in sharp contrast to the gentleness of the red hand stroking Mrs. Robins's head. She kissed the cat's ear and murmured

tenderly, " Little soul of a lamb ! Mother Pussy ! "
before putting her down on the floor. " That Mickey,"
she remarked. " He's been playing with the paper all the
afternoon. I'll come for the tea-things now, Miss Rhoda."

" It will take you a long time to get straight in here,"
Rhoda remarked.

" Oh, no, not long. I'll 'ave all this cleared away in no
time."

Rhoda began to say, " Well, be careful not to break
things," but stopped herself. She thought, I'm as bad as
Mother and Aunt Ellen ! Why does everyone start to warn
and caution the confident people, the people who feel
equal to things ? Ivy will break one or two, of course, but
she'll do it just the same whether I tell her or not. It's
damnable, all this discouragement, and, the worst of it is,
you do it more if you've been discouraged ! She nodded.

" All right, Ivy. I'll come and see if you want any help
later."

She went upstairs to her bedroom. It was beginning to
look habitable. The dressing-table and washstand were
in place, Ivy had made the bed, and a wooden case of
books had been carried up, and stood in the middle of the
floor. One of the men had untied the thick cord and
thrown back the lid. Rhoda's fingers itched to unpack her
books and put them on the white painted shelves waiting
for them. The last few days, so entirely devoted to practical
matters, had been exhausting. Rhoda pushed back the
covering newspaper. The very sight of the books was like
opening a window, remembering other worlds. There was
always that ! Reassurance warned her, her chilled spirit
revived, and she lost some of the sense of unreality which
had been with her all day.

I don't know what I'm making such a fuss about. It's bound to be a bit queer, removing from the place where you've always lived, but it isn't really the end of anything. In a few days I shall have lost this odd feeling of hanging between two worlds. We shall be settled in here, and ordinary life will be going on as usual. All the change and disturbance will be over. I shall see my friends again, and read new books, and I shall go and stay with Ursula, and there'll be things to do for Delia before her wedding, and Maurice and Evelyn and Tatty coming in and out, and everything going on normally. I shall be sensible again.

It is so easy to deceive yourself sometimes with this talk of being sensible, as though being sensible were always the safe, the colourless thing, and not, at least once or twice in a lifetime, the sudden spring of the imagination, the sharp dramatic action.

Rhoda moved to the window and looked out. She thought, I shall like this garden. In a few days I shan't feel restless any more. The autumn is beginning; people will be coming back from their holidays, concerts and theatres will be starting again. I shall be able to pull my life round me again like a blanket. This is that half-waking minute in the night when the blanket is slipping off, before you pull it up again.

She saw over the garden fence Delia and Jim coming along the road. He looked square and solid in his grey flannel suit; he carried his suitcase easily, not bumping it against his knees. They walked slowly, in no hurry to reach the house, enjoying their moment together.

Rhoda, leaning on the window-sill and watching them, thought, as though coming upon something which had been in her mind for years, That is what I really want !

The blanket had slipped off on to the floor. It was woven of custom and habit, of pride and the thing called modesty, of fear; of remembering Barry, and clinging to her love for him because it was a disembodied ghost of love. It had been safer to cherish that than to try again.

You can't live much if you want to be safe. When we all three went skating together on the dam, Maurice and Dell and I, Maurice and I began gingerly, trying not to fall, but Dell ran at it, and did fall, but she skated while we were still learning. I can see her now, a little sturdy girl in a blue reefer coat with brass buttons, calling to us to come on. I don't know why she was so different ! It's the only way with anything, to run at it and get your balance, to be like Dell and not mind, but, if you do mind, still to do it, even though you fall harder.

She was taking out the books and stacking them on the bed. A childish desire tickled her to open one and look for a sign, trying the *Sortes Vergilianæ*, like poor King Charles when he opened at the loss of his dead head. She disbelieved in fortunes in cards and hands, told by obliging friends who had learnt it from a friend who really knew, but they had a fascination for her.

There was a penny in her pocket. Heads I stay, tails I go ! If it came heads, she knew that she would stay with her mother as long as she lived, and afterwards have just enough money—that was a pity, probably; had kept her inactive—would be pleasant, busy, intelligent, have friends. Not like Aunt Ellen. Yes, like Aunt Ellen really. Only unlike her on the top floor. If I go I must go now, leave Mother, do some work, make new friends, hope for love. I can't remember who it was who said that life was never closed to you as long as you went down any avenue that was open. Tails I go! She laughed, suddenly ashamed of herself, and put the penny back in her pocket. She thought, I might be some sickening Buchmanite, seeking for a guidance! I expect the Vergil's in the other case, and if I found it, it would probably open at the catalogue of ships, and serve me jolly well right! I'm not much good, but I will at least make up my mind decently before to-night.

She heard below the sounds of arrival, doors opening and shutting, Jim's deep voice, Delia's laugh, her mother and Aunt Ellen fussing and being kind. She ran downstairs to join in the welcome.

CHAPTER XXVII

If, thought Rhoda, you could, just for a single minute, get inside another person, and look at yourself and everyone from them, what a difference it would make to all the rest of your life ! She could remember, as a little girl, realising one day that she would always be Rhoda. Surprised by this truth, hitherto unnoticed, she asked, " Maurice, what is it like to be you ? " They were lying out on a rug on the grass, both reading, and Maurice, who was absorbed, did not answer. She shut her book and looked at his square body in grey flannel trousers and white shirt, at his rough dark head and rosy, sunburnt face, with the tiny freckles on the nose. What was it like to be the person inside that? She shut her eyes, and stretched and strained her imagination, trying to become, just for one moment, the person inside Maurice. She could imagine herself in Maurice's body, looking at the body of Rhoda, a bare-legged little girl in a blue cotton frock, but still she was not Maurice, only Rhoda, who had moved outside herself into someone else. It was disappointing ! Where were you, she wondered, inside yourself ? Whereabouts in your body was the person Rhoda, or the person Maurice ? She laid a grubby hand on her chest, and then lower down on her diaphragm, feeling that she herself must be somewhere in the middle. " Maurice," she said, " *where* are we ? " Maurice, who was getting bored with his book,

answered her this time. He said, " On the lawn of course,
you fool ! Have you been to sleep ? Let's go and get some
strawberries."

But I should like just for one moment, thought Rhoda,
to be inside Jim, to be Jim, and see this family from outside
as anyone must who is coming into it. It would be better
to see it from Jim than from Evelyn ! He doesn't mind
us, and I think she did. It was harder for her; she made
the first breach. Besides, although she's so definite and
cool, she's not sure of herself. She's always afraid, really,
of not doing the right thing, not coming up to some
standard. I don't know if it's her mother's, or those
people she ran about with at Gillans Cross. Jim isn't
troubled that way. An unusually independent young man,
quite able to stand on his own. That's what mother and
Maurice don't like about him. Mother knows she can't
get at him anywhere, and Maurice expects more super-
ficial modesty and deference. Besides, although Maurice
has Liberal views, his feelings are Conservative; he wants
a lot of support from the herd, and he likes to feel that
other people want it. And this is a dogmatic young man, a
bit arrogant, though he'll probably grow out of that.

She looked up at Jim as he stood on the hearthrug,
appraising him. He caught her eye, and suddenly gave
her a grin so sweet and friendly that she thought, Yes,
it's a tough nut, but it's got a sweet kernel ! Dell hasn't
made a mistake this time. He knows that mother doesn't
like him; he probably knows Maurice doesn't; but I
don't suppose he minds much, and I dare say they will
when they get used to him being different. Hilary had
been aware of Maurice's dislike, had thought about it
and smarted under it. He had always been conscious

of Maurice's presence in a room; had talked with a more
cutting brilliance when he was there, or had made
nervous, and, to Rhoda's eyes, pathetically inept attempts
at conciliation, asking those questions about the industrial world which are asked by well-intentioned
theorists who have seldom spoken to an artisan, and for
whom the whole of England north of the Trent is a
distressed area. Maurice, on his part, thought the questions
patronising, and suspected the cutting wit of being
directed against himself. As uneasy in his own way as
Hilary, he had been just as nervous as Hilary was of him.
The sight of the two handling one another so gingerly
and unsuccessfully had sometimes amused Rhoda and
sometimes made her feel sorry for them. The relief with
which she saw her mother's unexpressed disapproval
slide off Jim was mixed with a faint surprise. That potent
displeasure which, ever since she could remember, had
filled her house and darkened her world was not more
to him than cold weather would have been to his strong
and vigorous youth. His presence in the house was like
daylight, revealing that the shadows in dark corners
were only shadows. Among her confused feelings, Rhoda
discovered a faint pity for her mother. She felt her dis-
comfiture at finding her weapons powerless. Yet she
thought, as she lay back in a big chair, and watched her
mother talking to Jim, that they ought to have been
powerless long ago but for a yielding weakness in them
all—in herself, in Maurice, in her father. A tyranny is
not all the tyrant's fault; it is the fault of those who
submit to be slaves.

She discovered surprisingly that she had made up her
mind. Before we go to bed to-night, she thought, I'll

tell mother I'm going. It would be unkind, perhaps, to
tell her to-day, on top of everything else, to let her know
on the first night in the new home that she was going
to lose her daughter. All the same, Rhoda knew that she
must do it. If she didn't do it to-day, she never would.
Only free people, she thought, can afford to be kind, and
I'm not free ! She could do it to-day, when she was
shaken out of her ordinary life, strung to an unusual
clearness of perception. If she let the opportunity go,
put it off until to-morrow or next week, everyday life
would enclose her again with its soft meshes, its deceiving
reality that for her, she now knew, was only half reality.
Probably it was only half reality for everyone, unless
it was a channel through which their whole being flowed.
Everyday life had been her friend, helping her to go on
after she had lost Barry, through the colourless years,
through her father's illness and death; but it had been
her enemy, too, because its various demands had hidden
her from herself, its manifold activities had made her
think that she was living.

She was very tired after a day's hard work and hanging
about. She lay back and closed her eyes. A twittering
of birds came through the window from the apple trees
in their new garden. The voices of the four in the room
also became a confused blur of sound; Aunt Ellen's
fluttering and jerky tones, Delia's clear young voice,
her mother's decisive and slightly sharpened words, all
running together above the bass of Jim's deeper tones.
She dozed off, slipping from wakefulness into a heavenly
peace that relaxed every stretched nerve in her body,
and filled her to the brim with tranquillity.

When she opened her eyes again, the group by the

fireplace had separated. Probably they had gone to arrange
the dining-room, for she could hear the noise of furniture
being pushed about. She thought that she was alone in
the room, until a movement at the far end made her look
round. Her mother was standing at her desk. She had
opened it without pulling out the runners at the sides
to support the lid, a thing which she often did, and which
had never failed to annoy her husband. It was character-
istic of her that she should expect the desk to serve her
purpose at once without remembering that she was
putting too much strain on the hinges. She bent down and
fumbled in a pigeon-hole, opened a little drawer and shut
it again with a quick, impatient movement. She was looking for something that she could not find, and in a minute
she would turn round and blame somebody, Rhoda,
since there was no one else there. Rhoda's nerves quivered,
shrinking back from the irritable tones, the small outburst of temper. Coward ! she said to herself impatiently.
If she felt like that about so small a thing, a moment's
fretful outburst, how could she manage to tell her
mother that she was going to leave her ? She might tell
her now, while they were alone together, and then it
would be done with; she would have burnt her boats,
and the worst would be over. She was not likely to have
another chance of seeing her alone until bedtime.

Her body was taut in the corner of the chair. Her
mouth felt dry, and she moistened her lips with her
tongue. It was like the moment some years ago, before
her first frightened attempt at lecturing. I'll do it before
she speaks to me. Her mother had stripped the elastic
band from a bundle of letters, and was looking through
them. Go on, you fool, said Rhoda's reasonable mind,

tell her now ! Untouched by reason, her feelings fought,
the two opposing desires locked in a grip that paralysed
her. I must get away. I want my own life. She shan't
keep me ! I can't leave her. I can't hurt her. I love
her.

There were two women standing at that desk, turning
over some letters and accounts. One was Rhoda's enemy,
who held her back from freedom, who had demanded
too much unselfishness, and taught her fear, who had
set up a policeman in her mind to say, Keep off the grass.
The other was her mother, who loved her and whom she
loved, to whom she had run all her early life for safety
or protection. The feeling of indecision was so painful
in itself that it almost obscured the issue. Something
like this had happened before. A small Rhoda in a
Holland smock and straw hat stood on the steps of the
French window, watching her father go off down the
drive. He was going to a sale of work in the vicarage
garden. He turned again at the bend of the drive, and
smiled and beckoned to Rhoda to come with him. Her
whole body was one eager longing for the outing
in his company, for the bran-tub and the toy-stall and
tea in a tent, but her mother had been angry and said,
" Very well, take the child ! You don't want me, I
know, if you've got her ! " Rhoda stood on the step,
aching to run after her father, guiltily tied by remorseful
allegiance to her mother. Her father walked on further
away from her. Tears smarted under her eyelids; the
deprivation was almost more than she could bear. She
went back into the cool drawing-room, shaded by sun-
blinds from the heat. Her mother was lying on the sofa
with a headache, her eyes closed. She opened them and

saw the disconsolate small figure. She smiled and said
gently, " Run after him, dear, if you like." But it was her
own permission Rhoda wanted. She did not go. Afterwards she had felt ashamed of herself without knowing
why, some dim perception that she had been silly disturbing her consciousness of having been good.

Now she saw the issue more clearly. If I don't go,
it won't really be for mother's sake; it will be to keep
my own mind comfortable. I'll tell her before she speaks.
The air in the room seemed to be waiting for her mother's
voice or her own. It was like being in a nightmare,
struggling against this opposing half of her that dried
her mouth and held the words back in her throat. With
an effort that was like a birth-pang through the whole
of her divided person, she said huskily:

" Mother ! "

The door opened and Aunt Ellen came in.

" Nan dear, I thought you were having a rest. You'll
be so tired. Why don't you sit down in your chair for half
an hour ? Where's Rhoda ? Oh, there you are, dear !
Could you just come and show us where your mother
wants the chest of drawers ? It makes such a difference
having Jim. He is so strong. He seems a very good-
natured young man, Nan."

The last words were a deprecating protest against a
dislike which Ellen felt. How often had she made in-
effectual protests on behalf of Nan's " detestables,"
never quite daring to admit that she liked them, but
trying to insert a softening clause ! Natalie's voice was
sharp with irritation and weariness as she replied:

" Oh, yes, I think he's quite good-natured. Oh, Nell,
I can't find the list of things to go into the sale anywhere,

and I ought to post it off to-night ! I've had so much to think of ! "

The peevish, usual complaint, so familiar a part of everyday life, brought Rhoda back to the surface. Ashamed, but relieved, she replied rather crossly, " I've got the list in my writing-case. If I'd known you wanted that, I could have told you where it was."

Aunt Ellen, looking from one to the other, said soothingly :

" There, Nan. Rhoda will get it, and we can post it as we go over to Maurice's. Look, I'll bring you an envelope and your pen and you can sit down in this chair and address it."

Her bright, kind fussing over her sister troubled Rhoda, impatient because her mother accepted it so readily, impatient with Aunt Ellen for offering it, even faintly jealous of her for playing the part of a better daughter than herself. She exclaimed, "I'll get the list," and escaped out of the room.

CHAPTER XXVIII

At least once a week Maurice had driven round
by his old home on the way back from the office, had
called in for a cup of tea and a few words with his mother
or Rhoda. Very often when his father was alive he had
driven him home and come in with him. On those brief
visits without Evelyn he had seemed to his family to be
more like his old self. Natalie had usually said so after he
had gone, pleased because she had at least the illusion
that he was hers again. It was on these visits that he said
what he thought about a good many things, including
Evelyn's mother. They all agreed with him about her,
she was really a rather dreadful woman; but sometimes,
as she listened to him, Rhoda felt a qualm of uneasiness
for him. He seemed to find a relief and satisfaction in his
indictment of Mrs. Amber, in pouring scorn upon a
whole attitude to life and way of looking at things which
she personified. But Evelyn had been brought up in that
attitude, and had not departed from it. What was it,
Rhoda wondered, that he was really complaining of and
straining against as he strolled on the lawn and stood by
the fireplace before going away from his old home to
his new one ?

Maurice was thinking of those brief visits as he locked
his desk in the office, and prepared to leave. The new
house was on the other side of the town; it would be much

more out of his way. He would go there often, of course,
run in for a few minutes and find his mother knitting by
the fire, and Rhoda with a book under the light, but it
would be going to see them in a new house, not going
home. A chapter was over. It was absurd that he should
feel so much as though he were cut adrift, for he had left
home five years ago, when he married Evelyn, and went
to his own house.

Yes, he thought, but I didn't really leave it. He started
the car and drove out of the yard. His old home, his
family, his parents had still been the background of his
life. He had felt himself their son getting married, their
son taking his wife home, taking their little grand-
daughter to see them. He had never quite ceased to feel
like a visitor in his new, clean, chintzy house. His house !
It was Evelyn's, and he was staying with her. With dismay
he perceived that he had always been staying with her.
His engagement, honeymoon, and married life had
been a prolonged and lovely visit. A visit could be a
delirious pleasure, full of novelty and exhilaration and
delight; you might feel that you wanted it to go on for
ever, and that home would be dull after it, but you came
home. If you were told in the middle of the most agree-
able visit that you would never go home again, you would
feel dismayed and disconcerted. That was what was
happening to him now. He was making a belated change
over which he ought to have made five years ago. He
was realising for the first time that his visit was his
home.

He turned off the tram-lines and drove through the
side streets, determined to go round by the old house
once more. He said to himself that he ought to go and

see that everything had been left all right, and that the place was shut up after the men. The devil of it was if you realised that your visit was permanent, and at the same time that you were an unwelcome visitor whom your hostess was obliged to put up with. Not altogether unwelcome, Maurice thought bitterly. I'm a husband. I do. I'm much more necessary than the new things she wants for the drawing-room. I made her a bride, and I've supplied Tatty, and I suppose next year I shall supply another one. Oh, God ! Like having the house repainted in the terms of the lease every three years ! What a way for a child to be born ! Tatty at least had not been born like that. She had been born of their needing one another, coming together by a natural rhythm with no thought of her. But Evelyn said, " We won't order another till next spring." She had said it at the end of the summer holiday with her mother, and he had never been able to get out of his mind since then the idea that she had talked it over with her mother, settling it between them as they might settle to send for the plumber. Talking like that about it was what Evelyn called " everyone being so sensible about sex nowadays." But sometimes, thought Maurice, " being sensible about sex " meant not knowing a single damn' thing about love ! Evelyn's mother occasionally talked with a smile that curled his spine about " men's stories "—" the things you men talk about when we aren't there." Well, he'd heard plenty of bawdy stories, some funny, mostly dull, but no one of his friends had ever said to him, " I'm going to start ordering a baby next spring."

He turned in at the gates, drove up between the trees, and stopped the car at the front door. The door was open,

but the shutters were fastened across the downstairs
windows. The upstairs windows, blank and without
curtains, were all shut. The house that had always been
so welcoming had no welcome for him, it was a shell,
empty of the life that had filled it for a hundred years.

He pushed the door wide open, and walked into the
hall. His shoes made a loud noise on the bare stone floor.
There was an echo somewhere in the back of the house
near the kitchen. He stood still, but the echo did not
stop. Someone was in the house, moving about and
coming towards him. An absurd, a preposterous, fancy
came into his mind that it might be his father. He did
not believe in ghosts, certainly not in ghosts that walked
so audibly, yet it would have seemed no more than
natural if his father had come through the archway at
the back of the hall, and glanced at him with his quick,
welcoming smile, and said, "Hulloa, old boy. Had a
good day?" He had said that on the evening before he
died, when Maurice came home, on his way from the
office, and found him sitting out on the lawn looking at
his herbaceous border. They had talked for a minute
or two about business, and then Maurice had hurried off
to take Evelyn out to dinner, thinking that his father
seemed much better. That had been their last talk, for
by the time he got there, in the early hours of the morning, his father was dead.

The feet must have walked perhaps twenty paces while
Maurice recalled that evening—dinner and bridge, the
drive home with Evelyn, sleepy by his side, the telephone
ringing in the night across his dreams, his father's dead
face, and someone downstairs. Ivy, he thought, half
dressed and crying, thrusting a cup of tea into his hand,

most of it in the saucer. The footsteps were lighter than a man's. His absurd expectation vanished as Rhoda came into the hall. She was wearing a coat and hat, and carrying a suitcase and a bunch of keys. He thought that she had been crying. He was always very fond of her, if a little inclined to take her life for granted. He went up and put an arm round her.

" Do you hate leaving it, Roddy ? So do I."

She shook her head.

" I don't, Maurice. I don't really mind."

Her eyes filled with tears.

" It isn't that. It's that I've been realising how I've gone on with daily life in this house all these years, and never done anything at all ! "

" Why you've done lots of things. You're always busy ! "

" Oh, yes, that, but I haven't moved. I've stayed shut up in life at home, a child's life. Don't you see, Maurice ? I haven't grown. Dell has. Dell has gone out into the world and worked for her living and mixed with all sorts of people, and now she's going to marry Jim and start a new family; she's following the natural order of things. She's kept pace with Time, but I haven't. I've slipped behind it, and if you once do that you're all wrong. It's so hard to catch up. If you're wrong with Time, you're wrong with everything."

" I suppose I'm wrong with Time too. I want to put it back. I've been wanting to all day. I was thinking, when I came in here, that we were happier in this house when we were young than we ever shall be in our lives again. I mind the house going so much because I shall be cut off from that."

" But, Maurice, dear, you ought to be. Don't you see we ought to have moved out of here years ago—with our minds and our feelings, I mean? I know you did actually move into another house, but that isn't enough. I haven't even done that, but I'm going to."

" You mean, you'll go away and leave Mother? "

" Yes, go away and work, and see life and do things."

" Couldn't you see life here? "

" I could, of course. I do; but I want to take more part in it. I can't do that here, because I've got into a safe, narrow channel; I've been running down it all my life. If I'm going to do anything at all, I've got to begin by getting out of it. Do you think I'm wrong? "

" No; I think it's brave of you."

" Only half brave. If I was altogether brave, I could stay here and be free. If you're a whole person, you can be free anywhere. It doesn't matter where you live or what you do."

" I know. But we aren't whole, you and I."

A settle, which was to go into the sale, still stood near the fireplace. Maurice sat down on it, flinging one leg over the end, as he had often done when he came in from cricket matches or from skating, when he came home from work, when he was ready for dinner first and waited for the others in the hall. Seeing his dejected face, Rhoda forgot herself, stirred by old affection and a pity that was touched with impatience. She said: " It's no use regretting anything. It's like a chess problem, where you have to play handicapped with a lot of pieces lost. There's nothing to do but make the best job of it you can with the pieces you've got left."

" Why aren't we free, Roddy? "

" I don't know. At the moment I don't feel as though it mattered."

" I do. I've got a daughter. If I knew what went wrong with us, I might be able to avoid it for her."

And if I can do that, he thought, it doesn't matter about me ! I'll rub along.

" I think perhaps we were too well brought up, too much protected and cherished and looked after and instructed. We'd probably have been better kicked out into the street as soon as we could walk, and left to look after ourselves and fight other children and get out of the way of the traffic."

" Dell was brought up the same way as we were."

" Dell was different stuff, not so soft."

" I should hate to kick Tatty out into the street," Maurice said vehemently.

" Well, Evelyn won't let you."

A silence fell between them at the mention of Evelyn's name. No, Evelyn would never let Tatty run out into the street, not only because she loved her, but because running out into the street was outside her way of life, which was a neat gravelled path, Rhoda thought, in a well-kept suburban garden. Anything else was for her not only dangerous, but slightly wrong, a moral and social risk. The enclosed life was the decent life ; she would walk on her garden path and keep Tatty there. And Maurice ? Maurice would keep her in a garden, too, because he wanted to keep her safe and happy ; he loved her so much, but not quite enough to let her go free and suffer his own misgivings for her. And they were both trying to do their very best for her, would have made any sacrifices for her ; were already preparing to make them, to send her to an expensive boarding-school which would be a continuation of the enclosed garden. All that they could they would do for her, and the harm that they did her by their fears and withdrawals and rigidities, by love gone wrong between them, would be done without their knowing. It was no use saying anything.

" I ought to be getting back, Maurice."

" You've got the car here, I suppose ? "

" Yes."

" How are you getting on ? "

" Oh, very well. The bedrooms are more or less ready, and quite a lot done downstairs. Jim's just arrived. I've left him helping."

" Oh, he's there, is he ? " Maurice sounded rather sulky. He did not like the idea of Jim in the middle of his own family, doing the man's jobs, taking his place. Rhoda answered his unspoken feeling.

" He's right for Dell, Maurice. She's very fond of him."

" I suppose he is." He kicked the settle, and grumbled : " Well, anyhow, he's better than the last one ! "

" Poor Hilary ! I rather liked him."

" A terrible fellow ! " Maurice said finally.

" Not really. Only too clever for his sense."

" I can't think why Dell likes such extraordinary people ! "

Poor Maurice, Rhoda thought, always wanting people to be like himself and his family, to share their ideas and see things as they saw them, never quite willing to accept a world in which most people were very different and thought quite otherwise. That removal whose necessity she was beginning to realise was harder for him than for her, for she had been prepared a long time ago to accept other people's realities, other ways of living and loving. Looking at his sulky, downcast face, she said:

" Cheer up, Maurice ! You won't see a great deal of him, and he and Dell have the same sort of mind and feelings, the same slant on life. They're harmonious. That's a great thing, surely ? "

He lifted his face, and she saw in his eyes a look of pain that startled her. She felt as though she had broken down his defences and caught him unawares, spying out a nakedness that he had hidden even from himself. For a second she saw his young, impotent, and despairing spirit. He opened his lips, and she thought that he was going to say something. He jumped up and exclaimed:

" I must go. Evelyn will wonder where I've got to. See you later ! "

He ran out of the house to the car, as though he were escaping.

CHAPTER XXIX

ON HIS WAY HOME Maurice was conscious of an impatient desire to see Evelyn, as though the unhappy doubts and regrets which had been in his mind all day could be dispelled by her actual presence. He found reassurance in the fabric of their daily life together: their joint decisions about what they should do and spend or save; their exchange of gossip; their shared interest in Tatty. He left the car at the gate, thinking that he would want it later to take Aunt Ellen home.

Evelyn and Tatty had come back from their party. Evelyn was in the house, but Tatty had begged for a last ten minutes in the garden, and was moving about on the lawn. She ran with skipping steps, kicked up one foot behind her, stopped, turned, then darted off again, as pleased with the mere movement as a kitten scurrying and pouncing. Her face was interested, absorbed; she talked to herself, or played some game in her own mind. Maurice stood still on the front doorstep to watch her. Funny little thing! What in the world was she playing at and thinking about? Like Carol Wilson that afternoon, he was struck by the mysterious strangeness of his own child. They knew so much more about them now, Evelyn said, there was so much that they could do for them. With unwearied patience and care she had stuck to the routine hours of sleep and fresh air, weighed and measured vitamins, given reasonable explanations of baby fears. But Tatty herself, the person growing, the spirit housed in that healthy, well-cared-for little body, which of them knew anything about that ? How could they tell what their blundering care might do ?

Tatty paused on the far side of the lawn, put out one tentative finger, and just touched a bee, browsing deep in the crinkled coral rosette of a hollyhock. As the bee flew past her face with an angry buzz, Maurice heard her clear chuckle of mischief. After all, he thought more cheerfully, we can't be doing her much harm. Anyhow we do the best we can for her ! Hadn't they made her their first consideration since she was born, altered the whole routine of their lives to suit hers, thought of her first when ordering meals or making plans or arranging holidays ? Whatever else he and Evelyn were divided about, they had always agreed to do what was best for the child.

Tatty turned round and saw him. She called out, " Daddy ! Daddy ! " and came flying across the lawn. She hugged his knees, pressing her cheek against his coat, while he ruffled her dark hair. She stepped back from him, opening the little woollen coat she had been made to put on, and showing the pale pink Shantung frock beneath it.

" Look, Daddy ! My new frock ! "

She spread out her brief skirts and looked up at him, eagerly and innocently inviting admiration from the person whom she loved best in the world.

" You are a vain child ! " Evelyn said, in a cool voice, from behind Maurice's shoulder.

Maurice turned.

" Hulloa, darling ! I didn't know you were there ! Why shouldn't she be vain ? It's a very pretty frock."

Tatty dropped her skirts and stood abashed, chilled by a feeling of her mother's displeasure. Maurice, too, felt it, and said in a conciliatory tone:

" Did you make it ? "

" No, not that one. Mother sent it to her for a present."

Something in her had risen up annoyed and disapproving at her daughter's baby vanity and upward, feminine glance. The look and smile with which Maurice had responded hardened her still more. She said, as Tatty ran off:

" She's far too much interested in her frocks for such an infant."

" What does it matter ? She'll get interested in something else soon. Besides," Maurice added, laughing, " you can't blame her. She looks so pretty in them ! "

That remark flicked the feeling of which Evelyn was unaware, and made her say sharply:

" You're late back, aren't you ? I wanted you to come and see about drinks."

He followed her into the dining-room, and knelt down by the big cupboard under the bookcases which they used for a cellar.

" I went round by the old house."

He won't go on doing that, thought Evelyn. She had always resented those brief visits, always said to him, in a cold voice: " You're late back, aren't you ? " Jealousy of his family, of his old life and his own people, surged up in a keen pleasure because there was an end of his old home. She stood behind his kneeling body, fiercely glad as of a victory in a drawn-out campaign.

His head was in the cupboard, but he spoke to her over his shoulder:

" Roddy was there, locking up after the men. Do you know, she wants to go to London, and take on Delia's job ? "

" She did say something about it to me this morning, but of course I knew she didn't mean it."

" Oh, I think she does."

" It's nonsense ! " Evelyn said. " How can she go and leave your mother alone ? "

Her feeling against his family sharpened her voice. In the reaction towards them which the day had brought uppermost, he was moved to defend Rhoda. He said:

" Well, you left yours."

" That was to get married."

Her tone was complacent, or he fancied that it was. It flicked not only his feeling for his sister, but a deeper and more personal trouble, a feeling that Evelyn had wanted him as an accessory to her career; a bitter suspicion that anyone else would have done. He was accusing her rather than defending Rhoda when he cried out roughly: " Getting married isn't the only thing in the world ! "

He was thinking that it was very little without love. Evelyn, who had another antithesis in her mind, shrugged her shoulders, and replied:

" Oh, women take up careers when they can't get married, and want something to do."

" I suppose that's the sort of thing they said at Gillans Cross ? "

He used the place as a scapegoat, but the scorn and distaste in his voice cut at her like a whip, rousing her to an indignant defence of the people and the life that

had made her youth a toil and strain and exacted so
much of her. She said, in a challenging voice:

" You didn't like Gillans Cross, did you ? "

" No, I didn't. It was vulgar and smart and greedy and
stupid ! "

" They were my friends, the people there, and
Daphne's and Mother's."

" Friends ! " Maurice exclaimed. " If you'd got into a
hole they'd have dropped you the next day ! "

That stripped off the gay covering of parties and pretty
clothes and gaiety, and probed down to the hidden fear
which Evelyn had felt from her fifteenth year onwards,
but had never acknowledged. It made her feel, not only
that she might easily have been a failure, but that Maurice
despised her success. He had no idea how deeply he had
pricked her. He saw the blood rush up under her fair
skin till her face was as red as a furious child's. Her cool
composure broke up; it was a younger, more human,
Evelyn, that he often saw nowadays, who cried angrily:

" I know you despised my friends and all the things I
liked ! I believe you despised Mother and Daphne ! I
dare say, really, you despise me ! "

She saw his movement of denial, half angry, half
alarmed. She went on in a rising torrent of temper:
" You and your family despise a lot of people ! You think
you're so damned clever and intelligent and full of good
taste, knowing all about books and music, and being
sentimental about politics, but you don't know anything,
any of you ! You're soft and ignorant ! You don't know
what life is like, and what people are like. You don't
understand that you've got to fight to get what you want.
You've had an easy time all your lives, and lived shut

up in your own ideas, and you don't know a thing ! "

" I dare say we don't come up to the standards of Gillans Cross." He still clung to the place, instinctively trying to unload on to it his irritation and distaste. " You've said a lot about despising, but it sounds more as though you despised us ! "

They were glaring at one another, both scarlet and furious, when there was a light patter of steps, and the door was pushed open. Tatty stood in the doorway.

" Daddy——" She stopped, looking at them with startled eyes. She was aware at once of the vibrations of their anger. She stood quite still, her dark hair swinging to rest against her cheeks, and one small brown hand fidgeting uneasily with her pink skirts.

Evelyn turned away from Maurice, her colour fading. She said sternly:

" What do you want, Tatty ? It's bedtime."

Tatty came doubtfully forward, staring at them. Maurice got up and put the bottle of sherry on the sideboard. He said, steadying his voice:

" Helloa, Tat-rabbit ! We're out of beer, Evelyn. I'd better get some."

" There are two bottles of cyder. Won't that do ? "

His strung nerves, sensitive to every touch, made him fancy that she thought anything would do for his family party. Conscious of absurdity, he could not shake it off. He said sulkily:

" No. Jim and Dell both drink beer. I don't think they like cyder. I'll run round in the car to the shop and get some."

He moved towards the door, stopped, half turned, and looked at Evelyn. He said diffidently:

" It won't take five minutes to run round there. Come
with me ? "

Evelyn's temper was cooler than his, but, once up, it
lasted longer. She had very seldom quarrelled with
Daphne, but in all her life she had never apologised to
her, nor been able willingly to accept an apology.
Her voice was hard, and her face unyielding, as she
answered :

" No, thanks. I've got several things to see to."

The child stood between them, fidgeting and looking
from one to the other, her face anxious and distressed.
She knew that her mother was angry. Evelyn did not often
speak to her crossly, but she was familiar with that cool,
stony displeasure, and frightened of it. Above her head
the glances of her parents crossed like swords.

" All right," Maurice replied. " I'll take Tatty. Come
along, Tats ! Come in the car and help me to fetch some
beer."

He held out his hand to her, smiling. Tatty skipped,
and made a joyful movement towards him.

" It's her bedtime, Maurice."

" We shan't be ten minutes."

" I don't want her to be late. She's tired after her
party."

" No, I'm not, Mummie ! No, I'm not ! "

" I want her." Maurice's tone was defiant, his eyes
stubborn. He had tried to make friends again, and Evelyn
had rejected his advance. Sore with her lack of response
during the last few months, he wanted to hurt and provoke
her. If they had been at a dance, he would have gone off
with another partner under her nose. As it was, he picked
up Tatty. The child's arm went round his neck ; she

pressed her soft little cheek against his, and looked down
at her mother with eyes full of mischief.

"You seem to forget that Mary has to come into the
room and wait on your people, and she's got to get Tatty
into bed first. Put her down, Maurice ! Tatty, say good
night and run upstairs ! "

Maurice's arms tightened round the child.

"They can wait on themselves, or I'll wait on them.
They aren't fussy. Anyhow it's quite early, and we shan't
be long. I want Tatty for a few minutes. If there's anyone
that does want to do things with me, I may as well have
her company."

"Don't be absurd, Maurice ! She must go up to bed
at once."

Over her father's shoulder Tatty looked down at her
mother's face. She wriggled uncomfortably in his arms.

"Back in a few minutes," Maurice said.

He walked out of the house, carrying Tatty, and put
her down in the car on the seat next to his own. He
touched her cheek with his hand.

"You like coming with Daddy, don't you ? We must
have some fun together sometimes ! "

The protest was as near conspiracy with Tatty against
her mother as he had ever allowed himself to come. He
was still very cross. He got into the car, slammed the door,
kicked the self-starter, and dragged the gear handle.
Tatty was quiet, but, in his pre-occupation, he did not
miss the chattering delight with which she usually started
out on the smallest expedition in his company. He thought
angrily that only Tatty really loved him, and wanted
him for his own sake. He was part of the furniture of
Evelyn's life, and that was all. It was more important to

her to have everything in the house in the most minute order before a casual family party than to make friends with her husband after a quarrel. Appearances always mattered more to her than feelings; she hadn't any feelings, thought Maurice, working himself up. She didn't care twopence about him, and probably never had.

As they turned the corner of the road and passed out of sight of the house, Tatty burst into tears. Maurice stopped the car.

" What's the matter, darling ? What is it ? " He put his arm round her and drew her towards him, but she pushed him away. " What's the matter ? " he repeated. " Tell Daddy ! "

Tatty sobbed bitterly, but made no answer.

" Have you got a pain ? " After all, she had been to a party.

She shook her head. Large tears were streaming down her scarlet cheeks, and the sobs became almost convulsive. Maurice was astonished and dismayed, his own troubles entirely forgotten. " Tell Daddy what's the matter, darling ? " he pleaded again.

Her voice came muffled and choked:

" I want to go home ! "

" But we're going soon. We're only just going to the shops."

" I want to go now. I want Mummie ! "

She must be feeling ill, Maurice thought, or perhaps she hadn't been upstairs when she came in. Anyhow it was evidently a case for her mother. She did not often cry, and he had never seen her cry like this before, with this violent hysterical sobbing. He turned the car. He did not want to take her back, he would feel a fool after running off with her in defiance—but her distress was all-powerful. She sobbed less violently as they drove the two hundred yards to the gate. Maurice lifted her out, and she flew up the path. He followed her to explain, feeling sheepish.

Evelyn was arranging flowers in a bowl on the hall table. He heard the snip-snip of her scissors, and saw the shaggy, curly head of an early chrysanthemum poised above the bowl. Tatty ran to her, threw her arms round her, and pressed her hot, wet face against the rubber apron which Evelyn had slipped on over her frock. Tatty would remember the smell of the rubber, and the slippery, cool feel of it long after the rest of the evening was submerged in her mind.

" She began to cry and wanted to come home. I don't know what's the matter," Maurice said.

Evelyn put down the flowers, and knelt on one knee with her arms round the child. She did not ask her what was the matter, but smoothed the dark hair away from her hot face, and said:

" You're tired, aren't you, my lamb ? It's bedtime. Hush ! Come along, we'll go upstairs, and I'll give you your bath while Mary's busy."

Over Tatty's shoulder she said to Maurice, with friendly indifference:

" I should go along and get the beer, Maurice, and hurry back. She's had too much party, that's all. There, old lady ! Come along."

Her tenderness to the child released a constriction in Maurice's heart; he knew how helplessly he still loved her. He stood just inside the front door, watching as she carried Tatty upstairs. A few minutes ago, Evelyn had been odd man out in the family, while he and Tatty, close allies, defied her authority. Now the balance of the household had changed, the two feminine creatures had drawn together, and he felt himself alone, pushed aside as someone who had blundered. It did not occur to him that the balance was likely to shift a good deal once there was a rift in the primary combination. He went out again to the car, and drove to the shops, pondering over Tatty's unaccountable behaviour. She loved going to the shops or anywhere else with him. It was the first time that he could remember that his little, eager, happy daughter had turned back from any sort of fun. He was so much distressed that he bought her a box of coloured chalks, and a packet of scraps for her scrap-book, and hurried home to apply these consolations.

CHAPTER XXX

IN THE DINING-ROOM, Delia and Jim moved chairs
and tables, lifted the drawers into a chest, reduced the
packing-cases to order, and began to unpack the table
silver and cutlery. While they worked, they talked hard.
They were accustomed to make the most of their time
together, for they had never had much of it. Jim, being
an energetic young man, had found it quite possible to
combine his private bacteriological researches with his
job as house surgeon, but difficult to combine the two
of them with being engaged. It was the first time that any
clash of interests had disturbed his single-minded pursuit
of his purpose, and the discovery that everything was not
straightforward, even when you knew what you wanted,
had come as a valuable if a trifle belated part of his
education. Neither he nor Delia had any money to spare;
they were saving hard to furnish the flat, and the small
private lab, about which she was nearly as much excited
as he was. It was an engagement shorn of all its pretty
frills, and sometimes Delia wished that Jim could have
taken her to a dance, or bought her flowers or given
her a useless present. Such things had not been part of
his upbringing as they had of hers: his father was the
vicar of a big Tyneside parish, and his pretty, thrifty
Scotch mother had learned easily and early to dispense
with luxuries. For Delia and Jim, during the last eighteen

months, time had been the greatest luxury. Life was a continual effort to meet and be together, in spite of other urgencies. In fact, thought Delia, we couldn't have stood it much longer without getting married.

It would have been an awfully difficult engagement, she thought, if we hadn't felt certain. But she had felt certain since that day, nearly two days ago, when a Dr. Roberts telephoned to the lab to make an appointment with Vicary for that afternoon. She had thought, as she answered the telephone and made a note of the time, that he was rather abrupt, and she had looked him up in the books and found that he had had no dealings with them before. Then she had thought no more about him until the afternoon when he was shown into her little room, and stood there looking at her across her typewriter, a square-shouldered, solid young man with reddish-fair hair, and the face of someone determined to get his own way in the world, and not yet aware of the inevitable necessity for compromise. He had learnt much more about that during the last two years !

When their spate of talk about their own affairs subsided for a moment, Delia, who was putting away spoons and forks into a baize-lined drawer, said:

" Jim. I want to get Rhoda out of this ! "

" Away from home ? "

" Yes. To try my job at the lab. You know they asked me to look out for someone to take my place. And she's had secretarial training, and kept it up with one or two odd jobs, voluntary work and so on."

Jim, bending over the packing-case, straightened his back.

" Does she want to get away ? "

" She's not happy. She's got nothing really to do. She's got past the age of just being a girl and having fun. People who've all known her for years count her out as someone who won't, now, be attractive or fall in love and get married, and who hasn't any particular work of her own, so they get her to help with all their bits of work, and different committees. Perhaps that sort of thing was enough for people thirty years ago, but it isn't now. And it's not good enough for Roddy ! "

" Certainly not," agreed Jim. He liked Rhoda, although he had seen very little of her. His impression of her was of somebody difficult to know, but worth knowing; of a sensitive and intelligent person, rather shy, but with a suppressed gaiety that he had seen bubble up once when he and she and Delia had lunched together in London. He had been pre-occupied and tired, and had really wanted Delia alone; he had not noticed her sister very acutely, but now he recalled a faint surprise at seeing her younger, prettier, more talkative than he remembered her at home. She had been, he thought, like somebody set free.

" I think she was fairly happy while Daddy was alive. She adored him. But you know, Jim, Mother is damned difficult to live with ! "

He could well believe it. Her polite hostility had not disturbed him, but it had not made him love her, and he replied, with candour : " Yes, I'm sure she is."

" She doesn't like anybody to be anything except in relation to her. Daddy was *her* husband; Aunt Ellen was *her* sister; we were *her* children. She didn't like Maurice, who was *her* son, to go off and be Evelyn's husband. She doesn't like you because I'm going to be

your wife. But Rhoda's still her daughter, and she means
to keep her. You see, she was brought up with that
picture in front of her. Her own mother was like that,
my grandmother. Aunt Ellen was always *her* daughter.
I remember, on Roddy's twenty-first birthday, we had
a dance at a hotel, and, of course, we asked Aunt Ellen.
Grandmamma sent her in a taxi, and sent the taxi to
fetch her home at eleven, because she didn't want to be
kept awake any later. She bought a new dress for her,
but she forgot to give her any money for the evening,
so Aunt Ellen had to borrow sixpence from us for a cloak-
room tip. And next time we saw Grandmamma, she
said : " Of course I missed Ellen on Thursday, but I was
anxious to spare her for Rhoda's dance if I could. I
so much wanted to hear all about it."

Jim laughed as he piled the empty cases one on top of
another, but he said :

" Yes, they were like that."

" Mother isn't as bad as Grannie, of course; she isn't
as potent. But she was brought up in that pattern, and
she tried to make it again in her own house. Oh, Jim,"
exclaimed Delia suddenly, " stop me, for God's sake,
if I try to make it in ours ! "

Jim shook his head. He looked at her lovely, glowing
face as she turned to him, half smiling, half serious, the
dark hair pushed back behind her ears, leaving her forehead bare, and showing the fine curve of cheek and jaw.
He could not imagine that there could be much wrong with
any pattern she made in their house. It was with the sweet
and friendly smile that Rhoda had noticed that he said :

" I shouldn't worry, darling. It's rather an antiquated
pattern nowadays."

" Oh, Jim, that's the way Hilary and Sally talked !
It's only antiquated to some people in some places !
Everything's moved so quickly lately, that only the quick
people have kept up with it. Why, there are people with
1930 minds and 1914 minds and 1890 minds living in the
same house ! "

Besides, she thought, people always wanted to reproduce the pattern. If she had married Hilary, wouldn't
he have wanted to make their house or flat as much as
possible like his own home, like the tall, narrow London
house that looked as though nothing in it could be moved ?
Wouldn't he have wanted his children to grow up little
Hilarys ? Wasn't Evelyn bringing up Tatty in the faith
and fear of Gillans Cross? Even the people who laboured
to get away from the pattern were guided by the pattern,
chose its opposite because it was behind them.

" I expect I shall give our children too much rope,
and they'll grow up flabby for want of discipline ! "

" I'll take a hand, then. You're gloomy this
afternoon ! "

" Not really. Only I think I'd forgotten, till I came
back here, how tied up people are ! I don't want to see
Roddy drowning before my eyes. I've been talking to her
to-day whenever I've had a chance, but I don't believe
she'll break away. She's got such a strong current in her
against doing anything for herself. I can't persuade
her."

The young doctor sighed.

" It's difficult to help people much if they won't help
themselves ! "

He would not have said that three or four years before,
when he had hoped to cure all the ills of humanity by

sense and knowledge. The sigh and the remark were the measure of his gained experience.

"You'll back me up, won't you, Jim, if you get a chance? If she talks to you about it? It's this awful unselfishness she's learnt, just the same as Aunt Ellen must have learnt it. I suppose our grandparents began it. It suited them to have dutiful children and workpeople who lived on the same wages while they got richer and richer."

"They were pretty bad about it, Dell, but I don't think they began it. The world's always been full of people who abused power, and other people who let them. They've both got such a strong emotional appeal, grabbing and giving up, getting what you want or being self-sacrificing, that their advocates can shout down the people who just want fair play every time." He wrinkled his broad, young brow as he pronounced authoritatively, "You can always get a following for piracy or a crusade, because people can get hot over either of 'em. It's because fair play's *cool* you can't get a mob to run after it. It doesn't satisfy primitive greed, or the Christian ideal of self-immolation. But it's the only single damn' thing with any sense in it, all the same, and it'll always be there in the middle while the pendulum swings backwards and forwards, so I expect we shall worry out something decent in the end."

CHAPTER XXXI

Evelyn came out of the front door to meet her husband's family as they trooped up from the gate. The close waves of her silvery-gold hair covered her head like a polished cap. Her dark blue dress, long-sleeved and high at the throat, showed the lines of her slim body, and set off her delicate fairness. Rhoda, seeing her, felt tired, plain, and dirty after the day's removal. Evelyn greeted them all with proper cordiality, welcomed Jim prettily, and said to Mrs. Powell:

" Will you go in and say good night to Tatty, Grannie ? She's staying awake on purpose to see you. I promised I'd ask you. I expect she'll want to see Aunt Ellen too. She's always excited when she hears Aunt Ellen's coming."

It was astonishing, Rhoda thought, that Evelyn should always be so nice to Aunt Ellen; taking more trouble about her, really, than Delia ever did. It was one of those unexpected bits in people. You would have expected Evelyn to despise Aunt Ellen, so despicable by all the standards of Gillans Cross. Rhoda did not realise that Evelyn felt safe with Aunt Ellen, the one member of Maurice's family whom she did not suspect of criticism. She did not know that as Evelyn, so pretty, fair, competent, and polite, came down the path to meet them, she was afraid that her mother-in-law might guess that she and Maurice were not getting on, and had quarrelled that evening; she shrank from the combined intelligence of Rhoda, Delia, and Jim, and foresaw that most of their conversation would be about things that did not interest her, and that she would sit silent while Maurice took his share, making her feel that he belonged to their world rather than to hers. She wondered how many of them thought that Maurice would have been better and happier if he had married a different wife. She came down the path to meet them feeling as though she were receiving a hostile army. Unimaginative though she was, she was not immune from the law which compels half the world to spend its time being afraid of the other half, turning its eyes away from the unalarming and equally alarmed reality, and writing an agitated chapter in its personal novel. Evelyn wrote in her personal novel that all Maurice's family knew that they were getting on badly, and were blaming her for it, thinking her the wrong person. As it happened, Mrs. Powell was thinking that it had been kind and thoughtful of her to ask them all, Rhoda was trying to suppress a grudging sense of inferiority that seemed to her ungenerous, Delia was thinking that it would be nice to sit down at a table to a proper meal, and Jim was frankly admiring Evelyn's looks. As far from knowing one another as people who speak different languages, they went into the house together in a companionable bunch, talking cheerfully.

Maurice had not recovered his self-possession as quickly or completely as Evelyn; he was uneasy, alternately constrained and unnaturally jovial. He gave them all a drink, and then withdrew into the window with Jim, and tried to talk to him. It was not a great success. Jim had very little small talk; he was apt to answer an

idle question with " Yes," or " No," and let it go at that.
He was untroubled by any feeling that silence was rude
or indecent. Odd sort of bedside manner this fellow must
have, thought Maurice. He's got plenty of confidence,
but he doesn't take much trouble to make himself agree-
able. What does Delia see in him ? It seemed to Maurice
quite unnecessary that any more outside people should
be brought into the family. He had his wife and child,
his mother and sisters. He would have drawn a ring
round them all, keeping them to himself, and shutting
off intruders.

Evelyn was showing the proofs of Tatty's new photographs to her grandmother, Aunt Ellen and Delia looking
over her shoulder. Rhoda stood apart from the two groups.
She was so tired that one glass of sherry had given her a
momentary feeling of unreality, as though she were on a
stage during a play and the actors were going on with
their parts around her. She looked at Maurice and Jim,
standing side by side with glasses in their hands. How
easily and willingly in any English gathering the sexes
fell apart, men and women grouping themselves with
relief among their own kind ! To get out of your own
group into the other was surely the great excursion and
adventure, the removal on which life depended, but which
so many people could only accomplish timidly and
temporarily, with part of themselves left behind.

" Come and look at these photographs, Rhoda,"
her mother called out. " Which does Maurice like ? "

" That one," Evelyn said. She and Maurice had
already disagreed about the proofs. Maurice liked one
in which Tatty looked exactly like Rhoda. Evelyn preferred one which showed her looking down at a doll.

It was certainly the prettiest picture, but Maurice maintained that it was not Tatty, but might be any little girl with short, dark hair. He kept out of the controversy now, listening while Aunt Ellen lavishly praised them all, and his mother, Delia, and Rhoda debated their merits. Anything to do with the child of the family was of paramount interest, and superseded all other considerations.

It was queer, Rhoda thought, how important you were when you were young. Your necessities must be provided, you must not be disappointed, whoever else went to the wall. For the first few years of your life the mere fact that you had managed to be there at all gave you a tremendous importance. Once Aunt Ellen must have been an astounding event to her parents, the centre of a household's love and care, of a family's interest. There was a portrait of her—a pale little girl with fair hair, in a frock trimmed with braid, and a tartan sash. She had not been pretty, but, when her parents had had that portrait done, they had loved her and wanted to have it. Nobody now would want a portrait of Aunt Ellen. It was a difficult journey that people made from a small world in which they were so precious out into the large world in which they were not necessarily precious at all !

" She's awfully like Rhoda in all of them," Delia said, handing them back.

Evelyn put them into their envelope again without answering. All at once she hated the photographs, and nearly hated Tatty. Tatty was the Powell's child. She had loved Maurice, had been sick and frightened and ugly, had spent a night of confused pain, had grown thin and tired nursing her baby, and given up her time to her, all to rear another Powell, an alien creature. Like

Rhoda ! She looked at Maurice now, talking to Rhoda, happy and at ease. They did not stumble upon continual differences, not of opinion, which matters less, but of taste and feeling. Like Rhoda ! Evelyn's mood swung over, she clasped the photographs in a tight grip. No, she's not ! They shan't make her one of them ; they shan't have her ! She's my little girl ! She had not been able to make Maurice to her pattern, but she was determined to make Tatty to it, to set her stamp on the soft, new wax. And if we have another one, she thought, I hope it will be like my family ! She was aware of a swift yearning for her mother's congenial company as she said to Mrs. Powell :

" Let's go into the dining-room, shall we, and have something to eat ? "

Rhoda dropped thankfully into a chair. Her body felt incapable of one more effort, but her mind was sharpened and alert. Ordinarily, sitting down to a meal in Evelyn's house, she felt flat, sure that they would talk about nothing interesting. Nothing, she thought, could be very interesting at Evelyn's table, because all the conversation was in her key. Her view of things was sensible, practical, matter-of-fact, one-dimensional. Everything looked to her, thought Rhoda, as a box looked to you when you were small and were told to draw it, one square front facing you, no sides, no top, no light nor shade nor angle, nothing behind it. But why do we let her ? Maurice and I are not very clever or successful people, but we know that there is always more than the front of the box. Why is it so easy for the people who see less to override the people who see more ? It had been just the same, she remembered, at home. Her father coming in with a tale of some chance encounter, some new, odd glimpse of an acquaintance or stranger, telling it with that attractive eagerness that he never lost, his eyes sparkling; her mother quenching him with a word that reduced the adventure to a boring anecdote. Maurice and I both saw her do that over and over again, and were annoyed. But why do we all let them do it? When the life and spirit and colour are there in things, why do we give in, why aren't we loyal to them? And why, oh why, did Maurice, who saw it, and minded when mother killed it, go and marry someone else who kills it too? It's just like me, going to have the same life as Aunt Ellen, though I'm sorry for her and don't want it. There is such a thing as a family curse! It makes you repeat the things in your family that you don't like! But I'm not going to. They're too much for us, mother and Evelyn, because they're single-minded and we're not, but for once I will be. I'll break the curse.

A conversation was going on between her mother and Evelyn and Maurice about the removal, the things that had gone into the new house, and the things that would have to be sold. I don't, thought Rhoda, want to hear any more about houses or furniture for the next six months! Jim was holding a dish of potatoes for her, and, as she turned towards him to help herself, he said to her:

"When are you coming up to London again? You haven't been up to see Delia for a long time, have you?"

"No. I haven't been up for months. I wanted to, but I've been so busy I couldn't manage it."

Suddenly she thought, that's not true! I could easily have managed it for a few days if I'd tried. Impatience swept her, because she so often did not do the things she wanted. Selfish always to do them, yes ! Bad to be like Evelyn, seeing only the things she wanted, the front of the box again, no more of it, but the opposite was just as bad, feeble, stupid, disloyal to the life in you !

" Jim, do you usually do the things you want to do ? "

" I have a good try," remarked Jim cheerfully.

" Would you push other people out of the way to get what you want ? "

His mind went swiftly back to a scholarship won after close competition with a friend in the same form, to the two great friends who had applied with him for the same hospital appointment.

" Yes," he said. " Sometimes. It can't be helped, can it, if you're going to do anything at all ? "

He looked at the delicate, downcast face of his future sister-in-law. She had, he was sure, too much capacity for self-sacrifice. And, of course, having that, she lived with somebody who had too much capacity for demanding it ! Nature's jig-saw puzzle, it didn't matter a damn what happened to the pieces so long as they went into the puzzle. It was only each bewildered and resentful piece that thought Nature cared, saw itself as the centre of the puzzle with others fitting into its curves and hollows. All that probably seemed too hard for this gentle young woman, who had no doubt been taught as a child to believe that God was watching the fall of every sparrow. And for all I know, thought Jim, he may be, but he certainly leaves it to the sparrow.

He wondered how he could say to Rhoda, without distressing her too much, that if you don't fight for yourself you die, and, if you do, you are always liable to damage other people. It seemed to him as plain as the inevitable laws governing people's bodies. He saw so many bodies every day damaged by departures from those laws. The laws were inexorable. He shed no tears over it, he was young, healthy, in love, interested in his work, but he had enough imagination to see that Rhoda was beginning to realise it, and probably did not like it. While he wondered what to say to her, Maurice leaned across and spoke to her.

Maurice was still feeling sore and injured after the quarrel. Evelyn did not love him nowadays at all. She snapped at him; she repulsed him; she would not come anywhere with him because she was always fussing about things. She talked him over with her detestable mother, he was sure. She was annoyed when he wanted Tatty's company; she was as cool and hard as a smooth stone. He hastily blotted out of his mind a picture of her kneeling on the floor with her arms round Tatty, her face tender and the child's wet cheek pressed against hers. No, she was altogether cold and unloving. He whipped up his anger, hardening himself against her. They were all talking and leaving him out. He felt a childish sense of injury. He looked round the table and saw Rhoda sitting very quiet. Of course she was bored by all this endless talk about removing and furniture, just as he was ! He felt drawn towards her, deeply aware of the kinship between his mind and hers. He leaned across and spoke to her in a loud, assertive voice that conveyed his sense of injury, and a suggestion that he was tired of the conversation going on round him. He said :

" Have you written your lectures for next winter, Roddy ? I suppose you'll be doing them again ? "

The abrupt sound of his voice, unheard since the
beginning of the meal, caused a sudden silence to fall
round the table. Rhoda looked up, startled out of her
thoughts. Aunt Ellen said, in her flat, kind, commonplace
tones :

"There ! It must be twenty minutes past, or twenty
minutes to !"

She peered at the ornamental clock on the mantelpiece.

Rhoda looked at Maurice, and said :

"I don't know. I don't think so. I may not be here.
I'm thinking of going to London and trying to get Delia's
job."

Her knees trembled under the table. She dared not
look at her mother. She had done it, all in a minute, badly,
stupidly, unpardonably, as she now saw at once, springing
it on her like that in the middle of all these people, without
warning. She had done it cruelly in the way frightened
people did do things. Her heart beat in great thumps,
and she felt sick. She caught Delia's look of warm, loving
congratulation, and Jim, at her side, said cheerfully :

"Oh, good ! Then we shall be seeing a lot of you."

Maurice and Evelyn both said something, but she did
not hear them. She was listening for her mother's voice,
and trying to look at her face. Her mother had not spoken.
Suddenly Aunt Ellen said :

"But, my dear ! What will your mother do without
you ?"

Damn, thought Delia; I hoped nobody would say
that ! She looked at her mother, and saw the pink colour
which she knew on her cheek-bones. Mrs. Powell shrugged
her shoulders, and said :

" Oh, mothers don't count when they get old ! But
Roddy hasn't gone yet, have you, darling ? Moving
makes you feel very unsettled just at the time. It's too
early to make plans for the winter. Evelyn, this sauce
is delicious. I shall never teach Ivy to make it like
this."

Clever ! thought Delia. She means to keep her. Rhoda
sat quiet, feeling exhausted and stupid. Her bomb had
fallen, and had not exploded. Her mother had covered
it up, buried it hastily under ordinary life, so that the
suggestion seemed fantastic, and the family group sitting
round the table, the little house in which she and her
mother were going to live, the only reality. But I've let
ordinary life cover up everything all these years, thought
Rhoda, and I won't again. I want independence and work
and experience and people and doings, and I really
want love. I could have them here, probably, if I could
get out of the rut, but so long as I'm with mother I can't.
I've got to go."

She felt suddenly sleepy, as though it would be an
intolerable bother to hold up her head for the rest of the
evening.

They were all talking again, Maurice talking to Delia,
her mother to Jim, Evelyn to Aunt Ellen. Suddenly
Maurice jumped up.

" Listen ! There's Tatty ! "

Only his quick ears had heard her screams, but, as
soon as they stopped talking, they all heard her, and the
noise redoubled as he opened the door. They heard him
run upstairs.

" Does she often wake at night ? " Mrs. Powell asked.

" Oh, no," Evelyn said composedly. " She got too

excited at her party to-day, I think. We had tears when she came home."

The door of Tatty's little bedroom was always left ajar. Maurice pushed it open, and switched on the light. Everything in this house seemed wrong to-day, he thought. Tatty was sitting up in bed, her cheeks hot from sleep and wet with tears, her dark fringe ruffled. She was silent for a minute, staring at her father with great, drowned eyes. He went across to the bed, sat down by her, and put an arm round her.

" What's the matter, sweetheart ? Funny dreams ? "

To his astonishment she pushed him away.

" I want Mummie ! "

" Mummie's busy. She's got Grannie here. You mustn't bring her upstairs. Besides, I'm here. It's all right. Look, the light's on, and you're quite safe with Daddy."

He wiped her face with his handkerchief. Such soft little cheeks, and such a small, warm body in his arms, she touched the tenderest place in his heart.

She wriggled out of his arms and threw herself down on the pillows.

" Go away. I want Mummie ! Mummie ! " Her voice rose to a wail.

Maurice stood up, wounded and astonished. She had never turned from him in her life before. Without knowing it, he had always been delighted by her obvious preference for him, by the way she ran to him first with her small joys and discoveries. He looked down, perplexed, at the little heap of dark hair and pink pyjamas.

" All right," he said. " I'll fetch her."

Evelyn came up, kind and competent, reassuringly displeased. She gave Tatty a drink of water, shook up her pillows, kissed her, and told her not to be silly. She did not ask her what was the matter, and certainly Tatty could not have told her out of what dreams of running off with her father, of her mother's angry face, she had woken up to feel her mother her only safety. She lay down on the pillow with wide-open eyes.

" Couldn't you stay with me a little, Mummie ? "

" No, of course I can't. Grannie and the Aunties are here. I must go and look after them."

" What did they have for supper ? "

" Never mind now. I'll tell you in the morning."

" Could I have a hanky ? "

" Yes. But I shan't give you anything else. You must go to sleep."

Tatty sighed, perhaps a little sorry that she had sent her father away. He was easier to keep than Mummie.

" I think I've got a pain."

" I don't think you have. Lie down at once and go to sleep. I'll leave the light on for a little bit, and then I'll come up later and turn it off. You mustn't be silly like this, you know. You're such a big girl, now."

" Almost a lady," said a conversational voice from the bed.

" Yes. Good night, darling. I'll come up in about half an hour."

On the landing outside, Evelyn paused for a moment before going down. Poor Maurice had come down so crestfallen because Tatty didn't want him, but the fact that she had sent him away and demanded her mother assuaged some bitterness in Evelyn's heart. She stood on the landing, hearing the murmur of voices from the room below, hearing the clink of silver and glass from the

kitchen where washing up was going on, hearing from
Tatty's room behind her a sigh, and a creak of the little
bed. This was her house, and she was the centre; she was
hostess, mistress, mother, and wife. She was necessary.
Why had she been worrying about them all—her mother-
in-law, who was old and past being necessary; Rhoda,
whom no one needed; Delia and Jim, who were young
and untried? Here in the centre of her house, her child
going to sleep behind her, the work that she directed
going on behind the scenes, her husband depending on
her, she could afford not to be afraid of anyone! She
slipped into her bedroom, powdered her face, touched up
her lips, took a reassuring glance at the room full of her
own possessions, and ran downstairs.

CHAPTER XXXII

"IT'S BEEN A LOVELY EVENING," Aunt Ellen said, walking by Maurice down the garden path. "So very kind of Evelyn to have us all ! And it's so kind of you to drive me home. I don't like taking you out so late, though ! I could just as well have gone in a bus."

Maurice, opening the gate for her, roused himself to answer. Aunt Ellen's voice dripped over you like rain ; it was easy to stop listening and go on with your own thoughts.

" Oh, no, I like some fresh air last thing at night. I'm sure you must be tired, too, after helping them all day."

" I've enjoyed it ! " Aunt Ellen replied sincerely. " It's so nice to be useful. But I do wish you'd let me just jump into the bus at this corner ! It goes nearly to my door, you know."

" That," said Maurice, " is settled. You aren't going in a bus."

He liked Aunt Ellen, but found it irritating that, while she was so ready to give kindness, she made such a fuss about receiving it, almost shrinking away from the smallest favour or service. I suppose, he thought, it's because she's had so much practice in bothering about other people, and they've bothered so little about her, she's never had a chance to get used to it. His imagination was stirred to-day by the break with his old life and the disturbance in his own mind. He was less inclined to take Aunt Ellen or anything else for granted.

"Is that a decent place where you live?" he asked. "I mean, do you really like being there?" It was the first time he had given it a thought.

"It's very comfortable and convenient," Aunt Ellen said cheerfully, "and the people are very kind."

Something in her voice making the best of it touched Maurice.

"What do you do with yourself all day?" he asked. What did Ellen do? Looked at the morning paper, knitted for a babies' welcome, mended her clothes, read such novels from the library as seemed to her neither alarming nor indecent, went for little walks, wrote a few letters in a stiff, pointed hand, gave up her chair to old ladies and picked up stitches for them. They called her "my dear," and restored to her a shadow of her life with her mother.

She said in a bright, brisk tone:

"Oh, I've always plenty to do!" She belied her cheerful assurance by adding, "Mamma always said that it was your own fault if you couldn't be happy and busy all day long."

"They always said that!" Maurice exclaimed impatiently. "People of their age and time, I mean. Everything was your own fault!"

"Well," said Aunt Ellen, "isn't it?"

"Oh, of course it isn't, Aunt Ellen! It's the qualities you're born with, and circumstances."

"I suppose," said Aunt Ellen diffidently, "it's your own fault if you don't do your best with the qualities in the circumstances." She laughed, "Mamma used to say

to me when I was growing up, ' You'll never be a beauty,
Ellen, but you've got nice hair and you must keep it well
brushed.' And I did; I brushed it for ten minutes every
night and every morning. I was always very proud of it."

They were crossing a main road at the junction of some
tram-lines, and Maurice, intent on his driving, did not
answer. Ellen, blinking dreamily at the green lights of the
robot, let her mind slip back. The long sweeps of her
brush fell on her thick hair, polishing the surface to a
silky sheen. It was winter, and frosty. Separate hairs
sprang up, electric with frost, and clung to the brush.
Ellen was just grown up; she had come back from a party,
and her white dress lay over a chair. She looked at herself
in the glass, moving a candle forward. If only she had not
such brown skin, such salt-cellars above her collar-bone !
If only her hands did not get so red, and seem to be so
much *there* at parties ! She never thought of them at home,
but as soon as she walked into a ballroom they seemed to
swell and grow larger; they hung like lumps of lead on
the ends of her arms. Why was it so difficult to talk at
parties, especially to young men ? Ellen wanted so much
to please them; it was her duty. Wasn't that what she was
sent to parties for ? She knew that it was. What distressed
her most of all was that, when she did not please them,
she fell in her mother's esteem. But she could not please
them; her fluttering attempts disconcerted them, or she
was tongue-tied, unable to think of a word to say, pitying
them desperately for having to dance with her. It had
been like that to-night. She had not enjoyed herself a bit.
Her mother would come in a minute and ask her, and she
would try to pretend that she had, and would not succeed.
Backwards and forwards went the brush; the hair sprayed

up and dropped again behind Ellen's serious, downcast face.

And then her mother did come in, carrying a glass of hot milk that she had heated on her spirit-lamp.

" I thought you would have a cold ride home in the cab," she said. She put the glass down on the dressing-table. Ellen waited for her to ask questions; nerved herself to sound as though the party had really been great fun. But her mother only touched her hair, and said, " You'll never be a beauty, Ellen, but you've got such nice hair ! You must keep it well brushed." Mamma's rare praise was a tonic to her daunted spirit, a blessed appeasement to her unsatisfied heart. Even now that her hair had grown thin and dull and grey, Ellen brushed it for ten minutes every night and every morning.

They had crossed the main road, and were driving through side streets.

" Tatty's been in trouble to-day," Maurice said, more to himself than to Aunt Ellen.

" A little bit upset, perhaps, poor little girl ! " How nice it was, Aunt Ellen thought, that Maurice was so fond of Tatty ! She exclaimed impulsively :

" It gives me so much pleasure to come to your house, Maurice, and see you so happy with your pretty wife and your dear little girl."

Maurice sighed, but did not answer. He ought to be very happy. Most people thought he was. The difference between everything being all right and everything being all wrong was so small and yet was the whole thing, all your real life. I'm a fool, thought Maurice, for if having a wife and child and home and work isn't real life, I don't know what is ! Yet the conviction remained that those

things in themselves were no more the whole of real life
than sleeping with anybody was the whole of being in
love. Maurice felt incapable of discussing his own affairs
with Aunt Ellen, and changed the subject.

"It's surprising about Rhoda, isn't it? I didn't know
she wanted to go off on her own. I hope she'll like
it."

"I'm afraid your mother will miss her dreadfully."

Aunt Ellen's tone was reproachful, but she brightened
as she remarked:

"Rhoda has always been such a dear girl, so very fond
of her mother and father. I can't believe she will go off
and leave her mother. I think she was just feeling unsettled.
I don't think she would really do anything selfish."

Maurice was moved to protest.

"After all, Rhoda's life matters as much as Mother's."

Aunt Ellen simply did not believe him. It would never
have occurred to her for a moment that she mattered as
much as her mother. If it had been suggested to her, it
would have sounded like blasphemy. It had been in the
air of the household in which she was brought up that
no one mattered as much as its master and mistress. This
unspoken law had applied to Ellen just as it applied to the
servants and gardeners, and more remotely to clerks and
travellers in her father's office, workmen in the works.
Only Nan, the spoilt, delicate baby, the successful beauty,
had managed to make herself matter very nearly as much
as her parents, and had carried on the tradition to a
household of her own.

"No, I'm sure Rhoda didn't really mean it," Aunt
Ellen said hopefully. "It would never do. Your poor
mother couldn't be left all alone."

" Well, couldn't you go and live with her instead of Rhoda ? "

Maurice made the suggestion casually as he stopped the car at the gate. He jumped out and opened the gate for her. Now, he thought, Aunt Ellen would want to thank him for five minutes and say how sorry she was to have brought him out, and how she hoped he wouldn't be very late getting home. To his surprise, she thanked him briefly and almost abstractedly, and hurried into the house.

Ellen had a key, but, while she was fitting it into the lock, Miss Russell opened the door for her. She liked to know when people came in, and, if possible, what they had been doing. Ellen stepped over the threshold into the familiar passage. It had a smell of enclosed air, warmed by radiators and still faintly flavoured with dinner. There was an ugly table at one side with a plant on it in a pink pot; an ugly hat-stand beyond it, and a stand for umbrellas.

" Have you had a busy day, Miss Lister ? " asked Miss Russell. " You got the removal over and everything in all right ? "

" Yes, thank you."

" You'll have had some supper ? "

" Oh, yes, thank you. I've been spending the evening at my nephew's."

" How was the little girl ? " Tatty and Evelyn had once been to tea with Aunt Ellen at Lyndoch.

But Miss Lister was not disposed to be communicative to-night, even about the little great-niece.

" She was very well, thank you. Good night, Miss Russell."

"Good night, Miss Lister," said Miss Russell, disappointed. "I'm sorry it's too late for the bath, but you know old Mrs. Somers does complain so if the water makes a noise after ten o'clock."

"Yes. I know. Good night, Miss Russell."

Ellen opened the door of her room and switched on the light. It was a square room with a fawn-coloured wallpaper which had a small frieze of autumn leaves. It was furnished with a bedroom suite which Miss Russell had bought under the impression that it was modern furniture. There was a small gas-fire, with a soap-dish full of water in front of it. The dressing-table was covered with Aunt Ellen's own things, embroidered mats worked for her by Natalie for Christmas; heavy, old-fashioned silver hairbrushes; an embroidered handkerchief sachet, and a photograph of her parents in a silver frame. On the mantelpiece were her more recent photographs—Maurice's wedding; Evelyn with the baby, Tatty, in her arms; Tatty alone at two years old; Rhoda; and Delia, taken for Hilary when she was first engaged to him.

Ellen looked round the room. If it could really happen, she thought. If she could really be living in a house again, able to go into the kitchen and make a cake, or do some flowers for the table, or look through the linen for the laundry and see what wanted mending ! If she could live with Nan and do things for her and look after her as she always had ! She took off her tweed coat and hung it up on the door. She had lived cheerfully in Lyndoch, stressing its advantages and reminding herself often how much more fortunate she was than a lot of other people. But all to-day she had been in a house, doing useful things.

She could not pretend to herself this evening that her root-less life in this place satisfied her. Nobody needed her here, and she contributed nothing except her weekly payment. When there were difficulties, they were not hers to deal with. If she were in a real house, and several people turned up to tea when the maid was out, how gladly she would run into the kitchen and cut plates of bread-and-butter and make toast ! What fun it would be to re-cover the cushions, or plant bulbs in the garden !

She stripped off all her clothes except her vest, and stood with her lean, elderly body exposed to the cool air, pouring water out of her jug into the basin. There was no hot water in the bedrooms at night unless you fetched it for yourself, and the bathroom was locked after ten, so if you came in late you could not fetch it. Ellen did not mind cold water, not in the summer, anyhow, on the rare occasions when she went out in the evening. She was care-ful always to remind herself that Miss Russell had a lot on her hands. All the same, she did mind that comfort was doled out and grudged to the visitors at Lyndoch. Because this was not a real house, but a place of hire and bargain, people were supplied with the minimum of everything that they would put up with. Miss Russell, her friend and her niece who helped her, wanted to do enough to satisfy their clients. The three maids and the cook wanted to do enough to satisfy Miss Russell. None of them wanted to do any single thing as well as possible.

Aunt Ellen, who had felt this before, admitted it to-night. Scorn for mean living and mean giving raged in her unscornful soul. She pushed the thick china jug away from her across the mottled marble top of the washstand. It was seeing so many of her mother's old things to-day that had made her resent the coarse thickness of this lodging-house china. She had unpacked the Queen Anne silver teaset that she had so often rubbed up so that it should shine especially for a firelit tea, and the delicate glasses with clouded spirals in their stems that she had always washed with a little ammonia in the water to give them added brightness. She did not want the things as possessions; they had never been hers. She wanted to use her skill on them, to have something to do and somebody always at hand to love. As she climbed into bed and turned out the light, she said to herself again, Oh, if it should happen ! She felt an extraordinary certainty that it would happen. To-day, blowing the dust of years off their youth, had brought her and Nan together again, had made them realise how much they still belonged to the things they had shared before the younger ones, Rhoda and Maurice and Evelyn and Delia, were born. You never altogether remove out of the first house you live in, Ellen thought sleepily, and when you begin to get old you move back to it. It's right for Rhoda to go ; there's a whole new world for people her age that she ought to belong to ; but Nan and I belong to an older one, and we ought to be together, for we're the only two left in the family that knew it. Ellen slipped her hand under the pillow to feel if her watch, her handkerchief, and the key of her little writing-desk were all safe in their usual place. Finding that they were, she sighed with fatigue and a new satisfaction, turned her face away from the window, and went to sleep.

CHAPTER XXXIII

M AURICE drove home at his leisure by a longer way, that took him outside the town. The lights of his car picked out fields and hedgerows instead of street lamps and houses. Through the open window a fresher air flowed in against his cheek. The quiet and darkness around soothed him; he would like to drive on and on like this, over the uplands, through the dales, up to the hills, where the air would strike colder and grey stone villages, asleep, would slip by him. He did not want to go back to his own home.

Lucky Aunt Ellen, he thought with envy, to believe that God was in His heaven and Mamma were always right, and you must do your duty in that state of life to which it should please God to call you ! It was difficult to imagine what it would have been like to have lived in an age that had those certainties behind it, that could comfort itself in the troubles of this life by the sure hope of a future one. After all, Maurice thought, that's the biggest difference ! They thought it was a stage on the way, and we think it's probably all we'll get. That's at the root of everything we think and do. The people who would have been busy improving other men's souls are now improving their houses and their children's playing-fields. If you think everything's going to be levelled up in heaven, you don't worry so much about inequalities down here; but if life in a beastly house and a dull job and short commons of

everything is all some poor devils are going to get, and
there's no certainty of any compensation for them in
another world, then it's much more serious. The focus of
our sight has shifted from the future to the present in the
last thirty years.

He turned the car on to the ring road that skirted the
town. About a mile away on his right, hidden by a curve
of rising ground, was Stone Hall, empty, shut up, and
silent. The thought of it troubled him, as though, now
that his connection with it was cut, he was cut off from the
last stability in his life. In that house, as a little boy, he
had been taught the same certainties as Aunt Ellen; his
parents were there, omniscient and all-powerful, and
Heaven awaited him if he was good. Now his father was
dead, his mother was a peevish, elderly woman who
irritated him in spite of his affection. Heaven was
extremely doubtful, and even goodness was no longer the
firm and simple thing it had been; it was a delicate
balance, renewed afresh in every situation, instead of the
solid block of principles and behaviour which he had been
taught in the nursery. Things ought not to have been
made so easy, thought Maurice, if they were going to turn
out so complicated ! When you had learnt a few solid
rules in your youth, it was disconcerting to grow up into
a world that did not fit them, a world in which you had
to use your wits and sense and feelings over every single
thing !

But perhaps, after all, he thought, there has to be that
removal for a person or a civilisation. Some time or other
there has to be a growth out of certainty into inquiring
ignorance, out of safety into adventure, out of things as
they ought to be into things as they are. Perhaps Rhoda

was right, and we both ought to have left home long ago
with our minds. When you were little, your home was the
world, and you were its centre. It was a long time before
ever your parents appeared to have any life of their own
apart from being your parents. The small Maurice standing in his mother's bedroom and looking at her big wedding photograph had asked in a puzzled voice, " But why
wasn't I there ? " Perhaps after all, Maurice thought, how
much of a person you were depended on how far you were
able to grow out of that warm, childish world, how
genuine and deep was your removal.

He was leaving the country behind him and coming
back into the town. He thought of Evelyn, who would be
asleep perhaps when he got home, or, if not, would be
lying in her bed, turned away from him, so that, when he
switched on the lamp by his bedside, he would see only
the gleam of her pale hair above the sheet. I wish, he
grumbled to himself, that everyone didn't have those
blasted little single beds nowadays ! He remembered a
blissful week-end in his own old home in the big old-
fashioned bed in the spare room, when Evelyn had come
into his arms without any arranging and calculating, and
he could wake up and touch her, feel her warm and sweet
by his side, so that he had really felt as though he was
married. Evelyn had not liked it ; she said that everybody
had single beds nowadays. She had talked as though it
were almost indecent to have anything else. Well, he
reminded himself, she often talked about anything that
people did not have as though it were almost indecent.
He must be fair to her ! If they felt differently about
things, he mustn't try to force his ways on her.

The admission that they were different had crept

unnoticed to the surface of his mind. For the first time he acknowledged that he had not married, as he had supposed, the other half of himself, but a stranger whose spirit was out of touch with his. " With my body I thee worship." That had been so true on the wedding-day that he had trembled as he said it, and it was true now, only the temple doors were closed. But he had thought then that it meant a complete fusion of two people, and it didn't. For the first time he let himself see it, and although the sight was painful, the relief was great, as of someone moving out of an unnaturally cramped position.

She wants to make me into her sort of person, he thought, and I can't be. But I believe I'm just as bad. I want to make her see and feel things as I do, and she can't. That was the devil of being married; you could get on so much better with everyone else who disagreed with you ! But I'll try, thought Maurice, to make a better shot at it. Perhaps Grandmamma was right after all, and everything was your own fault, or anyhow it was your own responsibility to do the best you could in whatever circumstances you found yourself.

Evelyn was awake, and heard him shut the front door. She listened as his footsteps came upstairs, and heard the click of the switch as he turned out the hall light from above. He went into the spare room, which was his dressing-room except when they had a guest. He shut the door very softly, afraid of disturbing the sleeping house. Ten minutes later, Evelyn heard it open. His light footsteps crossed the landing. There was no sound of a door opening, but a board creaked under his foot, and she knew what he was doing. The door of Tatty's little room was never shut, so that they could hear her. He had pushed it open and had gone in, and was looking down at her. He had always looked at her last thing before getting into bed since she was a tiny baby, sleeping in a cot in their room. From the very first he had been as absurdly thrilled with her. When he first noticed her fingernails, the day after she was born, he had behaved as though no child had ever had fingernails before. Evelyn herself loved Tatty, but without any touch of astonishment or awe. Tatty was her baby, and babies were like that. What a long time Maurice was ! She could see him looking down at the sleeping child in the light from the door, his face softened and tender. A strongly possessive feeling stirred in her, quickening her growing resolution.

When Maurice came cautiously into the room, her bed-side lamp was still on, and she was lying high up on the pillows, her fair skin a mother-of-pearl pink in the shaded light, her hair shining. Maurice was surprised, and a little disconcerted to see her awake.

" Hulloa ! " he said. " Have I disturbed you ? I tried to be quiet."

" No, it's all right. I wasn't sleepy."

He smiled at her, and said frankly :

" I'm sorry I was so bad-tempered this evening."

That sudden and unexpected apology disarmed and softened her, making it easier for her to do what she meant to do, what she had determined to do to try and put things right between them. She pushed back the bedclothes, and said to him with a gesture of invitation :

" Maurice. Come here, darling."

Later, when they were each lying in their own bed, Maurice, drowsy after the physical release, thought clearly. But she didn't really want me ! He felt ashamed, further off from her because she had not refused him, but he was too tired to think, and soon fell asleep. Evelyn lay wakeful. Maurice was hers again, signed and sealed as her own, not his family's nor Tatty's. Perhaps it wouldn't be a bad thing if they started another baby now, before Tatty got used to being an only child. If they had one next summer, and not, as she had planned, at the end of next year, her mother would be able to come and stay with her; she always went to Bordighera for the winter months. All at once Evelyn wanted her mother with a desperate longing; she wanted to talk things over with her, to hear them all reduced to matter-of-fact terms by that sensible, practical, businesslike mind. Maurice was her husband and she was fond of him, but she did not understand him. She sometimes thought that to live with him was like living with someone who saw a ghost in the room when you only saw the furniture. She longed to-night for the company of her mother, who saw the furniture so clearly and was so certain that there was nothing else there that all other possibilities faded. Perhaps, she thought, I could run up and have a week-end with her this month. Her mind ran forward to her mother's little flat; she reached out to her congenial company, and, with her mind full of plans for seeing her, fell asleep.

CHAPTER XXXIV

R HODA drove the car home, Jim sitting by her in silence. It didn't matter whether you talked to Jim or not, Rhoda reflected gratefully. You knew that he wouldn't worry either way. It was a relief to have anyone like that about. Her mother always resented it if anyone in her company was quiet. She said, " What are you thinking about, Rhoda ? " or " A penny for your thoughts ! " She was annoyed if Rhoda's mind slipped away into places where she could not follow it; she tried to recall it, just as she was anxious that Rhoda should come back soon from a visit or a party.

Rhoda heard her mother in the seat behind her talking to Delia. She was appraising Evelyn's hospitality. The fish was very good, but the potatoes were not quite done enough. Maurice had been very quiet all the evening; he did not seem cheerful nowadays. That dress suited Evelyn; she had bought it last time she was in London with her mother. Tatty ought not to scream at night like that; she was getting a little bit spoilt; it was time they had another baby, a son.

" Grandmothers are greedy," Delia said. " They have all the fun of them and none of the bother."

She was thinking about Rhoda. Will Rhoda be able to stick to it ? What will Mother say to her as soon as they are alone together ? How will she get at her ? She's clever !

She's nearly always got what she wanted. If she'd ever been taught to use her brains for herself, instead of depending on other people, she'd have been a very capable woman. I'm afraid she'll be too much for Roddy; she'll get at that damned conscience of hers, and make her promise not to go. I rather wish I was going in with them now, and not driving Jim over to the Carters'. But I'm afraid Jim's right, really. You can't do very much for other people.

Rhoda stopped the car at the gate. Jim helped Mrs. Powell out, took the latch-key, and ran in to fetch his bag. Delia swung herself into the driving-seat. The car turned, sweeping the house wall with its lights. Rhoda and her mother were left alone.

They walked up the narrow, flagged garden path, and hurried into the house. A faint, clean smell of new paint met them as they went in at the front door, which Jim had left open. He had switched on the light for them. Already the house had lost its first strangeness. Their familiar things were in it; they had eaten and drunk it in, been away from it and come back to it. It was beginning to be home.

Natalie Powell dropped her fur and scarf on the table in the hall. What a house for her, she thought, a nasty little house not as good as Evelyn's ! I wonder Maurice can bear the idea of my coming here ! It always seemed to her that her troubles must be the same size to other people as they were to her. No conception of the inverted magnifying-glass through which other people saw them had ever penetrated her mind. She had wept for a bad headache or a dress that did not fit, and had demanded of Tom, if not tears, at least the same intensity of feeling.

Long before that she had been sure of Ellen's equal
distress when she broke her doll, or when a bad cold kept
her from a party. She had forgotten Rhoda's outburst at
supper for the moment when she exclaimed, half tearfully:

"Oh, Rhoda, I don't think we shall ever like living
here! I don't know how Maurice can bear the idea! I
don't know what your father would say if he saw it! I'm
sure Ellen must have felt miserable when she thought of us
coming home to this house." As Rhoda did not answer,
Natalie repeated, her voice rising on an imperious note,
"Don't you hate it, Rhoda?"

Then she remembered. She drew back from the idea
that Rhoda might hate it. Her voice had Aunt Ellen's
tone of bright, automatic consolation as she said hastily,
"Never mind! I expect we shall get used to it and be
very happy and comfortable here."

"I don't think I mind what sort of house I live in so
long as it's not too ugly. I rather like this one. You go on
upstairs, Mother, and I'll boil some water for your bottle
and bring your milk."

Rhoda went into the kitchen, switched on the electric
kettle, and poured some milk into a pan. She sat down on a
high-backed wooden chair that had once belonged to her
nursery. The kitchen already looked occupied; it bore
traces of Ivy. A cupboard door was open; a gay tradesman's calendar, with a picture of a child feeding swans
on a lake, hung above the table. On the mantelpiece were
a porcelain cat with a broken ear and a cracked jug of
striped china. They had both been thrown away before
the removal, and rescued by Ivy from the rubbish-heap.
On the one cushioned chair, Mrs. Robins and Mickey
lay close together, the kitten's black head pressed against

his mother's side. Relaxed by sleep, shorn of his bold
daytime personality, with limp paws and slack body and
soft cheeks, he was a little kitten again.

Oh, Mickey, thought Rhoda, you're going to-morrow !
You'll be bumped about in the basket and you won't like
it, but you'll get to a house, and hands will stroke you
and there will be a saucer of milk. You'll taste it, and it
will taste the same. You'll sniff all the furniture with your
black nose, and you'll look all round the room with your
big green eyes, and then you'll see something, a string
hanging out of a drawer or a bit of paper on the carpet,
and you'll pounce and spring and play, and it will be all
the same to you. You won't remember your mother, and
she'll look about for a new tomcat to sing to her in the
dark, and fight other cats for her, and then she'll have
another family of kittens and she won't remember you !
Cats were all right, they lived in here and now. The
trouble about human beings was that they wanted things
to last ! So often not what they saw or did to-day, but
what they had seen and done yesterday, was the pre-
occupation of their lives. They wanted childhood to go
on, passion to endure, youth to remain, friendship to
retain its full ardour, and life not to end. They fought a
losing battle against time, and had the sadness of people
in a lost cause. They knew that flowers die and leaves fall,
but they could not carry that knowledge into their own
lives ; the acceptance was beyond them. Sighing for the
blossom, they missed the fruit, growing and ripening.
Regretting the fruit, they did not see the delicate tracery
of bare boughs against a winter sky.

The milk was rising to the top of the pan. Rhoda
jumped up, poured it into a mug, and filled the hot-water

bottle from the boiling kettle. She stood for a moment by
the table, fingering the screw of the hot-water bottle,
which was already as tight as she could make it. She did
not want to go upstairs. She did not want to see her
mother looking small and forlorn, alone in a strange
bedroom. It would be cruel to say anything about leaving
her to-night. Yet she knew that she would have to be
cruel. The urgency which had caused her to break out at
supper drove her now. It could only be done to-day, in
this day that had rooted her from her old foundations,
this day when she stood apart from her everyday life and
saw it clearly.

She looked round the kitchen before turning out the
light. She found suddenly that she was trembling, and the
hand that lifted the milk shook so that it was difficult for
her to steady it. With an effort she pulled herself together.
It was such a small thing, to go upstairs and discuss a
reasonable plan reasonably. Maurice and I, she reflected,
do a lot of thinking, but we leave an awful gap between
that and getting anything done ! After all, to people like
us, thinking things out is fairly easy ! It's almost a form of
self-indulgence. We think out what we ought to do, and
then feel as though we'd achieved something, and don't
notice that we aren't doing it. I could sit down here and
think out a whole lot of truths about life much more
easily than I can go upstairs and tell Mother I really do
mean to go to London ! I could think of a lot of good
reasons for leaving it till to-morrow, or any time in the
next few days, but for once in my life I won't. I'll get
something done.

CHAPTER XXXV

N ATALIE WAS UNDRESSING in her strange, new bedroom. She had not yet got used to having her bedroom
to herself and sleeping alone. It still seemed unlikely that
this should happen, improbable that Tom should not
come in, wind up the clock, draw the curtains, and get
into the bed beside her. For years after they were first
married she had secretly disliked sharing a bedroom, and
shrunk from having her husband next to her in the big
bed. She had been glad when they followed the changing
fashion and bought two single beds, although she would
never have admitted to herself or anyone else that she did
not like the physical proximity. Married people did sleep
together, and presumably enjoyed it. As a very little girl
she had slept in a cot in her parents' room, and had
woken up to see their heads, side by side, on the frilled
pillows. Sometimes, with a feeling of privilege, she had
been lifted in to snuggle down into the warmth between
them. Without thinking about it at all, she had been
aware of their pleasure in one another and in the close
companionship. That was being married. It was after she
herself was married that she had begun to dislike being
kissed, had moved away from Tom's hand when he
stroked her hair or touched her cheek. Then she had
almost wished to have her bedroom to herself, had been
relieved, without acknowledging it, when he went away

on business. Habit had long ago overlaid those feelings;
she missed his constant and cheerful kindness, his voice,
first thing in the morning, saying, " Well, what sort of
day is it ? " as though no sort of day would come much
amiss to him, all were so sure to be full of affection and
interest, of contacts with his fellow men.

She did not at once begin to undress, but fiddled with
the things on her dressing-table, moving each one a
fraction of an inch. Her room bore fewer traces of the
removal than any other room in the house. Rhoda and
Aunt Ellen had worked to make it like home for her before
bedtime. Her furniture was as nearly as possible in its
accustomed places; her silver was unpacked; her various
odds and ends were arranged as usual on the chest of
drawers and mantelpiece. Only some of her clothes were
not yet unpacked, and her pictures and photographs were
stacked on a chair in the corner. She looked at these with
a little frown, vexed that her bedroom was incomplete.
Surely, she thought, they could have found a few minutes
to hang those ! The room feels like an attic with these bare
walls ! I hope none of them are broken.

She moved across to the chair, and began to examine
the framed photographs. Maurice's wedding photograph
lay on top. She looked at his young happy face, Evelyn's
rather set smile, the bridesmaids, the usual bevy of flowers
and hats. A flood of old feelings revived, pleasure because
Rhoda and Delia looked so much nicer than the two
friends of Evelyn's who paired with them; resentment
because her son was leaving her for a strange girl;
distaste for the girl's family and upbringing. There had
been other feelings too, hopes for Maurice's happiness,
a half-stifled sympathy that stirred in her as she saw the

young bride walking up the church with her bright hair
gleaming through the veil. Then, for one generous
moment, she had thought, I hope Maurice will be kind
to her ! but her strongest feeling was surprised indignation
that this girl could take Maurice from her. On the whole
the feelings revived by the wedding photograph were
not pleasant. Having seen that the glass was not cracked,
she laid it face downwards on the bed.

The four faces of a family group looked up at her,
herself, Tom, Rhoda, and Maurice in the set positions
ordained by the photographer. She was sitting in a tall
chair, her puffed sleeves spreading out on either side of it,
her face looking small and pointed above the high,
boned neck of her dress. Maurice, in a sailor suit, leaned
against her knee, turning the pages of a book. Tom sat
beside her, on a lesser chair, holding the three-year-old
Rhoda in his arms. There had been trouble about the
arrangement. The photographer had wanted Rhoda to
sit on her knee, but Rhoda was frightened of the camera
and of the stranger, and clung to her father, and Tom,
who yielded to his wife about everything else, would not
put the child down. Even in the stiff photograph—they
would never take a family like that nowadays, thought
Natalie—Rhoda was visibly cuddling her small person
into her father's arms ; his clasp was loving and protecting, and he was looking down at her with amused
eyes. Natalie had sulked on the way home, and in the
evening had told him that he spoilt Rhoda, and finally
had flared into a rage that neither she nor he understood,
but that ended as usual in tears on her part and perplexed attempts at comfort on his. No, the associations
bound up with that photograph were not much more

pleasant than those associated with Maurice's wedding. Natalie laid that, too, on the bed.

Beneath it was a small, yellow photograph of herself with Rhoda, an eighteen-month-old baby in her arms. It was fading fast, it had not been a very good photograph. She remembered well the occasion on which it had been taken, out in the garden on a spring morning, by a young son of their chemist who had set up a camera and was going round to try and get commissions. Rhoda had been very ill with congestion of the lungs, and was just allowed out again. For a month Natalie had hardly left her. For three nights during the crisis she had not been to bed. The child was uneasy with the nurses, and would only take food from her mother. The doctor had told Natalie that her devotion had kept her alive. Natalie did not know that those weeks had been one of the happiest times in her life; she would not have believed it, but it was so, for she had been single-minded. All conflicts had been resolved, all trifles had lost importance; she had never once thought of herself. She who was given to small ailments and self-pity had cheerfully done without sleep or fresh air, her irritable and fussy ways had vanished, leaving an unbounded patience and gentleness. She had never once noticed whether anyone was considering her at all, and her household had never loved her so truly.

She stood in her new bedroom, looking down at the faded print in her hand. She remembered that morning. She had taken Rhoda out for the first time into the clear sunny air. While she had been upstairs in the sick-room, spring had come without her noticing it. The stiff, short-stemmed tulips were blooming in the beds underneath the windows, the lilacs were in blossom, the garden smelled of wallflowers. She had walked up and down in front of the house, talking softly to the child in her arms. The young photographer had come up the drive, and she had let him take them, feeling that her hold upon her daughter was still precarious. Rhoda had come out a sad dark-eyed baby, but Natalie's face in the photograph was as no other portrait showed it—thin, but warm and tender, the face of a woman, not of a spoilt girl. Tom had loved the little picture, and had kept it in his dressing-room until he died, when she had hung it above her own mantelpiece. It had power to recall a mood that had not lasted, but even now, looking at it, she did not remember old irritations and resentments; she thought, My little girl! As she laid the picture down on the bed, there was a knock at the door, and Rhoda came in with the hot-water bottle and a glass of milk.

She came in taut with defiance, her nerves strung to meet and resist a demand which she always felt. Something softened and gentle in her mother surprised her, and at the same time frightened her more than any irritable protest. She was prepared to resist unfair claims; she had no armour against affection. She put the milk down on the dressing-table, and pulled back the bedclothes to push the bottle inside. She made an idle remark about the cats, they had settled down and seemed happy. Her heart was beating fast, and she heard the tick of the small French clock on the mantelpiece. She struggled against her own weakness. If I don't say something to-night, I never shall. What I said at supper will all go for nothing, be just a passing fancy, one of those impulses that take you when you are strung up and shaken out of your ordinary life.

She turned round from the bed. Her mother was standing by the dressing-table, taking down her hair. The soft hair, grey and pretty, fell down on to her shoulders, still kinked from the tight coils in which she wound it for the day-time. Looking past her, Rhoda saw her face in the glass, and met her eyes. She said, " Mother ! " It sounded almost like a cry of distress. Natalie, turning round from the glass, said, " What is it, darling ? "

" I must go away and get some work ! " Now that she had begun, it was like releasing a dam, the words tumbled out of her. " I'm not really doing anything here. I'm just existing. I'm not happy. I think it's selfish, but I want to go away, try life on my own, and do more things, see different kinds of people. I don't want to get old, like Aunt Ellen, without having had any life at all ! I've got stuck here; I can't do anything different ! I hate to leave you now, just when everything's changed. I ought to have done it before. I was lazy. I didn't think until to-day; leaving home shook me out of it, and stirred everything up. Oh, Mother ! " The tears were running down her cheeks. " I want to go ! "

The thick crust of possessive selfishness cracked across Natalie's heart. Once again in her life she forgot herself, she saw nothing but a child of hers in desperate need, and the loving woman in her, cramped, retarded, but never quite dead, rose to meet it. She saw, in that moment, more than her daughter, knew what she wanted and missed, saw her a forlorn little girl, saw her needing to be loved and have children; to work and be valued, to be set free to go her own way without misgivings. The passion with which she had fought for her baby's life rose up in her again, an unselfish passion, so that in that moment she only thought of her daughter and wanted to wring happiness from the world for her, and to give it her at all costs. She put her arms round Rhoda, and drew the wet face on to her shoulder. She said:

" Of course you must go ! I want you to. It's a good time now, while we're making changes. Aunt Ellen would always come and stay with me, you know. Hush ! There's nothing to be unhappy about. You're tired out. You must go to bed. Don't cry, darling. There ! My little girl ! My little girl ! "

CHAPTER XXXVI

As Delia said good night to Jim at the Carters' front door, she remarked:

" I'm rather glad you'll see Lucy and her household. You'll see the sort of thing I want Roddy to escape from."

It was a house like Stone Hall, Jim thought, as he followed the maid across the hall, but it had a different feeling. It was not only that the furniture was uglier, and there were more undistinguished oil-paintings in heavy gold frames. You felt that the doors of the house had been closed for the last twenty years, and no wind of new ideas had ever blown through them to disturb the settled air. Jim was shown into a big room on the right of the hall. It seemed very full of furniture; you had to skirt several small tables and cabinets of china to reach the fireplace.

Lucy Carter and her father, who were sitting one on each side of the fire, got up to meet him. He saw an old man, tall and square-built, but now stooping, who greeted him with a dignified kindness. The daughter, also square-built, had the same sensible, high-coloured face, and her blue eyes were of the same shape and colour. Seen close to, the rosy colour in her cheeks was made up of a network of tiny veins under a fair skin much exposed to wind and weather. There were fine lines across her forehead, and a good deal of grey in her thick brown hair, but the general effect of the face was very young. You

would have called her a girl unless you had looked closely.
Her manner to Jim as she shook hands was cordial, but a
little flustered, as though a young man were a strange
visitor in the house and she could not quite take him
naturally. It was the manner of someone who never had
taken young men naturally; the old-fashioned schoolgirl
flutter had crystallised into the good manners of a kind,
middle-aged hostess like a fly in amber.

They had some sandwiches and various drinks on a
tray, and gave him a whiskey and soda. The old man was
drinking Ovaltine, and Lucy sipping hot water. They
asked about the removal, and inquired courteously if
Mrs. Powell was very tired.

" It must have been most trying for her," the old man
said. He looked round his big over-full room. He was
thinking how much he himself would dislike removing.

" It's a shame ! " Lucy cried. " That lovely garden cut
up into rows of horrid little red houses, and the old house
pulled down ! If they built anything as good as the
things they destroyed, it wouldn't matter so much, but
they don't ! All the old solid things are going, and cheap,
shoddy things coming instead ! I do so sympathise with
Mrs. Powell and Rhoda. Of course," she added hastily,
" Delia won't feel it so much, as she's been away such
a lot."

Lucy had often felt that Delia was away too much and
left everything to Rhoda. She herself had often wished
for a sister. Her imaginary sister would be someone like
herself, who lived with her and shared the responsibilities
of housekeeping and looking after her father, and the
pleasures of walking and tennis and good works. It was
the one secret wish that she admitted into her dutiful

cheerfulness. When she bought a new hat or a new jumper, she imagined herself going into her sister's room, unwrapping it and trying it on. Father was not interested in clothes, and you could not, in Lucy's code, show your new hat to the housemaid. A faint sigh escaped her unawares.

" I think they'll find the new house much more convenient," Jim said. It was no use saying that neither the Powells nor the Carters were entitled to live in large houses and lovely gardens just because their grandfathers had built them, and that a world in which they had thirty acres of ground while eight families shared a lavatory was badly in need of a few removals. It was no use saying anything here, Jim felt. Thick, solid, impenetrable, the atmosphere of privilege filled the house. The Carters, he guessed, were kind people, who concerned themselves with good causes and gave away a lot of money, but it must be theirs to give, and others must receive it. Any other conception of life was outside their imagination. A momentary dismay filled his heart. They were an extreme case, no doubt, but how much of prosperous England was really with them, willing to be kind, utterly unwilling to be fair ? These were not people who lived in the country, or in an artistic or literary circle. They were in the middle of the industrial world, and had lived in it all their lives ; its gross inequalities and injustices had surrounded them both from childhood, and they had never seen them, or had seen them as unfortunate necessities. How slowly things happened in England !

Lucy took her father's cup away from him, moved his footstool, and shifted the screen between his face and the fire.

" I shall come and see Mrs. Powell and Rhoda as soon
as they're ready. I want to be one of their first visitors.
You know, I've known Rhoda all my life."

Lucy really liked Rhoda, and never quite admitted to
herself that half an hour alone together found them both
searching for something to say.

" I think Rhoda won't be at home much longer,"
Jim remarked. " She's going to try for Delia's job in
London."

" Oh ! " exclaimed Lucy. " Delia is coming home,
then ? But I thought——" She stopped.

" We're getting married in December, so Delia won't
be going on at the lab. They asked her to look about for
someone else, and Rhoda thinks of having a try at it."

" But who will stay with Mrs. Powell ? "

" She's got her sister quite near, you know."

" But surely Rhoda won't leave her alone ! " The
square, rosy face opposite Jim was full of startled indignation. " I think it's very selfish of her," Lucy exclaimed
bluntly.

" I don't think Rhoda's selfish."

" I've never thought she was, but I should if she went
away now, and left her mother alone in a strange house
with everything different. I don't believe she'll do it."

" She's probably feeling unsettled," old Mr. Carter
said kindly. " They've had a lot of trouble lately. I expect
Rhoda wants a holiday."

Once again Jim thought that it was no use saying anything. It was another privilege that went unquestioned
in this house, the parents' claim upon the unmarried
daughter, the daughter's duty to the parents. The old
man was fond of Lucy; his voice and look and smile

showed it. If she had been unsettled, he would have suggested at once that she should have a holiday, and then come back to him. There could be no possible reason for her doing anything else; this was her home, and he would have plenty of money to leave her. Privileges always have their victims, thought Jim.

Lucy felt the difficulty of discussing his future relations-in-law with him, and, like her father, concluded that Rhoda would not go. Her candid, ingenuous eyes had never really looked at any other point of view except her own. She changed the subject, and tried to discuss plays with him. It was not a very profitable discussion, for he had been too busy to go to theatres, and Lucy, as she explained, did not often see the No. 1 Touring Companies that came to the town.

" Father doesn't like going at night now, and, when there's a matinée, I so often have a committee meeting or something I must go to. Besides," she added, " there are such a lot of rather unpleasant plays. I like something cheerful."

The faint complacency in her tone, as though she did something virtuous in staying away from the theatre, irritated Jim. He wanted to shake her, but it was no business of his. Besides, he reflected, it would have to be such a good hard shake, a harder shake, perhaps, than you had a right to give anyone. She had grown up to school-leaving age, a pre-War school-leaving age, and then stopped.

Lucy, knitting steadily, was thinking that Delia would have this sort of young man, rather brusque, a little casual about important things. Delia herself was like that; she had fallen in love with her own kind of person. It was very odd, thought Lucy, to think of anyone falling in love with this young man. For that matter, she often thought it odd about any young man. Many of them were " nice " —anybody Lucy liked was " nice "—but they seemed ordinary, and rather ugly. None of them, to her mind, were likely to arouse the ardour and ecstasy which she associated with a girl in the sixth form at school, the object of her single brief passion. I suppose, thought Lucy, it's funny I've never fallen in love ! Yet she was convinced that people talked a good deal of nonsense about it, thought it more important and exciting than it was. Some of it would be very difficult to put up with ! What would it be like to be Delia, living so close to Jim and sleeping with him ? A faint, personal curiosity stirred in her as she looked at Jim. She flushed suddenly over her candid forehead, and said to her father:

" I think Dr. Roberts must be tired. Shall we ring for Alice to show him his room ? "

When he had said good night and gone up, she sat staring into the fire. Her father shut up the biography that he had been reading and laid it on his little table.

" We ought to get those plants up from the station to-morrow."

" Yes, dear. I haven't forgotten. Collis can go for them in the morning."

" Do you know where I put that notice of the library meeting to-morrow ? "

" Yes, it's here, in your desk."

She kept all his papers for him, reminded him to pay his bills, and watched his engagement-book. His memory for small things was growing uncertain.

" Thank you, my dear."

He bent down to kiss her good night as usual. She clung to him with sudden fervour.

" I wouldn't ever leave you ! I love you more than anyone in the world."

He blinked at her, his faded blue eyes kind but surprised. He patted her cheek, and said: " Good night, Lucy, my dear." He walked heavily across the room, stumbling a little, his ankles stiff from long sitting. The door closed behind him. Nothing, Lucy thought, was as sad as growing old. In a few years she would not have him any longer. Already he had drawn away from her into the narrow world of the old, her doings did not interest him much, nor her small concerns trouble him. He needed all his waning vitality for his own. She fought against every sign that he was getting older; she was sometimes almost cross with him for forgetting things and being tired.

I don't know how Rhoda could think of it ! Indignation comforted Lucy, giving her a platform to stand on, confirming her in her own way of life. She won't really do it, she decided. She's not that sort of girl, not selfish like Delia. To condemn Delia as selfish was also in some obscure way a comfort. Lucy switched off the lamp and went upstairs to bed.

CHAPTER XXXVII

DELIA fastened and bolted the front door behind her. The light was still on in the tiny hall. She slid out of her coat and threw it on the table. It had been a long day; she was tired, and also, as she suddenly realised, hungry. She debated whether she was more sleepy or more hungry; whether she would go straight up to bed, or go into the kitchen and try and find some milk. She heard a door open softly on the landing upstairs. A whisper floated down to her.

" Dell ! Is that you ? Come in before you go to bed."

" Come down, Roddy," Delia whispered back. " I'm hungry. I'm going to look for something to eat."

" All right. I'll come too. I want to talk to you."

Delia felt more wakeful. She explored the small larder, found eggs and milk and butter and bread, and carried them into the kitchen. She began to break the eggs into a basin. Rhoda came in, wearing a thin rose-coloured dressing-gown. The dark curls, that were generally smoothed back behind her ears, hung loose.

" You look nice in that colour ! " Delia exclaimed. " You ought to have a rose-coloured evening dress. Were you asleep ? "

" No. I was listening for you."

" I'm going to scramble eggs. Would you like to make some toast on the griller ? "

" Are you as hungry as all that ? "

" Quite," said Delia firmly. " Family evenings are exhausting. Besides, this sort of day is so absurd anyhow that we might just as well have a meal in the middle of the night if we feel like it. There isn't any beer, is there ? "

" No, I'm afraid there isn't. We never have it unless we know Maurice is coming, and get it for him specially."

" You like it, don't you ? "

" Yes, but it doesn't seem worth while getting it just for me."

" I always think it's worth while getting things if I like them ! Let's make some tea ! What's the matter with Maurice ? "

" Evelyn, I think."

" How trying for her ! "

" For her ? " exclaimed Rhoda, surprised.

" Well, I know, but I do feel rather sorry for her. She'll never understand the things that Maurice makes himself unhappy about if she lives with him for a hundred years. For one thing, most of them aren't there."

Delia was beating eggs vigorously with a fork. The golden froth rose in the white bowl. Rhoda pulled out the tray from under the griller, and looked at her toast. The pale wedges of bread were crisping, and turning a golden brown; the kitchen smelt of toast. It was the old smell of schoolroom tea, when she and Maurice and Delia jostled one another in front of the fire, toasting their bread on knives, and scorching their cheeks and noses to produce irregular pieces of toast, burnt at one side, and grey with ash where they had fallen into the grate.

" Maurice and I are awfully alike," Rhoda said. " We're both in a muddle."

" You'll get out of yours. I don't know if he'll ever get out of his."

" I think he's further out than I am. He's more use in the world. He's got a job and responsibility; he's necessary. He's got a wife and child and home depending on him."

" I think that makes it harder for him. He's got a job that he can only put half his heart into, and a wife that he'll never be in touch with. He's taken too many steps that he didn't know about nor really want to take. He'll either have to face that or keep it out of his mind altogether, and as long as he's doing that he won't be square with anything."

" Well, I haven't taken any steps at all."

" No, but you will, and you'll know what steps you want to take, and where you're going."

Delia poured the beaten eggs into a pan and began to stir.

" It seems so queer," she mused, " that people don't really think more about living. If they're moving into a new house or buying their summer clothes, they think a lot about what they'll want and when they'll want it and how to get it, but they so seldom do that with their lives; they let them run on without any sort of plan. All that pseudo-D. H. Lawrence stuff about instinctive living and not thinking is such bosh ! As though when you're really feeling hard about anything you don't use all the brains you've got ! Why, when you're in love you think and plan and arrange to meet him and please him; you work out all sorts of possibilities; you're cleverer and more ingenious about it than you ever were before ! Yet people so often seem to think that using their intelligence isn't one of their instincts, and can't go with real feeling."

Rhoda turned her toast over and slid it back again. It was comfortable to be with Delia. Life in her company seemed a possible business, to be attacked fair and square; secret fears and inhibitions shrank to a more reasonable proportion. Somehow with Delia enjoying yourself seemed a normal thing, and not only normal but completely justified. So many people made a ticket-of-leave business of it; you might enjoy yourself for just so long, but no longer, because enjoyment was doubtful in itself, and to be free for long meant danger. An almost extinguished gaiety sparkled in Rhoda's blood. She would see things and do things, learn more of the rich, enchanting business that living really was. She would be free like Delia, unprejudiced and unafraid. She would taste and try, find out and enjoy, make more life in the world because she herself would be more alive. An unexpected liberation had set free her spirit. She said to Delia:

" I'm going to try for your job. I've been talking to Mother; she's willing to let me go. She thinks that Aunt Ellen can probably come and keep her company."

" Of course she can. She'll love it, and you'll come back for holidays and week-ends."

But, thought Delia, I am surprised! She bent over the pan, stirring, watching the yellow pool crinkle and solidify round her spoon. She had expected a scene, tears and reproaches, long arguments in which Rhoda would be worn out. Perhaps, she thought, I don't really know Mother after all! It was a humbling thought to her cocksure youth. We don't know anybody, really, she thought, only their house front, and often that gets in

the way of really knowing them. She lifted the pan off
the ring.

" It's ready now. Turn the cats off the chair, and let's
sit down and be comfortable."

" I don't want to disturb them. You have the other
chair, and I'll sit on the fender."

The tinkle of spoons and china had already disturbed
Mrs. Robins and Mickey. Mrs. Robins jumped down
from the chair, stretched her body with unhurried dignity,
first the front legs and then the back. She came across
to them and lifted her face, with the intense, spiritual
expression of a cat asking for food. Mickey, still only
half awake, settled himself alone on the cushion of the
chair like a statue of a lion couchant. He yawned, showing his pink tongue and small, sharp teeth. He blinked
his green eyes at them; the eyelids dropped. He lowered
his broad cheeks, with a gesture of resignation, on to his
doubled paws.

Delia lifted her cup of tea and said to Rhoda over the
top of it:

" Here's luck ! "

Rhoda laughed. She had not expected to end the day
like this, enjoying scrambled eggs with Delia in the
kitchen, and looking forward to a new life. She felt as
though she had been a long journey since the morning
through dark tunnels and difficult places, and had
emerged into sunshine and clear air. Her mother's permission had been like a weight lifted off the top of her
head; she felt a little drunk with new possibilities, exalted
by fatigue and the relaxation of a strain.

" Tell me some more about the lab ! " she said.

Delia, very willing, began to talk: the lab and the

staff; Vicary's theories and Dr. Dunt's love-affairs; the patients and their idiosyncrasies; the common life of people working together; the active mental life of people ih daily contact with new ideas, tumbled out of her. There was so much in the world, and she wanted Rhoda to share it; she talked with all the ardour of somebody persuading to a new faith. It was her faith that she was expounding, for you were put down here, she believed, in a life which was probably all you would get, and of which, after all, you knew nothing. What could you do but experiment, and try and find out by experience? You got no wisdom except by living. Rhoda listened, growing drowsy, but something in her own mind answered Delia's. Her father's willingness to embrace life was buried in her, deep under her mother's withdrawal from it. It was that eager spark at the bottom that had made her restless and unhappy, that had made her unable to accept her circumstances as Lucy Carter had done, that would make her able to get out of them.

Upstairs, Natalie lay in bed in her unfamiliar room, and heard the new sounds outside, a car passing on the road, a dog barking at one of the houses near, the creak of a tree in the garden. In spite of the strangeness, she felt at peace, in the release of tension that comes when someone accustomed to thinking of herself has forgotten herself. She was thinking about Rhoda with sympathy and understanding. It did not occur to her that to-morrow her mood would have changed; she would repent of her generous impulse, and reassert her claims, make complaints and demands again.

She had never meant to be a selfish woman, but it had always been so easy. The pretty, delicate baby spoilt by her parents, the adored younger sister spoilt by Ellen, had developed into the irritable and imperious young wife, spoilt by a loving and easy-going young husband who dreaded unpleasantness. Her world had made no demands on her, but had encouraged her to be exacting. There were times when she had a dim perception of the inverted wrong it did her. There was an evening long ago when she had made a scene because Tom had to go away on business on a day on which she wanted him to take her to a party. She had cried and sulked, refused to come down to dinner, stayed in her bedroom all the evening, and turned her back on him when he came up to bed. In the end, he had promised to alter his business arrangements and take her to the party. She had kissed him, and made friends, but as she lay awake by his side afterwards she had felt ashamed. Very much to her own surprise, she had found herself thinking, I wish he'd shaken me, and told me not to be a little fool ! If he had, she would have given in, and found that rare peace which only came to her when she could lay aside her fretting claims and exactions. It was with her now, although she was tired and lonely and strange in her new house.

She thought drowsily, I'll have Ellen here to live with me. It will be like old times.

The day that had detached Rhoda from her had drawn her nearer to Ellen, rounded the curve of her life towards its beginning. Her mind went back to those old times when she was a very little girl getting ready for a party. She saw the cream flounces of the flannel petticoats, with their edges scalloped in white silk, warming on the fender before the nursery fire. She saw Ellen, pale and serious in her velveteen frock, standing near her, holding comb

and brush and hair-ribbon, while their nurse brushed
Natalie's soft curls round her finger. She remembered
how they had jogged home from parties together in a
cab, bundled up in red-riding-hood cloaks, and how
often she had gone to sleep with her head propped on
Ellen's shoulder. The musty smell of the cab came back
to her; the feeling of the red woollen cape, rough but
soft, against her cheek. Her strange bedroom in the new
house merged into the cab, or into the night nursery at
home. The various removals of her life, marriage and
children, grown-up life and widowhood, slipped away
from her, and she was a little girl at home again with
Ellen, as she turned on her side and went to sleep.

CHAPTER XXXVIII

As Rhoda undressed in her new bedroom, the glow faded out of her spirits. She was cold and stiff with fatigue, the day seemed to have lasted for years. She jumped into bed, and relaxed her limbs thankfully between the sheets. She lay for a minute or two getting used to the new shape of her room, the window, a pale square on her right, instead of a pale oblong on her left, all the furniture nearer to her, as though someone had put their hands round the walls of her old bedroom, and squeezed them in.

When we're finished with it, she thought, it will be a dear little house. I suppose Aunt Ellen will probably come here, more or less permanently, and sleep in this room.

She discovered in herself an objection to this idea which surprised her. She would like to feel that her room was always empty, so that she could come back to it at any time. She realised that that was how Maurice had felt about his old home. He would never really come back to it, of course, but as long as it was there, lived in by his own people and waiting to welcome him, he had probably always felt that he could come back, that his retreat was not cut off. She had the same feeling, even though she was going away she wanted to be sure that she could come back at any moment. A truth which she had not yet had time to perceive came up to the surface of her mind, and she admitted it.

After all, I only half want to go !

But, she resolved soberly, I'm going. I've learnt a lot of things to-day. I know, now, that if I stay here with Mother it won't be because she keeps me, it will be because I want to be kept. It isn't necessary. Mother and Aunt Ellen will be very happy together, really more in tune than Mother and I ever would be. Aunt Ellen does spontaneously the things that I make myself do. If I stay, it won't be unselfishness, it will be because I'm a coward and unenterprising, humbugging myself with a duty that isn't there. I shall go, but I wish I was different ! I love and admire people like Delia who take their risks and adventures joyfully; I believe with all my mind that it's the way to live, the real goodness, but I'm not like that. In my heart I'm afraid of risks and adventures. I know now that I am. That's the thing that I've found out to-day, the real difference for me between this morning and to-night.

How much difference does it make, she wondered, to know where you are ? Probably not as much as you think when you first find it out, and feel the tonic glow of a new revelation. It must make some, because you are not working in the dark; it is an honest fight against heavy odds. You cannot become a whole person by seeing the division, but, if you know where it is, you can sometimes behave like one. At least there is a certain peace and decency in making no pretences to yourself, and on that basis only you can grow to a little more courage, a little more life, a little more experience.

Rhoda saw that she had not won a victory, but only the

first skirmish in a long campaign. A day can change two lives but not two people. To-morrow her mother would return to a more ordinary mood; she would complain and cry and think of a dozen reasons to prevent Rhoda from going. That would not matter so much as the reasons that Rhoda herself would think of. No pressure mattered except on a weak place. What you did was never anyone else's fault. For the first time Rhoda realised this, and accepted full responsibility, stepping over the threshold of childhood into maturity. A delicious drowsiness relaxed her mind and body, and, turning over on her side, she fell asleep.

THE END